CAMERON 8

THE FINALE

JADE JONES

www.jadedpub.com

ARE YOU ON OUR EMAIL LIST?

Sign up to Jaded Publications newsletter to be the first to hear about new releases, contests, and giveaways!

Text BOOKS to 44144

This novel is a work of fiction. Any reference to real people, events, establishments, or locales is intended only to give the fiction a sense of reality and authenticity. Other names, characters, and incidents occurring in the work are either the product of the author's imagination or are used fictitiously, as are those fictionalized events and events that involve real persons. Any character that happens to share the name of a person who is any acquaintance of the author, past or present, is purely coincidental and is in no way intended to be an actual account involving that person.

THE HIGHLY ANTICIPATED EIGHTH INSTALLMENT IS FINALLY HERE!!!

Cameron is back and unlike you've ever seen her before. From strip clubs to car theft rings, you've journeyed with her from girlhood into womanhood, but the drama isn't over just yet! New faces and new situations make this new installment the most riveting of the entire series! If you enjoyed "Wife of a Misfit" and "Soul and Diana", you're in for an even bigger treat! Join Cameron and the gang on another wild ride packed with action, romance, secrets and juicy drama!

NOTE FROM THE AUTHOR:

This novel takes place approximately 11 years after *"Soul and Diana 4"*. To better enhance your reading experience, I highly recommend reading the complete *"Soul and Diana"* series, as well as *"Wife of a Misfit"*. Thank you all for rocking with me as long as you have! Where would I be without my loyal readers? I hope you all enjoy *"Cameron 8"*. It's been a long time coming!

PROLOGUE
CAMERON

Thirty-seven. Tomorrow I'll be thirty-seven years old, and it's like I'm speeding into forty with no fucking safety belt on. It's crazy, 'cuz I could vividly recall being 19 and attending college, and enduring all of the shit Pocahontas, Tiffany, Kiki, and every other crazy bitch I'd ever tried to befriend, put me through. Hell, I could even remember every boyfriend, before *and* after Silk, and the way he shot himself in the head when I refused to take him back.

I'd been through so much, but luckily, I had a rider by my side. Jude Patterson, the love of my life, was as loyal as they came. After eleven years of marriage, we were now stronger and closer than ever. But it wasn't an easy journey, and it took a lot of time nurturing the solid and enduring relationship we had today. We'd been through our fair share of trials and tribulations—the biggest being the bartending bitch he'd impregnated behind my back. Lucky for him, we hadn't had any fidelity issues since then, or at least none that I was aware of. Anyway, I say all this to say, that 37 came pretty fucking fast. With 40 knocking on my door, I suddenly found myself wondering *am I getting old*?

Come to think of it, I didn't begin feeling old until my 36th birthday last year. That's when the gray hairs started popping up, and music that was too loud started to bother me, and getting out of bed in the morning became a bit more laborious, and the world as I knew it seemed to be filled with nothing but teenagers and their terrible ass music. That's when the questioned seemed to burn in my brain. Was this former stripper finally past her prime?

I never imagined a time when so many people around me would be decades younger, and I damn sure never thought I'd see the day when my own son towered over me. It seemed like just yesterday I had given birth to Justin, and now he was one year away from graduating the prestigious private school he attended. Words couldn't express how proud I was of him, and my daughter Journee didn't fall too far behind, either. She was almost 15 now, and currently enrolled in a private academy in Beverly Hills for exceptional and gifted students, where she faithfully made Honor Roll every academic year.

Jude was determined to put her in one of the best schools that the city offered, and all of her classmates were the offspring of famous actors, musicians, politicians, doctors, lawyers, and other people with high-end occupations. It cost us damn near $75,000 a year just to keep her in that school, but Jude religiously paid the tuition without batting an eyelash. He worked very hard to make sure our children had the best education he could give them, and for that, I was beyond grateful. He was a damn good father and an exceptional provider.

After everything we'd been through in Atlanta, he made it his mission to move us to California the minute Justin turned 10. He didn't want the kids following in our footsteps, and he felt like that could easily happen in a city like Atlanta, so we relocated. Plus, it was far better opportunities and colleges in California, in my opinion, so he got no argument from me there. Besides, we could really use a change of pace and scenery after all the shit we'd endured in Georgia.

Six years ago, we closed the deal on a swanky Mediterranean villa in Beverly Hills, and the rest was history. With Jude still running the business, we started life anew and were able to give the kids an even better life than Cleveland or Atlanta could offer them. So far, we were loving Cali.

They say *the west coast is the best coast*, and I *was* a firm believer of that, until every catastrophic thing that ever could have happened in my life did.

CAMERON 8

1
CAMERON

Event coordinators. Chefs. Caterers. DJs. I'd hired the very best for this birthday celebration and it was sure to be an unforgettable one. After all, it wasn't everyday a girl turned 37. I had to go big. Super grand ballroom, bougie finger foods and expensive wine good. I'd long outgrown my years of throwing basic ass birthday parties, plus all of me and Jude's friends and business associates would be there, so I *had* to leave a lasting impression.

Jude and I were like celebrities in our city, since my husband cleaned a portion of his cash through charities and campaign contributions. Most people didn't know that though. They simply thought Jude made his millions off investments and the magazine company he'd recently launched. The fact that he was really the king of moving weight was far from public knowledge. He and Soul were business partners now, and they had the drug game on smash.

Soul supplied the product, and Jude handled the distribution, laundering and financial aspect of the organization. Jude was a very sophisticated money launderer, and he cleaned the drug money by opening legitimate businesses, while pouring some of it into the government in exchange for their protection.

At first, I wasn't crazy about my husband selling drugs—especially with everything we'd been through in the past stemming from his life of crime. However, Jude kept that side of his life away from us, and he did everything he could to protect us, including hiring a 24-hour security team. They chaperoned us and kept guard of our Beverly Hills mansion 24/7. We never wanted the horrific things that happened in the past to repeat themselves.

I had just finished jotting down the list of music for the DJ when my phone rang. I was seated at the kitchen island, sipping my glass of bubbly and enjoying the madness of party planning.

"Hey, Taryn," I greeted the head of my catering team.

"Good afternoon, Mrs. Patterson. I hope I didn't catch you at a bad time," she said.

"Not at all. What can I help you with?"

"Well, I was confused with the *types* of assorted cheeses you wanted distributed. You didn't mention it in your order."

"Hmm." I scratched my chin. "What type do you recommend?"

"Well, we have French cheeses, Irish cheeses and *fresh* imported Italian cheeses."

"Mmm. They all sound so good. How about this? *You* just surprise *me*."

I could hear her smiling through the phone. "Sure! You got it, Mrs. Patterson."

"Thank you, Taryn! See you soon!"

I hung up the phone with her, downed my glass of wine and closed my planner. I would call it a day for now since I'd been planning all week. Besides, I wanted to clean up, and spend a little time with my hubby before going to the airport to pick up Madison.

Madison came and visited us every school break. She was 17, and kinda like my niece since she'd been around the family for so long. She and my kids grew up together and she even called me Auntie. I really enjoyed when she came over because it was sort of like having another daughter. After barely raising our own children, Jude and I mutually agreed that we were done having kids.

Climbing off the stool, I padded through the swanky home until I reached Justin's room. I'd been meaning to clean it for some time now, especially since it had the whole first level of our house reeking like sweaty gym socks. The boy was a pig, and I was reminded of that every time I walked into his junky ass living quarters.

"How can this boy even sleep in a messy ass room like this?" I asked, taking in the sight of it all. There were dirty clothes on his bed, shoes kicked everywhere, magazines scattered throughout and the smell of old, molding food coming from somewhere in the small space.

I took a deep breath, rolled up my sleeves and got to work on cleaning up the mess. Jude always said we should hire a maid, but I felt like that would rob me of my motherly duties, and everyone that knew me knew I loved being a mom. I cooked, I cleaned, and I tended to my family's needs before my own.

I was halfway done cleaning Justin's stink chamber when I realized what had his room reeking—apart from his dirty ass clothes. A stale pizza slice under his bed that was already turning green from sitting out too long. Just looking at the molding mozzarella had me second-guessing the assorted cheeses altogether. That's how fucked up that shit looked.

I really need to talk to this child about organization, I told myself. After all, *cleanliness is next to godliness.*

After throwing out the food, and putting his dirty ass clothes in the washer, I stripped his sheets and prepared to make his bed, but I paused when I noticed a journal stuffed under his pillow. I'd never seen it before, but then again, I didn't go rooting through my children's belongings. They were teenagers now, so I respected their privacy, and only investigated if I felt like I had a reason to.

I usually straightened up, and kept it moving. However, something about the journal had my curiosity peaked. Grabbing the small book, I flipped it open and looked through the pages. To my surprise, it wasn't filled with journal entries at all. Instead, there were lists of every hood in and around Los Angeles.

I scratched my head in confusion when I saw that most of them were crossed out. The only one that wasn't crossed out was Watts, California.

"What the hell is this?" I asked myself.

Justin went to a bougie ass high school with a bunch of high-society kids. Why the hell would he have a book with all the hoods in LA scribbled down?

I always knew that he was somewhat fascinated by the ghetto, but I kept him and Journee away from that lifestyle because I didn't want them to fall into the wrong crowd. I didn't always agree with Justin's friends, but as far as I knew, he was on the right path. He got good grades, and he'd only had one run-in with the law.

I prayed he wasn't doing anything that could get him into trouble. I'd have a fit if my first born was out here doing some shit he had no business doing. Hell, I'd probably kill his ass myself.

"You still cleaning this big ass boy's room?" Jude asked, appearing in the doorway.

"I have to," I said. "If I don't do it, it won't get done." I put the journal back up under his pillow and dismissed it for now. "Can you believe I just found a molded ass slice of pizza under his bed?"

Jude laughed. "I can believe it," he said. "You know he gets that messiness from your side of the family."

Now it was my turn to laugh. "You're right. I guess that's why I'm always cleaning up after your behind." My voice was dripping with sarcasm.

Jude walked over to the basketball sitting in the corner of Justin's room, picked it up, and spun it in his hands.

"Feels like ages since we hooped together," he said. "Maybe I'll see if he wants to play after school."

"That'd be nice. A little father and son time."

Jude put the ball back down. "You wanna know what would be even nicer, though? Chillin', watch TV, and rubbin' on my wife's juicy, fat ass booty," he said, spanking my ass.

2
JUSTIN

The final bell had just rung and I couldn't have been happier, as I slammed my locker shut and tossed my red Supreme backpack over my shoulder. It was finally Spring Break. I hated high school, and if I had it my way, I would probably drop out, if it wasn't for me only being 16. Don't get me wrong, I aced all my classes, I just felt like I learned more shit in the streets than I did in school.

After securing the combination lock, I pulled my phone out and hit my boy Drip to let him know I was on my way out of the building and would meet him in the back of the school. I was just about to put my phone away when I got a random text from my little sister Journee:

Aye, thirsty. Guess who's coming into town today? MADISON!!!!!!

My heart skipped a beat and I smiled and texted back:

You sound way more dehydrated than me sis.

I fronted like I didn't care, but truthfully, I was happy as hell that Maddie was coming to stay with us. She only visited during school breaks, so I didn't get to see her cute ass often. Needless to say, I was pressed than a bitch to handle this business so that I could spend some quality time with her. I'd really been missing her ass lately, and the Facetimes just didn't make up for her physical absence. I needed her next to me all-year long.

Damn, I hope this shit don't take all day, I thought to myself.

I was just about to walk out of the building when a few of my friends called out to me. "Aye, J. You hoppin' on the sticks later on, bro?" Lee asked.

"We puttin' money on that shit too, so you better get in where you fit in," another added, in an attempt to further sway me.

Usually, after homework, I hopped on the Xbox to play a few games of basketball with my friends, but tonight I didn't have time for video games or any other trivial bullshit, for that matter. I had business I needed to tend to. And that business didn't involve Lee, or any of them, for that matter.

"Nah, not tonight," I told them. "I got some work to catch up on, and moms won't even let me *touch* the fuckin' TV until I finish it," I lied. My classmates chuckled before pounding me and promising to hit my line later on. I was pretty popular at school, always had been.

"A'ight then, bro. I'mma go snatch these niggas' allowances," Lee bragged. "I'll catch you later." Lee was the captain of the basketball team and one of my closest friends in school. And while he was cool and all, I still kept him at an arms' length distance, because I never wanted him, or anyone else to find out about the shit I was into.

As I left out of the school building, I bumped into Aria, a pretty Latina chick whose father was a high-profile lawyer. She'd been on a nigga's dick ever since I moved to Cali, but I never gave her the time of day. Hell, I never gave *any* bitch the time of day. My head was so far up Madison's ass, I couldn't even *see* another chick. I'd had a crush on Maddie ever since I was 10 years old.

It was a love at first sight type of thing. No lie, I think I fell for her the second her father brought her over my house six years ago. She was my first kiss, my first love, my everything. On God, there wasn't a girl on the face of this Earth that could compete. Not even Aria, who was in the chess club, on the debate team *and* played soccer.

"Hey, Justin!" Aria smiled, sidling up beside me as though I'd given her a personal invite to start conversing.

To be so invasive, the bitch was actually cute as fuck. She had sun-kissed skin, chestnut eyes, auburn hair, and a fat ass. Aria was a good girl, and a lot of the niggas in school were on her, but she only seemed to have eyes for me. Too bad, the interest wasn't mutual. She was too much of a square for me, plus, I already had a girl.

"Any plans for the weekend?" she asked, with a hopeful look on her pretty, round face.

I really wished her cute ass would scram because I needed to meet my boy in the back of the school, and I didn't want her following my every gotdamn move. "Just playin' it by ear really," I said unenthused.

"Oh, well, I don't know if you heard, but Travis is having a party this weekend at his place—"

"I don't have time for parties," I said annoyed.

"Wow. Okay then, Mr. Grouchy," she laughed, tossing her hands up in surrender. "Then what *do* you have time for?" She batted her long, curly eyelashes in a seductive manner as she waited on a response.

"Not too much these days," I mumbled, scratching my head.

She was starting to get on my nerves. Here I was, preparing to get into some shit and this bitch wanted to stand around playing 21 Questions. I needed to be focused and level-headed for the shit that was about to go down. Annoyed that she was still following me, I sighed in frustration.

She either couldn't take a hint or just didn't care about it altogether, as she continued with her mindless chatter. "I swear, you don't seem to have time for anything, *or anybody*," she added surreptitiously. "You know, of all the years we've attended school together, I've never once seen you date anybody, and almost *all* the girls have a crush on you, *especially* the cheerleaders."

I couldn't help that a lot of bitches were on my head. I was a handsome young nigga. "Maybe I already have a special someone in my life," I told her. "Has that possibility ever crossed your mind?"

Aria looked disappointed. "Oh...I didn't know..."

"Yeah, well...you can relay that info to the cheerleaders," I told her. I was loyal as fuck to Madison. They say your first love is like your only love. I wouldn't know if that was true or not, because no one had yet to come in the way of me and Maddie.

"Oh...alright then..." Her eyes fell to the floor and if I didn't know any better I'd think she was about to cry. "Well, I won't hold you up. I guess I'll see you later. And hey, if you change your mind about the party, bring that *special someone*. I'd love to meet her...or him," she smiled before bopping off, her checkered uniform skirt blowing in the California breeze.

Damn, like that?

Looking over my shoulder at her as she walked away, I couldn't help but steal a quick glance at those toned, athletic legs of hers. They were long enough to climb, and they looked so smooth and soft to the touch. *Damn.* Soccer, chess and debating sure does the body well, I thought to myself. I could've been hit that if I wanted to, but like I said, I already had a special someone in my life, and she owned every part of me.

Once I reached the back of the school building, I pulled out my phone and hit my homeboy Drip. He answered on the second ring. "Fool, where yo ass at?" I grilled.

"Turn yo gay ass around."

I quickly turned around and found him smiling like a Cheshire Cat. He was rocking a white tee, baggy jeans, some scuffed up ass Chuck Taylors and a red bandana in his back pocket. His red Polo hat was on backwards. He was a Blood, who wore his colors proudly. At 6'2, Drip had a face full of gang-related tattoos, and was lanky as fuck in frame like a ball player. His real name was Deacon Tanner, but everyone called him Drip because he loved to sip codeine.

I always told the nigga he looked like Scottie Pippen in his prime because of his chinky eyes, slim face, hooked nose, and bird-like features. He used to have an older brother that looked just like him, but he passed away two years ago at the age of 21. He'd died in his sleep, high on lean, leaving Drip to look after their family. I never understood how he could keep drinking that shit even after his brother passed.

His mother was a prostitute, and legend had it, she was still selling pussy to anyone that could feed her drug addiction. She hardly ever came home, unless it was to wash her ass, and she pretty much forced Drip to take care of her other three children. He put clothes on their backs and food on the table, and for that, I really commended him. I was born into money, so I never had to work an honest day in my life. I didn't know what it was like to struggle because my parents were my providers, and they were damn good providers at that.

Drip and I came from two very different worlds, and we were pretty much polar opposites because of that. He was a high school drop-out, and I was on my way to graduating high school early *and* attending an ivy league college. We were like night and day, but it was our obvious differences that fueled our friendship.

"Who the fuck you callin' gay?" I asked, shoving the shit out of him. He was the closest thing I had to a brother, so we were always taking playful jabs at one another.

Drip dropped the blunt that was tucked behind his ear and went to pick it up, all the while cackling like a fucking hyena. Because of his bird-like features, he looked and sounded like a squawking hawk anytime he laughed. "Nigga, who the fuck you think I'm talkin' to? Stanley ass nigga. With that Harry Potter ass fit you got on! Nigga, you look gayer than a cock-flavored lollipop," Drip laughed. "Straight star boy shit."

Because I attended private school, I had no choice but to wear uniformed attire. White collared shirt, black tie, black slacks, and black dress shoes. It honestly didn't get much gayer than that.

I fake-yawned. "*Weeeeeaaaaakkkkk,*" I told him. "Bruh, you ready to make this move, or you wastin' more time on outdated jokes?"

"Depends on how much time we got."

Instead of answering, I headed towards my car, and Drip anxiously followed suit. I put this nigga on to all kinds of lick money, and he still ain't have a fucking whip.

"Damn, my nigga. Is that Valerie?"

"Yeah..."

"Man, I'm tryin' to give that white bitch some dick to spit on." He craned his neck to look at the busty white girl walking with her friends not too far from us.

"Easy, bruh. You stare any harder, your eyes might fall out your goofy ass head."

"Fuck that, bro, she could get worked," he said, licking his dark purple lips. Drip loved him some Snow Bunnies. He didn't fuck with black girls, at all. We'd been homies for years, and I'd never once seen him look in the direction of a sista. "Can't believe you never tried to beat the brakes off that bitch, homie."

I sucked my teeth. "Man, she a dub," I said, unimpressed.

"Keep it real, J Money. You couldn't handle the hoe if the bitch came with a manual," he laughed.

I just chuckled and shook my head at him.

"Damn, my nigga. You see the rack on that bitch??? Shit!" Drip motor-boated the air. "I'd drag my balls through broken glass just to stick my dick between them!" If he stared any harder, he was bound to get pepper-sprayed. "Bro, she gettin' donkey fucked if she ever gives me the chance." He was one of the most vulgar niggas I knew. "You think them titties real?"

"Is that a trick question?" I asked him.

"I know right. She still on the no pull out list," he laughed. "Man, on hood, these bitches make a nigga wish he'd never dropped out."

"Fuck school," I said, climbing into my Mercedes. "Shit's overrated."

Drip hopped in too, then fired up a blunt. My parents didn't like me hanging with him because they had to bail me out of jail when we got caught hotwiring cars in the mall parking lot a few years back. Although I was in private school and kept my head in the books, I was still bad as fuck. I don't know why. I guess it was in my DNA.

"*Stay away from niggas that ain't trying to do nothin' or be nothin',*" my dad would often say to me.

My mom would flip if she knew me and Drip were still cool, but ask me if I gave a fuck. Me and the nigga broke bread together, and he had been my solid since day one. As a matter of fact, he was one of the first friends I had made after moving to California.

Drip and I met 3 years ago, at a local basketball court in the hood and we'd been tight ever since. They say in the game all you need is a buck and a buddy. Drip was like my brother, regardless of my folks' personal opinions about him. They didn't know him, or his background, like I did.

"Yeah, you say that shit now, but you'll thank yourself later," he said. "Education is the most powerful weapon, young blood."

I snorted in amusement. "Okay, Brother Deacon."

"Misguided and undecided," he said, shaking his head.

"Fuck you, preaching ass nigga," I laughed.

He flipped me off. "To hell wit'chu, man, I'm just keepin' it a buck."

I was just about to pull out of the school parking lot, when my pops hit me with a text.

Yo! You on ya way to the crib? You trying to hoop?

My dad had recently returned from a business trip, and as always, was looking to spend some one-on-one time with his only son, but that shit would have to wait right now. Besides, what I was getting ready to do, I was doing for him.

I quickly texted back:

Went to Lee's place to chill. I'll be home later. Maybe we can hoop this weekend.

I then powered off my cellphone to get my mind right for the shit we were about to do. I wasn't in the habit of lying to my dad, but if I had to in order to protect him and his business interests, then so be it. A nigga had to do what he had to.

***

"So, is this the spot?" I asked, once we pulled up to a trap house in a sketchy part of Watts, California. There were a few clucks stumbling up the streets, and a few blocks down, a pack of old, ugly ass hookers hoping to catch a date. They looked like they hadn't washed their asses in ages, so I doubted they were having any luck with that.

If my parents knew I was on this side of town— they'd flip the fuck out. They knew that I was attracted to the allure of the streets, so they sheltered me and Journee in hopes that we'd never fall into that lifestyle. Sadly, it was all for nothing, seeing as how I still found my way to the streets.

Seated on the front porch steps of a worn-down, weather-beaten house with gated windows were a group of guys, who didn't look like they took kindly to new faces. And that's *exactly* what me and Drip were.

"Yeah, this is it." He ashed his blunt and put his double Styrofoam in the cup holder. He had me stop on the way over just so he could grab it. "My cousin said they be on the block hard-bodied. That nigga wasn't cappin'."

"Shit." I quickly tucked my uniform shirt in and straightened my tie, as I tried my best to look as unthreatening as I possibly could. "Well, we here now, homie. Might as well do this shit and do it right."

Drip tucked his diamond rosary chain in his shirt before he opened the door, and I couldn't help but laugh.

"Nigga ain't nobody gone steal that weak ass piece."

"Fuck you. I done caught ya ass eyeing it a fuckin' few times," he said.

"Yeah...to see if that shit was legit or not."

Drip gave me the finger, and together we climbed out of the car. The niggas on the porch looked ready to pop off at any moment. "Aye, B, you know these niggas? Ya'll know these niggas?" The apparent leader asked, sizing me up.

"Nah. But dem niggas ain't never did a drill or jumped off a porch in they life!" His homeboy with braids said, clowning us. "Niggas look square as fuck. I know *that* much!"

The apparent leader joined him in laughter. "Yo, who the fuck are these bozos?"

A fat ass, Pitbull-looking muthafucka beside him chuckled. "Bro, I ain't never seen these corn flake ass niggas before. They *must* be on the wrong coast."

I opened my mouth to respond. "I was actually—"

"Yo, pat these niggas down. These niggas lookin' real sus. What, ya'll opps or some shit?"

"Nah, bro, we ain't opps," I replied through my teeth.

His homie quickly stood to his feet and patted me and Drip down to ensure we weren't carrying any weapons. "They good, fam."

"The fuck is you square bear ass niggas doin' on my block? Ya'll muthafuckas wander to the wrong side of the hood, or some shit?" he asked.

"Maybe," I said. "That all depends on if you have what I'm looking for."

The leader lifted his shirt, flashing me his glock 19. "And what the fuck is that?" He sneered.

Drip was silent in the background, as he let me do all the talking. When it came to this street shit, I was the mouth and he was the muscle. "I don't want no trouble, bruh. My peoples pointed me in your direction. Said that you could give me what I needed."

"Yeah, lil nigga? And what the fuck is that?" he asked, in a nasty and overly-aggressive tone. It was like he was playing a game of my dick is bigger than yours. Like he was really some hot shot cocaine dealer, or some shit.

I didn't like getting bitched around by this nigga, but I had no choice but to roll with it for now. "I need some of that white shit. And a few of them crystals too," I said.

He spat at my kicks. "Nigga, what the fuck this look like to you? A drive-through window?? I don't know ya'll goofy, lame ass niggas. Why don't you do yaself a favor, and hop back in that Foreign before I give you a few rounds and show you how I'm *really* feelin'." He got all up in my face to show me he wasn't playing around.

I didn't bat an eyelash, or back down, despite the threat he'd made on my life. "I can pay twice what you regularly charge. Plus, I have references. Trust me, my nigga, I ain't on that fuck shit. I'm just tryin' to get right for this final I got. You feel me."

The apparent leader sized me up again as he contemplated whether or not to do business with me, or just straight up shoot my ass. "Okay then, who's this *reference* you speakin' on...?"

"Nick."

"Muthafucka, I know a lot of Nicks! Where the fuck is he from?"

"Ladera Heights. He's tall, got nappy ass dreads to the middle of his back and—"

"Shut the fuck up real quick," he said dismissively, while pulling out his cellphone.

I waited a few seconds, trying my hardest not to break a sweat right there in front of him as he placed the call.

"Yo, wuz good my nig. Aye, real quick, I got two funny ass niggas in my face right now, claimin' they know you. I'm pretty sure one is a long lost relative of the DeBarge family, and the other is some pterodactyl lookin' mofo with a big ass nose. Sound familiar, my G?" he asked, looking us over. "Speak up now, cuz I'm two seconds away from smokin' these weirdos, these niggas ain't valid in my hood, G." He spat at the ground in front of him, and his homeboy continued to grill me hard as fuck. "Oh yeah? A'ight then, cool." He hung up the phone. "I swear, he just saved ya'll clowns from getting the entire fuckin' clip," he said. "Now what the fuck do you want? You niggas done already wasted enough of my time."

"An eight ball, and a gram of the crystals," I ordered.

"A'ight then. Aye, B. Stay focused on these fruit of the loom ass niggas," he said to his homeboy. "Make sure they don't try any funny shit."

"No doubt," he said, mugging the fuck out of me. The leader disappeared in the trap, and I noticed two other guys inside through the screen door.

"You must go to one of them fancy ass prep schools, huh," his homie said, looking me up and down.

"Somethin' like that," I muttered.

"So, who are your folks? Are they famous or some shit? You *look* like the kid of a famous person," he noted, taking in my neat, tidy, and clean-cut appearance.

Ever since we moved to Cali, people always assumed my parents were famous. I never understood why. "Somethin' like that..."

The leader finally walked back out, before his friend could further investigate and served me. "Here you go, Bobby DeBarge. Don't take it all at once."

I quickly paid him and told him that I wouldn't.

"A'ight now, get the fuck outta my hood," he said, waving us off. "Ya'll muthafuckas makin' my block hot. And aye!" he called out to me. "Next time, come by yaself. We don't need no fuckin' goofies," he said, taking a petty, last-minute shot at Drip.

Drip kept his mouth closed, as he and I hopped back in the Benz and pulled off before they changed their minds and shot our asses just because. Luckily, Nick came through, but best believe, I had to break him off, so that he kept his fucking mouth closed about the shit we were about to get into later on.

"Man, ya boy a dub," Drip said, firing up his blunt again. "Anyway, how many niggas you see inside?"

"Only two. So that makes five in total. Could be more though. I guess we'll find out tonight."

Drip reached behind him and grabbed a loaded Uzi from under the seat. "I guess we will..."

3
JOURNEE

I closed the school locker and was happy as hell that I was finally getting a break from this place. I couldn't stand the private academy my mom had me in, or the stupid Sailor Moon uniform I had to wear. Plus, there were no cute boys in my school. I bet my mother would leap for joy if she knew that.

I would've given anything to go to public school. It was much more fun; the gossip was juicier and the boys were hotter. Don't get me wrong, the boys in my school were rich, but they all had about as much personality as a cardboard box. To put it short, they were lame as fuck.

Speaking of losers, my long-time arch nemesis approached me looking to start some mess. "Oh my God, Journee, are those last year's pair of Louis Vuitton boots?" Abigail asked, eyeing my shoes. She was a bougie ass white bitch who thought her shit didn't stink. Her dad was some big-named heart surgeon who gave her everything she wanted, and she never missed an opportunity to rub it in the other kid's faces.

Since I was rocking the monogram combo boots with the LV logos from last year, I became an easy target for her. While they were old, they were still super cute and comfy.

"Oh shit, they are!" Her friend Gina laughed. "They're so last year!"

You'd think these bitches would have better things to do now that it was Spring Break, but apparently not. "Maybe I don't wanna follow every trend," I shrugged.

"Or maybe you can't *afford* to," Abigail spat.

Suddenly, I snapped. "Or maybe you'd better get out my face, before I shove these size eights up your ass," I told her.

Abigail rolled her eyes and walked off with her homegirl. She wasn't trying to take that L. I didn't care if I was in school. These hands were rated E for everyone. After she left, I secured the combination lock on my locker. That was another reason why I hated this school. The kids were so snobby and materialistic since their parents were all filthy rich. I guess, in a sense, I belonged here.

Although I'd told Abigail off, I had a sudden urge to hit the mall and go shopping. *I can't have these hoes trying to flex up on me. I need to upgrade.* "Ugh. I wish Letitia was here so I'd have someone to hit the mall with," I complained.

She was out of the country with her family tending to her sick grandmother. Letitia was my mom's best friend's daughter. She wasn't my best friend per se, but she was cool to hang out with, and my go-to partner in crime. I refused to call her my BFF because we fought like cats and dogs. Truthfully, I didn't really have a lot of friends but I was still popular in school, because everyone knew my parents helped fund the campaigns of California's newest mayor. Abigail was the *only* bitch in school who gave me grief.

"Don't worry about them bored ass bitches. Personally, I think the shoes are dope," a boy standing beside my locker said.

I'd never seen him in school before. I was certain of it, because if I did I'd remember. He was really cute, with soft brown skin, slanted eyes, and full, pretty pink lips. His hair was long and braided into a ponytail and he had a Stussy skull cap pulled low on his head. Baggy jeans hung off his waist, and on his feet were a pair of Vans. He had a white hoodie on with a naked white woman printed on the front. That let me know right away he wasn't a student because he was violating every dress code policy in the book.

Before I could say anything, a white boy walked up to him and handed him a small wad of cash. In exchange, Slanted Eyes handed him a small bag of coke. As sad as it was, I was used to seeing drug exchanges go down right in front of me—in *and* out of school.

After collecting his fare, Slanted Eyes walked off towards the school exit. His drug dealing ass was soliciting and I *would've* ratted if it wasn't for him being so gotdamn fine. Suddenly, in that brief moment, I realized why I didn't like any of the boys in my school. It was because I was attracted to bad boys.

4
JUSTIN

Glancing in the rear mirror several times, I made sure we weren't being pursued as I headed towards the city. The street life kept me on my toes and I never ever wanted to get caught slipping. After verifying that we weren't being tailed, I pulled out a switchblade, cut into the small plastic bag, and rubbed a sample of the product on my gums.

Frowning in disappointment, I looked over at my boy. "Yo, this shit ain't even good, bro," I told Drip. "If these niggas were gonna slang dope in my father's hood, the least they could do is slang good dope." My father's shit was on point. He had the best filth in the streets. I knew because I'd snuck and tried some of it when I was only 13. These small-time dealers selling this bullshit felt like the *ultimate* disrespect to me, my father, and his legacy. Them niggas *had* to go!

"Let me try it," Drip said, taking the bag of dope from me. He sprinkled a little bit on the back of his hand and did a bump. "Shit." He rubbed his nose, which was probably on fire from snorting such bad blow. "You ain't bullshittin', man, this shit is straight garbo!" he said angrily. "We should've burnt that nigga right then and there, man. Ole cocky ass nigga. Aye, lemme see them crystals real quick."

I handed him the small plastic bag containing crack cocaine.

"Nah, see this shit 'posed to be shinin' like fish scales. It's like they cut it with fentanyl or some shit."

"Man, that shit is thraga!!! Straight garbage," I said. "And these hoe ass niggas got the nerve to be selling this shit in *my* father's hood. Hell nah. We gotta go lay these pussy ass niggas down."

"Aye, I already got the hot boys on standby. You know they ready for the bullshit, bruh," Drip said. He did another line to make sure he wasn't tripping the first time. "Man, what the fuck *is* this shit?"

"It's a one-way ticket to God's doorstep. That's what it is."

"*And* we need to find they muthafuckin' suppliers and lay them bitches down too! I'm talkin' hog-tied and hands burned down to the muthafuckin' bone!" Drip was an even bigger wild card than me, and he'd been bodying niggas for twice as long. Before we started massacring my father's competition, he and his brother used to be jack boys.

Most people could look at him and tell that he was rotten from the inside out, but for me it was the total opposite. No one would ever know just from looking at me that I was on that fuck shit. I was light-skinned, a pretty boy with a baby face and I carried myself like an ordinary nigga. However, my life was *far* from ordinary. In my downtime, I went looking for dealers that were bold enough to slang dope in my father's turf and disposed of them niggas. For two whole years, I'd been hiding this shit from my folks. They hadn't the slightest clue that I was 10 toes deep in this street shit.

My father was a real trap legend. After hearing about all of the incredible and heroic things he did to protect me, Journee, and Mom, I knew that I wanted to follow in his footsteps. I figured I could help by wiping out the competition for him. If there was no competition, there would be no enemies, and my father could continue to sell his product with no one dipping into his profits. If I had to clap a nigga to make that happen, then so be it.

Drip was my right-hand, my partner in crime, and the nigga that helped me street-sweep. He was from Compton, he was crazy as fuck, and he already had mad bodies up under his belt at only 17. Drip showed me he was down early on, so I stayed loyal to the ones who had a proven track record with me. In return, he got 25% of whatever profits we made, and he was able to put food on the table for his family and loved ones.

So far, we managed to keep our heads above water. Shit was going smooth, and we'd never had any real problems. At least, not yet anyway. However, if we stayed on top of our game and moved strategically then I truly believed we would be alright.

After we got back to the city, I switched seats with Drip and let him drive us to the apartment his cousins lived in on the outskirts of Los Angeles. They were just as crazy as him, if not more, and they were always armed to the teeth and prepared for whatever shit we brought their way. I swear, I had some real killers and drillers riding for me. This game was nothing to play with. It couldn't be any scary shit going on. If you chose to live this life, then you *had* to know what you were doing, as well as the niggas on your team.

I planned to push the envelope until I cleaned every street, every suburb and every borough of all the posers and wanna-be dealers. I was driven by a sense of purpose that was almost terrifying. I would show my father that I didn't need school or an education. The streets would teach me everything I needed to know. I was born and bred to run his empire one day, and he would finally respect me as a man and stop treating me like a fucking kid.

The sun was just beginning to set when we pulled up to his cousins' building. They were already walking out, obviously ready to hit this lick.

"Aye, wuz poppin', scrap?"

"Wuz good, beloved?"

Chris and Nahmir hit me with the gang lingo, as I dapped them up once they came outside. "Shit, movin' and groovin'," I told them.

Chris was actually a female, and her real name was Christina, but she looked so much like a nigga that no one would ever know it. Nahmir was hood as fuck, but the nigga was smart as hell. He was into tech shit, and had even obtained an Associates in Mechanical Engineering, but he never did anything with it. He preferred being a stick-up kid.

Both of them were dressed in all black from their heads down to their feet, with black bandanas shielding their identities. They were bloods too, and wild as fuck. They were also the type of niggas you *wanted* on your team when it came time to do some fuck shit. Drip had texted them on the way over to let them know what was good, so they were all set to go once we pulled up.

"Aye, check this out, straight to the business. Them Watts niggas gotta go," I said. "They pushin' that trash ass dope on my father's turf, and you already know that's no-*bueno*. I gotta push up on these niggas. Let 'em know shit's serious out here," I told them, with a deadpan expression on my baby face.

Chris dapped me up again. "You already know how we comin'. You already know how we get down. We smokin' niggas like Backwoods. This ain't no muthafuckin' game," she said, ready to put a hole in someone's head. She reminded me of Snoop from the HBO series *The Wire*. She even looked a lot like her with her light skin, cherubic face, and long cornrows. "Whoever ain't with us gone either get down or lay down."

"Hell, you already know we 'bout business," Nahmir chipped in. "Let's go knock these niggas off."

Luckily, I was kicking it with the niggas that was *really* doing this shit. A lot of niggas were just talk, but not them. They were all about action. "Say less. Say less, do more." I quickly hopped out the Benz and popped the trunk.

Underneath the floorboard, inside a Goyard bag, was even more weapons from my gun connect. He was a young nigga from Oakland that kept me right. He had all the hottest, latest shit. Real guns that did *real* damage. After sliding on a black hoodie and ski mask, I kicked my dress shoes off and replaced them with a pair of dirty trainers, that I usually played ball in, and grabbed a chopper with the extendo clips.

"Boy, that ain't no toy," Chris laughed.

"Right. He might jump out the window and hang himself with that one," Drip instigated. Them niggas loved to clown me since I was from the suburbs. They always thought I couldn't handle shit.

"You might wanna rock with the nine-shot, homie," she teased, holding up a small ass handgun.

"Nigga, get the fuck outta here with that lil' pocket rocket. I need a nasty ass machine. Big boy shit," I said, pulling on a pair of plastic gloves to keep my fingerprints from being left at the scene of the crime. I couldn't afford to get bumped again. My parents would flip the fuck out if I ever went back to jail. After the gloves were on, I filled the cartridges and loaded them into the automatic. I planned on laying down every one of them niggas with this shit.

I ain't gone never let off these pussy ass niggas' heads. I'mma kill every single one of these fuck niggas. If you sold drugs on my father's turf then that was an automatic death sentence for your ass. Point blank period.

"Man, let's hurry up and get this shit over with," Drip said, grabbing his stomach. "That lean got me constipated than a bitch."

Chris and Nahmir grabbed their weapons of choice—a Colt .45 and MAK-90—and together we all piled into Nahmir's black 2002 Acura. I couldn't pull back up in the hood in my Benz, because that would only make us hot. I didn't need anything fucking up this play. We had to be on point if we wanted this shit to work. One wrong move could make all this shit go south, and I wasn't trying to take my last breath before seeing Madison—or before my mom's 37th birthday.

I swear, every time we did this shit, I found myself wondering if I'd make it home alive, but it was a risk that I took time and time again. I guess you could say killing and getting down on muthafuckas had become somewhat addictive. Sure, it was about my father's legacy, but it also made me feel like a man, at the end of the day.

"Hold up! I almost forgot something!" I said, mere seconds before they pulled off.

Hopping out the car, I ran back to the Benz, popped the trunk and grabbed my shit. Once I was set, I jumped back in the whip with my small, yet violent clique and together we braved the night, preparing ourselves for yet another lick. I prayed that everything went accordingly. We'd gone over the plan several times, so that everyone knew how to play their part. After all, good instructions equaled good production. And a team with no instructions would only lead to self-destruction.

You see, a lot of niggas talked this street shit, but a young nigga was really out here—good grades and all. I was only 16, but active in these streets. I'd be damned if *anyone* interfered with my father's business—which would one day be mine. I knew if my dad ever found out what I was doing, he wouldn't approve of it, but the shit I was doing was all for him.

5
MADISON

"Gooooddd afternoon, ladies and gentlemen, I'm pleased to announce that we'll be descending into Los Angeles shortly. About twenty or so minutes, give or take," the pilot said on the intercom. "Once again, thank you all for flying with South African Airways, and we look forward to accommodating you in the near future."

The passengers were so happy to finally land after a grueling 20-hour flight that everyone broke out into applause.

Leaning over in my seat, I looked out of the window at the California landscape below. I was so damn happy to be out of Ghana, I wanted to backflip. Africa was cool and all, but there was nothing like home; and home would forever be America.

I was so gracious that Auntie Cameron was taking me in for Spring Break, that I reminded myself to kiss her when I saw her. My life was so boring; my father was so strict, I didn't have any sisters and I was always stuck watching my bad ass brothers, Aseem and KJ. My dad was always working and my step-mom owned a restaurant in the city. They both lived hectic lives, so I always left to baby-sit and I hated it.

At first, I used to love having two little brothers, but that was when they were babies, and cute, and innocent. Now they were big and bad as fuck. When they weren't popping out of boxes and closets to surprise me, they were putting toothpaste in my shampoo and whip-creaming my face in my sleep. They were practical jokers, but sadly, the joke was always on me. I loved my brothers, but they could be so damn annoying. That's why I was happy to get a break from them every once in a while, but I knew that wouldn't last long. My dad had already agreed to start letting them travel with me once they got a little older. I dreaded the day.

I can't wait to find some legit fun shit to get into, I thought.

I was on the swim team in school, but that was about as much excitement as I got in my boring and meek life. My father kept a tight leash on me because he was scared that I'd fuck around, get pregnant and lose my scholarship. His worst fear was seeing me wind up like my biological mother, who was still serving time in a maximum-security facility in Georgia.

Milena had gotten pregnant with me young, then ended up falling for a pimp, and from there, her entire life went downhill. My dad wanted to see me go to college and be somebody. He wanted me to be his perfect little princess forever, but I was a far cry from it.

Pulling out my pack of cigarettes, I stuck a Newport behind my ear and counted the minutes down to the time I'd be able to smoke. Smoking cigarettes was a nasty habit I'd picked up from my dad. And even though I secretly smoked behind his back, it had yet to impede with my swimming abilities. I knew that I'd have to quit should it ever affect my performance.

"Hey, can I bum a smoke?" The woman to my left asked.

"Sure."

I let her take a cigarette, then shoved the pack back in my purse before I ended up donating to everyone in my cabin. It wasn't easy acquiring a pack of smokes when you were only 17. Pulling my phone out, I opened Instagram, and went to Justin's page. I stalked his photos like I always did and noticed he'd gotten a few comments since the last time I checked. Some fan girl named Aria seemed to stalk him more than I did, and that really bothered the fuck out of me. On quite a few of his pics, she'd left hearts and kissing faces.

"Who the fuck is this bitch? See, I'mma fuck him up just for that," I said to myself. Justin knew I was selfish when it came to him. It was already hard enough being in a long-distance relationship. Now I had to worry about some bird pushing up on my boyfriend. "I know how to fix his ass," I mumbled under my breath.

I added a pic to my Instagram of me and one of the guys from my swim team. I figured Justin would see it and get jealous. I loved Justin, but I also loved being petty. My step-mom always told me I was vindictive like my dad. Smiling at my own childish antics, I bit my finger and looked back out of the window. I couldn't wait to land in California. And more importantly, I couldn't wait to find some trouble to get into. My life in Ghana was so damn boring; whenever I came to the states I was just looking for action. Little did I know, trouble would soon find me.

6
JUSTIN

When we pulled back up to the trap house in Watts, I noticed the same group of niggas hanging out on the steps, smoking, laughing, and talking shit without a care in the world. They had the trap jumping, and hadn't even left their post, regardless of the fact that it was now nighttime. Sticking my chopper out the lowered window, I was the first one to start dumping.

"YA'LL BITCH ASS NIGGAS AIN'T ON SHIT!!!!!"

POP! POP! POP! POP! POP! POP! POP! POP! POP!

Shell casings dropped as I emptied the clip. I hit cars, trees, the barred windows of the trap and the fat fuck that had patted me down earlier, as well as two other cats that were sitting with them on the porch. My aim was impeccable since Drip and I frequented the gun rang.

POP! POP!

One of his shooters started firing in our direction, but they hit everything but us.

POP! POP! POP! POP! POP! POP! POP! POP! POP!

I let off several rounds, hitting the shooter and some other cat behind him. I didn't give a fuck who died. *Everybody* had to go! "Aye, look out for the law," I told Chris.

"You know I got'chu."

The guy who served me bolted inside the trap, and me, Nahmir, and Drip jumped out of the whip and sprayed up the block. We were determined to hunt down and kill every single one of them.

As we approached the front door, I noticed one of my victims still breathing, though barely. "Please, man...don't," he begged, his voice garbled in agony. Without a drop of remorse in his heart, Drip filled his face with several slugs.

POP! POP! POP! POP! POP!

"Oh, you runnin' now, bitch ass nigga?!" I hollered, sprinting up the cracked stone steps of the trap. I was the first to enter the old, worn down house since I was the leader of my terror squad. It had finally come down to leader vs leader. "You runnin' now?!" I laughed, changing the clip in my chopper. "Niggas always wanna show out till a nigga pull that thing out. You was talkin' all that big shit earlier!" I reminded him. "Now wuz good???" POP! POP! POP! POP! POP! I shot the ceiling for added effect, and to scare his ass out of hiding. "WHERE THE FUCK YOU AT?!" I was in straight kill mode as I searched for him. Unfortunately, I didn't see his ass anywhere, and I almost thought he dipped out the back door, until he popped out of nowhere.

"Here I am, fuck nigga!" He yelled, unloading his shotgun on me.

BOOM!

A hail of bullets struck me right in the chest!

7
CAMERON

"What's wrong, babe? Everything good?" I asked my husband, after noticing that he wasn't as into Sports Center as he was before.

Perched next to him, I had a book in my hand and my reading glasses on. Jude kept telling me that I should get LASIK once my eyesight began to slowly degenerate, but I hated the idea of someone slicing into my cornea— no matter his success rate with the procedure. Besides, I only needed my glasses to read, I could still function in life without them. My eyes weren't *that* bad. They just weren't as sharp as they were in my college years.

Jude sighed deeply and rubbed his chin. "I hit up Justin not too long ago to see if he wanted to shoot some hoops. Nigga said he'd rather chill with his friends," Jude admitted in a defeated tone. I could see the hurt in his eyes, and the disappointment of coming second best to Justin's friends once again.

"Well, you know he's getting older now." I then quoted him a passage from Corinthians. "When I was a child, I spoke like a child, I thought like a child, I reasoned like a child. When I became a man, I gave up childish ways. He's not a kid anymore, Jude."

"He's always gonna be my kid, no matter how old he gets," Jude stated with conviction. The skin around his eyes wrinkled a little as his brows knitted together. He was so damn sexy whenever he got worked up.

At 38, Jude had long given up the dreads lifestyle, and opted for a more clean-cut look. He had a low fade with the sides neatly tapered, and sprinkled throughout his head was a few silver hairs. I loved them because they represented wisdom and maturity. Jude had come a long way as a man and as a husband.

I thought about mentioning the journal, but decided against it. "Well, do you want me to have a talk with him when he gets back—"

"No, no," Jude quickly waved me off. "You're right. I guess I gotta respect the fact that he's getting older. He's not a little boy anymore. I just miss the days when he was...less independent, you know? He'd always be up under me, watching every move I made, with this proud look on his face." He smiled and there was a faraway look in his eyes as he reminisced. "That kid, I was like a hero to him."

"You still are, baby," I told him, weaseling my way into his lap. "And you're *my* hero too." I grinded against his erection.

Jude moaned and ran his fingers through my pixie cut, then kissed me. I was just about to give him the ride of his life when the doorbell suddenly rang. "Looks like we'll have to put a rain check on this," I said, climbing off his lap.

Jude growled like an animal, then squeezed and slapped my ass all aggressive-like. "You damn right we will," he said.

Even though a bitch was creeping up on 40, I still looked like I was in my mid 20s. I had a small waist, supple breasts and ass that only seemed to expand with age. Thankfully, it was the only place I put on weight. I worked out and did yoga four times a week to maintain my girlish figure *and* to keep my husband from having a wandering eye. As his wife, I lived by 2 simple rules to ensure his happiness: Keep his stomach full and his balls empty.

Padding barefoot to the front of the house, I checked the security monitor to see who was at the door. It was Conway, the head of our security team and my personal driver. I almost forgot that I asked him to swing by and run me to the airport. After inputting the security code, I opened the door and greeted him. "Hey, Conway."

Journee quickly brushed past him, carrying several shopping bags on her arms. She had a pair of Gucci sunglasses on, and was looking like a Real Housewife of LA. "And who told you that it was okay to hit the mall, missy? You check in with me first once you get out of school. You know that."

"Really, mom? I'm almost fifteen," she reminded me. She'd attended private schools for most of her life so she talked extremely proper.

Journee was a spitting image of me, right down to her attitude and demeanor, but a shade lighter in skin tone. She had a head full of naturally curly light brown hair with blond undertones, and she usually wore it in a fluffy fro, or piled high on top of her head. When it came to looks, she didn't take after Jude at all, and I was pissed when he admitted that he'd taken a paternity test behind my back, when she was first born. But that was neither here nor there.

"That doesn't change the fact that you need to ask me for permission. Fifteen don't make you grown," *I* reminded *her*.

"I was with Conway. I don't see what the big deal is," she whined. "Anyway, Justin's only two years older than me, and you damn sure don't make *him* ask for permission."

That's because Justin isn't an under-aged, overdeveloped, teenage girl. That's what I wanted to tell her, but instead I kept it to myself. "Hey, watch that tongue, young lady," I warned her.

Journee sucked her teeth and walked off with an attitude. I swear, that little girl was something else. Ever since she'd got some hips and ass, she'd been smelling herself.

"Afternoon, Mrs. Patterson," Conway greeted with a deep-dimpled smile. "If it's any consolation, I can assure you, she was in good hands."

I looked at him and shook my head. These kids of mine were going to be the death of me. "I know she was. And I'm sorry, how are you?"

"Can't complain. And you?"

I sighed dramatically. "I'm as well as can be expected."

At 6"2, Conway was tall and ball-head with honey-colored skin. He reminded me of Chi-town rapper Common, and even had a similar deep voice that sounded like melting butter to the ears. "You all set to go to the airport?" He asked.

He looked classy and dapper in a Ted Baker London suit, with a black silk tie. He looked like a hit man or a member of the mafia; not like someone who was paid to chaperone and protect my family on the regular. He'd been working for us for over a year now, and the kids absolutely adored him. He even attended school functions with me whenever Jude was out of town. He was like another member of the family.

"Yes. Let me just grab my purse and shoes."

"Of course, Mrs. Patterson. I'll be right here waiting for you."

"Journee, do you wanna ride with me to the airport to pick up Madison?" I called out to her.

"No, I'm gonna straighten up for when she gets here." That really meant that she was going to be on the phone with her little friends, and didn't want me overhearing her conversation.

"Alright then." I turned to walk away, then stopped mid-stride. "Did you see how traffic was looking?" I asked Conway.

He quickly peeled his eyes off my ass to meet my gaze, and cleared his throat. "Uh, yeah. The city's a bit congested, but don't worry. I'll just take an alternate route. We should get there in no less than half an hour."

"Excellent." I walked off to fetch my belongings, and I was almost certain that I felt his eyes on my ass once again. I knew that he was only just a man, at the end of the day, but I still made a mental note to have a talk with him later on about boundaries. After grabbing my purse, phone and key fob, I went into the living room to let my husband know that I was headed to the airport to pick up Madison. Unfortunately, Jude was preoccupied with his own affairs.

"What do you mean you misplaced the books? Did you look everywhere??? Okay, okay. Calm down. Right now, I need you to relax. Take a deep breath, hang up and call me on my business line."

"Is everything okay?" I asked, once he hung up the phone.

He ran a hand over his weary face. "Eve lost the ledger," he said frustrated.

"What???" The ledger was filled with all of his accounts, transactions and cocaine sales. If it just so happened to fall into the wrong hands, the damaged could be irreparable. "Are you serious?! See, that's what happens when you let a child in grown folks' business."

Jude sighed and pinched the bridge of his nose. "Not right now, Cam. I got enough shit on my plate, without you adding to it."

Jude already knew how I felt about his little 22-year old female accountant. It was like Essence all over again, but he swore up and down it was just business between them, and that he'd never step out on our marriage again. Eve was King and Evelyn's only child, and since he'd left his empire to Jude, he felt it was only right to give his daughter a position in the company. For those who don't remember, King was the nigga who had Jude, and his cousin Aso, stealing vehicles for his intricate car theft ring some 13 years ago. Enlisting Eve as his accountant was Jude's way of paying homage to King. Her father laid the foundation for him, so he felt like he couldn't leave his family hanging. Thankfully, Jude left the car business alone, since it wasn't much money in it anymore. Now he was partners with Soul, and they'd completely taken over the drug game.

"Alright. I'mma leave it alone, for now," I said, pecking him on the cheek.

I went to walk off, but Jude grabbed my arm and tugged me back to him. "Nah, you gone leave it alone for good." He kissed my lips. "You're my wife, the apple of my eye, the center of my universe. There's nothing another bitch could do for me that you haven't already done."

***

Opening my oversized Louis bag, I pulled out my foundation powder, and lightly touched up my face. I didn't want to walk in the airport looking a hot ass mess. This was LA, so you never knew who you would run into. Next, I applied a thin coat of MAC lipstick. It was a warm burgundy color that really complimented my cinnamon skin tone.

Screwing the cap back on, I tossed it in my bag and snapped it shut. As soon as I looked up, I caught Conway staring at me through the rearview mirror. The second our eyes connected, he quickly looked away in embarrassment. *Yeah, we'll definitely have to sit down to discuss boundaries*, I reminded myself. Don't get me wrong, Conway was fine as fuck. But I was a happily married woman and almost 13 years his senior. There was nothing he could do for me, other than drive me from point A to point B.

"Careful now, Conway. The last security guard we had couldn't keep his eyes off of me either," I told him. "And it didn't end too well for him." I thought about Jag and all of the bullshit he had put me and my family through. I would've hated for this to be a repeat.

Conway just laughed. "I hear you, Mrs. Patterson," he said. "I hear you loud and clear."

8
CONWAY

She was my boss's wife. The significant other to the man who signed my paychecks and still, that wasn't enough to keep my eyes from wandering, every so often. I couldn't help it. Her clothes shouldn't have clung to her curves the way they did. She shouldn't have been so fucking sexy and irresistible.

Damn.

What the hell have I gotten myself into, I asked for the hundredth time.

My grip on the steering wheel tightened as I fought to focus on the road and not on the bulge in my pants. I swear, every time I got around Cameron, I seemed to lose all rationality—and ability to control my erections.

Sure, she was older than me and married to a nigga that could easily have my dick severed, but that just wasn't enough to keep me from wanting her. Everything about Cam was a turn on for me. That pretty peanut butter complexion, that Hollywood smile, that short but sexy pixie cut she rocked, and her smell. Good god, don't get me started on her smell. Her perfumes always smelled edible, and I couldn't help but wonder if her feminine fragrance was just as inviting. Suddenly, eating her pussy jumped to the forefront of my mind, and I had to quickly clear my throat to get the dangerous thought out of my head.

"Is everything okay?" Cameron asked from the backseat.

"Yeah, just got some dust or lint trapped in my throat," I lied.

Cameron grabbed a bottled water from the car cooler and passed it to me.

"'Preciate it." I took the bottle from her, cracked it open, and took a swig. *Damn.* I swear, she had a player unfolding.

What the fuck did I sign up for? If I didn't get a hold of my shit and quick, then my lust was bound to get me killed, or worse...exposed.

9
JUSTIN

"Quit all that muthafuckin' hollerin' and shit!!!" Chris yelled to the nigga locked in the trunk.

Instead of killing the leader, we robbed and torched his trap, then took his ass hostage so that we could find his source. Not only were we bodying drug dealers, we were knocking off their suppliers as well. The nigga in the trunk must've thought shit was sweet because he continued thumping and calling out for help.

Chris punched the seat as if he could feel it. "Keep fuckin' wit' me!!! Boy, I'll bust ya ass right now, nigga!"

Thankfully, he finally quieted down. I was happy too, because he was starting to give me a fucking headache.

"J Money, you good?" Drip asked, after noticing me rub my chest for the tenth time that night.

If it wasn't for me making them stop so that I could get my bulletproof vest, I'd be a dead man. Other than some minor bruising and soreness, I hadn't sustained any real injuries. If it wasn't for the vest, I'd be on my way to hell with the rest of the niggas we just laid down. "Yeah, I'm straight. Chest sore than a bitch though."

"Aww, man, he good," Nahmir said, cruising through the streets of Los Angeles. "You already know dat nigga Killa J don't play! That shot ain't do shit but put a lil' hair on his chest," he laughed.

"That nigga can take a bullet better than a bitch can take dick," Chris cackled, grabbing her crotch, like she actually had one.

"Nigga a man now," Nahmir laughed.

"Nah, he ain't a man till he gets his dick wet," Drip corrected him. "And unfortunately, my nigga J, is *not* about that life," he laughed.

"Damn, my nigga, is that facts though?" Nahmir asked, all wide eyed in disbelief.

"Complete fiction," I said.

"Nah. That shit is all facts, no printer," Drip laughed.

"Don't tell me you out here laying niggas down, and never even laid down with a bitch before," Chris said.

"That's facts," Drip said, continuing to instigate.

"Nigga, you smokin' rocks. I've laid down with bitches. I've laid down with plenty bitches," I lied.

"Nigga, you big cappin'. You ain't official," Chris said. "When the last time you had a bitch? Keep it a hunnid."

"Blood, I been knowin' you for years, and you ain't *never* talked about pipin' a bitch a day in ya life!" Drip said. "Do you even know what pussy *look* like, my nigga?"

"Nigga, eat a bag of dicks," I told him. "Of course, I know what pussy looks like. It looks just like them fuckin' lips of yours flappin'!"

"Poindexter ass nigga never hit no bitch," Nahmir laughed. "Nigga still beatin' his chicken."

"What about that Aria bitch? Yo, you never killed that shit?" Drip inquired.

"Yo, get the fuck off my dick mileage, nigga! Why the fuck do I gotta report back to ya'll asses every time I smash a slut? Is *you* fuckin', my nigga?" I asked Drip.

"Man, you already know how I give it up," he laughed.

"Yeah, whatever."

Drip opened his mouth to respond, but the sudden wailing of police sirens cut him off.

"Oh, shit!" Chris yelled. "Oh, shit! It's Five-Oh!!!"

We all started panicking.

Of all fucking nights, the pigs were actually pursuing us! The nigga in the trunk must've heard the sirens too, because he quickly started thrashing and calling out for help again. I was just about to lose my shit when the squad car zoomed right past us. They weren't coming for our asses at all. They were on their way to a completely unrelated incident.

Damn, that was close.

"Alright now, I don't wanna bust you wit' this thing!" Chris hollered, waving her strap. "Shut that shit up back there, pussy ass nigga! I'm not gone say it again!"

***

"I'mma ask you one more fuckin' time!" *WHAM*! I smacked him in the face with my gun so hard, I felt his eye socket crack. "Who the fuck is you coppin' the birds from?!" We'd been at this shit for the last hour, but the hoe ass nigga wouldn't rat.

"I swear, man..." He spit out two of his teeth. "I swear, I don't know who he is!"

"I say we put 'em back in the trunk. Let that muthafucka sit in there a month straight, or till whenever he's ready to talk," Chris said.

"The trunk though?" Nahmir said, looking at her like she was crazy.

Chris shrugged. "Well, beatin' the brakes off the nigga ain't accomplishing' much of shit," she said. "I always thought starvation was one of the cruelest forms of torture."

"Nigga, you don't know shit about torturing people," Drip said. "And neither does Justin. That's why this fuck nigga ain't talkin'. With them baby ass punches, nigga. Who the fuck taught you how to swing? A kindergartner?" he asked me.

"By all means, my nigga, have at it," I said, stepping out of the way. "Since you talkin' big shit."

"Man, back up and watch a champ work." Drip walked up, grabbed the drug dealer's hand and snapped two of his fingers back. He cried out in agonizing pain. "That's for talkin' 'bout my nose earlier, pussy nigga! Now tell us who the fuckin' plug is!!!!"

"I swear, man! On my son, on everything, I don't know the nigga! He be havin' these triplet niggas drop the dope off. It's three of them mufuckas—they look the exact same! They make all the runs for him! We never see the supplier! That's on everything I love!"

He sounded sincere enough, but Drip still broke another finger for the hell of it.

"I SWEAR TO GOD I'M TELLING THE TRUTH!!!" he cried, snot pouring from his nostrils. It mixed in with his tears and he looked so damn pathetic; the total opposite of how he looked earlier when he was talking all that shit.

"Well, that ain't much help," Nahmir said.

I cracked the guy in his head with the butt of my gun, knocking him out cold. We couldn't risk killing him now just in case he *was* lying.

"Fuck it. We'll try this again another day," I said. "In the meantime, I could use a drink. Who's with me?"

"Hell yeah, blood! I'm wit' that. Now you talkin' my language," Drip said. That nigga was forever trying to get fucked up.

***

"Bro, this shit knock." I turned up the music to the mixtape we were listening to, once we got back into Nahmir's ride. I prayed that they dropped the topic of my dick mileage, because the shit had made me hella uncomfortable, but Nahmir just wouldn't let up.

"Nah, fuck that shit, bruh." Nahmir turned the music back down. He must've sensed that I was trying to avoid the subject altogether. "I gotta know, big dawg," he said. "Is you out here layin' wood or nah?"

"Look, I don't give a fuck what you think. I don't got shit to prove to you, dick mouth McGee," I said, pouting like a kid.

"You a nut ass nigga, B," Chris laughed. "Just answer the question!"

Nahmir's eyes lit up with amusement. "Fuck all that bullshit, bruh. We're getting your dick wet tonight!!!" Nahmir said excitedly.

He got off on the exit and weaved through a couple streets until he reached Skid Row, where a block of rundown hookers was waiting for a date. I could've smacked the fuck out of him when he stopped in front of a crackhead who looked like she'd been on that shit for eight days strong. The bitch's lips were so dry, if she smiled her shit would bleed.

"Aye!" Nahmir rolled his window down and called out to her. "What's the ticket, mamí? My man needs to get right."

She smiled, showing off her rotten, fucked up grill. I swear, I wouldn't have put my dick near her yuck mouth if someone paid me to! I could only imagine the foul, venereal diseases she was carrying in that bitch alone.

"Twenty. But I'll fuck the whole crew for forty," she said. Her breath smelled like a bag of dicks, and the bitch made my balls itch.

"Hell nah, man! The fuck is you on?!" I asked him.

"Yeah, you insultin' my man," Drip agreed, sipping his lean.

"Yeah, he needs to get his dick wet. Not have that bitch fall off," Chris laughed.

"Whatever, man. She can spit all over my mic any day," Nahmir said, licking his lips.

"Man, we need to hit that strip joint downtown," Drip suggested. "There's a much better variety of bitches than the cock-junkies on this block."

"Yeah, these ain't nothin' but a bunch of nut buckets," Chris agreed.

"Shit, I'm down," I said.

"That sounds like the move."

Chris tossed a couple coins at her as we pulled off, and she ran after the car cursing us out as we all laughed. It felt so good to be young, dumb, and reckless. Sadly, I never realized that shit would eventually get us caught up. Too many good times could easily lead to a bad time. Instead of realizing that, I had deluded myself into thinking I was untouchable.

10
JUDE

It was close to midnight when I finally touched down in Atlanta with a few bloodthirsty rogues in tow, and needless to say, I wasn't all too happy about it. Today was officially my wife's 37th birthday, and here I was, in Georgia, of all fucking places. I knew that Cameron wasn't feeling the shit, but I didn't really have much of a choice. Until the book was found, my back was against the wall.

After Eve called me about the missing ledger, I hopped on the first flight out to Atlanta to settle matters myself. I couldn't send anyone else to do the shit, because the contents inside of the ledger were sensitive, and I really didn't need anyone else to know that it was missing. Oftentimes, the hardest people to trust were the ones you were surrounded by. And the least of people I could trust got smaller every day.

You can't get love without hate.

As my head accountant, I didn't know how Eve had even let something like this happen in the first place. That ledger should've been by her side at all times, like a fucking bible! I knew that she was young, and being irresponsible was a part of being young, but this was just flat out careless.

Sighing in frustration, I pulled out a cigar. *Heavy lies the crown.*

Together, me and my security team walked out of Hartsfield-Jackson International Airport, and were met at the South entrance by a personal driver in a black on black Escalade with tinted windows. A security guard opened the back door for me, and I hopped in, then sent a text to my wife letting her know that I had landed. Next, I pulled out my business phone and called Eve to see where she was. It was taking everything in me to keep from losing my cool with her.

"Aye. I just touched down. Where are you?"

"I'm at the office," she said exasperated, as if *she* were the one stressed out.

I didn't know why she sounded like that. If the ledger fell into the cop's possession, I could easily be thrown in prison for the rest of my days. There was more than enough incriminating evidence in there to lock me up and throw away the key. I was already on their radar to begin with. The only thing keeping me free were my ties to certain politicians, and even *that* could only go but so far.

"I haven't left since I lost the ledger," Eve said. "I'm too afraid to. I keep thinking if I leave, someone else will find it, and God knows I don't want that to happen."

"Smart girl," I said.

"No, I'm not. I'm fucking dumb as a box of rocks. What type of accountant loses the ledger?"

"I won't argue with you there," I said pointedly.

"You must be so disappointed in me, Jude."

"We'll talk about that when I get there," I said, hanging up.

"Where to Big Dawg?" The driver asked.

"Buckhead."

"You got it, chief."

I had an office building out there for an urban magazine company that I owned called Opulent. It was one of my first business ventures, and a damn successful one at that. I had a degree in business management, so I decided to finally put it to some use by making a few smart investments. Not only did it serve as a means to launder money, it provided some of the hottest celebrity gossip, music reviews, and news about the hip-hop industry. Eve managed the place, and for the most part, she'd been on her shit, until now.

Thirty minutes later, we pulled up to the modern and newly constructed glass building, and my guard stepped out to open the door for me while another escorted me to the front entrance.

"I got it from here," I told him.

"Yes sir."

Firing up a custom Cuban cigar, I took the elevator to the 33rd floor where Eve's office was located. The place was completely empty. On the way up, I stared out the glass doors, admiring everything I'd built and how far I had come. I had made millions of dollars, legally and illegally. And to think, seventeen years ago, I was broke as fuck and in prison. That gavel had changed my life and made me move different. Nowadays, I moved with precision.

You've done well for yourself.

I smiled in spite of my current dilemma.

Ding!

The elevator doors slid open, and I fixed my blazer and promptly made my way to Eve's office. "Hey! Eve?" I called out. She didn't answer right away, so I went ahead and started looking through drawers and file cabinets myself. The fucking ledger had to be in here somewhere. It just had to! "Eve?" I called out again.

I opened the top drawer of her desk and found a miniature calendar, a couple of highlighters, a passport, and an old, worn photo of her and King, just weeks before he was killed. Once it was obvious that I wouldn't find what I was looking for in there, I slammed the drawer shut and exhaled. "Damn. Where the fuck is it?"

"Right here..." Eve said in a seductive tone.

I looked up and saw her standing in the doorway asshole naked in nothing but a pair of red bottom pumps. The cigar fortuitously dropped from my lips and landed on the office desk still lit. I was completely awestruck and at a loss for words by what I saw. A few of the ashes seared my right hand, but I quickly swatted them away, not taking my eyes off Eve for a second. She looked incredible, mouthwateringly incredible. Make me forget that I was a married man incredible.

Damn.

Shorty always had a nice visual, but she looked even better than I imagined naked. Her breasts were round and perky, her nipples high and erect on her chest, and her stomach taut and firm. Below that sat her shaved mound, the lips so fat, I could clearly see them from the front without her having to open her legs. Her pussy looked delectable, and I found myself yearning to taste her like a forbidden fruit.

"Well…" She sashayed over to the desk, sat on top of it and stretched her legs as far apart as they would go. Her juicy pussy lips parted like the gates of heaven. Her insides were glossy, pink, and beckoning me to sample it. "Are you just gonna stand there, as stiff as a mannequin?" She pushed a finger inside her pretty, pink pussy and moved it around until she found her spot, then she commenced to finger fucking herself at a slow and steady pace. The shit had my dick so hard, it was protruding from my slacks. "Or are you gonna get some of this good pussy?" she asked, sliding her finger out. I watched as some of her juices seeped onto the surface of the desk. She then pushed that same finger inside her mouth and sucked off all the wetness.

"Eve, I—"

"C'mon, Jude, it's only us in here. No employees. No security," she smiled. "No wife..."

Cameron quickly flashed through my mind, and suddenly, the guilt of being alone with a naked woman consumed me. "Eve, I can't," I said, regretting the words the second they fell from my lips. As badly as I wanted her, I didn't want the consequences that came with having her. Cameron and I had been on track for so long. I couldn't fuck that up. Not only that, but I loved my wife. I couldn't betray her trust. I'd already been down that road before and it was a rocky one. It took years to regain that unwavering level of trust back from her, and I'd be damned if I lost it again over some bitch.

Eve made me eat those words when she slid her hand down the crack of her ass and started rubbing her brown, little hole. *Fuck my life.* The shit turned me on so much, I almost said to hell with the ring...but I couldn't. "Eve, stop...I know what you on, but we can't go down that road, baby girl. I'm a married man," I told her. "You know we can't do this shit." My dick was still rock hard, as I tried to talk some morality into her. I hardly had a drop of it myself right about now.

"And why can't we?" she asked.

"Cameron—"

"Ain't here," she finished. "So, why can't we?" She slid her finger back in her dripping, tight, little pussy hole, and my breath caught in my chest. "What's stopping you?"

As if on cue, a stack of papers caught on fire.

11
EVE

Driving back to my residence, I reflected on the events from earlier and how I had come *this* close to fucking my way into a come-up. My mother had been grooming me to become the next Mrs. Patterson ever since I was 13 years old, but tonight I'd somehow let the opportunity slip through my fingers.

Maybe the way to Jude's heart isn't through his dick, I concluded with a smile. Perhaps, I would have to put forth more effort than just spreading my legs. Whatever the case may be, I knew that I had to try harder if I wanted to get him.

At 22, I was still living at home with my mother, but I didn't mind because we were tight, and she was sorta like my best friend. Plus, she couldn't take living on her own after my father passed. She still had nightmares to this very day. His untimely death had affected her tremendously.

After he died, she started putting a plan in motion. A plan to see us living like royalty again. You see, it wasn't even my idea to seduce Jude. It was all my mother's. She knew that Jude was the most infamous drug kingpin in the game, and she was determined to see me sit beside him on a throne. She'd been waiting for the day to come ever since I became of age. That's how long Jude had been around the family.

Now that King was dead, she'd grown obsessed with living in the lap of luxury, and she'd do anything to have that lifestyle again. I worked as Jude's accountant; he paid me well, and even purchased the townhome we lived in but it wasn't enough for Mama. Hell, it wasn't enough for me either, come to think of it. We wanted more, and she felt like we wouldn't have more unless I was his *wife*.

"I still can't believe this nigga didn't smash!" I yelled at thin air. "How the fuck could any nigga resist sticking his dick in this? A bitch practically holding her pussy open for him, and he stands there like it's his first time. The fuck? What type of backwards shit is that? I cannot believe this nigga didn't fuck me."

What straight man in his right mind *wouldn't* have hit? I was a bad bitch in every sense of the word. So bad I could make a gay man rethink his sexual preference. Jude had to be smoking big rocks. That was the only explanation I could think of for why he didn't bend me over that desk and raw dog the shit out of my ass.

I knew he didn't miss the subtle flirting and looks I gave him on the regular. I'd been trying to get his attention for years now, and my patience had run so thin, that I thought throwing myself at him would work. But obviously I was wrong. Jude wasn't an easy nut to crack. At least, not now anyway.

As I headed towards my townhome in Marietta, I smiled at the way he'd struggled to keep his hands to himself back in the office. He had a strong will, but not strong enough to resist me forever. Eventually, he'd come around.

Still, I was sad that it couldn't have been tonight. I wanted to ride him so bad that I could just feel his dick in my stomach. I wanted him to give me a baby, and of course, a ring before all that. I wanted to wake up and go to sleep beside him every night. I guess to put it simple, I wanted to replace Cameron.

I knew the task wouldn't be an easy one, so if I had to share him in the meantime then I was all for it. *He'll come around,* I told myself again. *Oh, his ass will come around.*

One thing was for certain. Mama was *not* gonna be too happy when she heard about this failed attempt.

12
JUSTIN

After parking our car in a nearby parking garage, we headed to the classy strip club in downtown LA, called Fox's Den. We were all trying to have fun and get fucked up. Since Nahmir knew the owner, he let us all in even though me, Drip and Chris were all underage. We got fucked up on liquor and pills and every bitch in the joint was on me and Chris hard. Females loved Chris. Drip had all the white hoes going crazy, as always. Nahmir tried to buy me some pussy, but I kindly turned him down and when midnight rolled around, I told them niggas I had to dip.

"A'ight then." Drip dapped me up and hugged me now that he was $5,000 richer. "Keep yo feet on these niggas' necks, buzzo."

"You already know."

As I left the club, I was totally unaware of someone watching me. And it wasn't one of the hobos lurking through the streets of downtown. Calling up an Uber, I had a driver come swoop me, so that I could get my car from Nahmir's place. I was already out past curfew and I knew a tongue-lashing was coming from my parents. I wasn't too worried about it, though. I'd deal with it when the time came. I had bigger fish to fry, like figuring out what to do with the nigga in the warehouse, and how we'd go about finding his supplier.

It was 12:35 a.m. when I pulled up to the crib and all of the lights were on. Conway, our head of security, was stationed at the front of the house. He waved to me and I tossed up the peace sign at him. He then let me through the tall, iron gates, and I immediately got butterflies in my stomach when I realized Madison was inside my home, probably just as mad as my mom that I was still out. I knew her though, and she could never stay mad at a nigga for too long.

Turning off the engine, I climbed out—wearing my school uniform again—and hit the automatic locks. After checking myself out in the mirror to make sure I was cool, I dropped to the ground and did a few push-ups to make myself look cocky and impressive to Madison. She hadn't seen me in over seven months, and I wanted her to think I'd been hitting the gym on the regular even though I hadn't. I'd been too busy hitting the streets.

As soon as I walked in the house, I heard the girls talking and laughing in the kitchen without a care in the world. "Justin, is that you?" My mom called out, once the security system alerted her to my entrance.

"Yeah, Ma, it's me." I walked in the kitchen and found them eating ice cream straight out of the carton. My heart instantly lodged in my throat when I saw her. Madison Janelle Asante. She was so damn beautiful it made me nervous just being in her presence. She had coffee-colored skin, hazel eyes and a splash of freckles across her nose and cheeks. Makeup or no makeup, she was still everything.

She wasn't super busty or thick like a lot of the chicks in my school. As a matter of fact, she was somewhat on the petite side. Small boobs, small butt, small everything, but she still had curves where it mattered.

"Hi, Maddie," I said, dry as fuck. My tone didn't correlate the way I was feeling, which was the complete opposite.

She waved at me. "*Mema wo adwo*. That's how you say 'good evening' in Twi." That was her dad's native language.

"Ohh, that's nice," I said, faking interest. "By the way, that's how you say I don't give a damn in English."

Journee laughed and my mom scolded me for being a smart ass.

I only *acted* like I didn't fuck with Maddie in front of my folks. But of course, that wasn't the case. I knew that if her dad found out I was her boyfriend, he'd forbid her from coming here, and the same went for my mom. Soul was very strict and overprotective of his only daughter, and my mom wasn't too far behind. No way in hell she'd let a girl stay with us for as long as Maddie stayed if she *knew* we fucked with each other. She'd probably think we were fucking in every room in the house behind her back every chance we got. Unfortunately, for now, me and Madison had to keep our relationship under wraps. Journee was the only one who knew about us.

It was kinda sad really. I wanted the whole damn world to know she was mine. I wanted everyone to know

Madison was with me. She deserved to be shown off like the prize she was, and yet I couldn't. It really sucked, but it is what it is. Luckily, we wouldn't have to do this for too much longer. She would be 18 soon, and we planned to get a place together, and attend colleges in the same city. Our parents couldn't say shit or do anything about it since we'd be grown.

"Hi, my ass!" My mom snapped me out of my thoughts. "Why the hell are you waltzing your ass in so late? You know your curfew is 10 pm. It's almost one in the damn morning!"

"Ma, chill. Cut me some slack. I just lost track of time," I said with an attitude, like it was no big deal.

"You 'bout to lose them teeth if you don't take some of that bass out your throat," my mom threatened.

Journee and Madison giggled.

"And is that," she paused. "Liquor and weed I smell on you?"

Of course, we were blowing loud at the club, but I wouldn't tell her that. "No—"

Before I could fully get the word out, she was all up in my face sniffing me like a police dog. "Bullshit, boy, let me smell your breath," she demanded.

I looked at Madison and my cheeks flushed in embarrassment. "*Maaaa*," I whined.

"Don't 'ma' me. Let me smell your breath, boy."

I modestly blew my breath in her face and she frowned.

"Okay, I had one shot. But I didn't smoke any weed, Ma, on God."

"Yeah, whatever you say, Justin. Just know your father *will* be hearing about this when he gets back in town."

"Where is he now?" I asked. He'd just texted me earlier.

"He had to catch a red-eye to Atlanta."

My dad was always in and out. One minute he was home, the next he was halfway across the country. He lived life in the fast lane. To me, that was goals as fuck.

"Don't worry, he'll be back in time for the party later on today," my mom said.

With everything that had happened tonight, I almost forgot it was my mom's 37th birthday. "Oh, happy birthday, Ma," I said, kissing her on the cheek. "You're practically knocking on forty's door," I teased.

My mom pushed me away. "*Mmhmm*, whatever boy. Just know I'm still getting in that ass later on. You can believe that," she said. "You better thank your lucky stars I'm in a good mood now that my niece is here."

Madison smiled like she was so sweet and innocent, when in reality, she was the total opposite.

I knew my mom wouldn't keep her word. No matter what I did, she always treated me like I was her perfect little son. I swear, she thought the sun rose outta my ass. It was the complete opposite with her and Journee. I swear, the two of them stayed beefing.

"I'm helping Auntie Cameron set up for the party tomorrow," Madison said cheerfully.

"Good for you, you wanna cookie," I said, unimpressed. I had to blow her off from time to time to keep up the facade we had going. I couldn't let my mom see that I actually cared about everything that came out of those beautiful lips of hers. "I'm finna hop in the shower."

"Good, because you stink," Journee said.

"And you're ugly. But you don't see me complaining."

"Justin!" My mom grilled.

I laughed and disappeared to the nearest bathroom to wash off the lies and deceit.

13
CONWAY

Twenty minutes after Justin pulled up, I noticed a black van with black tinted windows creeping down the street of the Beverly Hills residential that Cameron and her family lived in. The vehicle was hard to mistake—and avoid.

"What the fuck are they doing here?" I grumbled in frustration, killing the lights to the front yard using a handheld security system. I didn't want Cameron to see the van because I knew that it would immediately raise suspicions.

Leaving my post, I unlocked the gate to the mansion and briskly walked down the street, making sure to keep my head down low. The van pulled off to the side of the winding road, and when I finally reached it, the back doors swung open and I quickly hopped in before anyone could see me.

"What the fuck are you doing, man? Are you *trying* to blow my cover???" I fired off at my colleague, Frank García. He, and two other officers, were in the van tailing me like they had nothing else better to do. Taped to the interior of the van was a myriad of photos of all of Jude's workers, right down to the attractive head accountant.

"I'm just checking in, seeing how shit is moving. We've been building this case for some time now, so I'm kinda at the point, where I feel like it's necessary."

"Don't be such a wise ass. What you need to do is let me do my job before you fuck around and get me killed, Frank!" I hissed. "Haven't you ever heard of Kiki Camarena?" I reminded him of the undercover agent who was abducted and tortured while on assignment in Mexico. "Do you want that to be me, Frank? Do you really wanna see me be the next Kiki Camarena??? Kidnapped and tortured over a 30-hour period?! Having my skull crushed with a fucking power drill?!"

"Of course not, but the captain's getting impatient. He wants to see some arrests being made and I, myself, wouldn't mind seeing these scumbags go down already."

"Look, I'm doing everything I can to see him on trial and ultimately behind bars, Frank. I'm doing every fuckin' thing that I can. But it takes a lot of work gaining these people's trust," I explained. "Jude just promoted me to head of security, but this shit takes time. Putting together a sting takes time. *Tener paciencia,*" I said to him in Spanish.

"You've had over a year's worth of time, Diego," he reminded me.

"You say you wanna see these scumbags go down, right? Well, I'm making sure I've got enough evidence gathered to do that. I don't wanna just slap dismissible charges on these bastards. I wanna see them go away for a very, *very* long time," I explained. "The only downside is these guys aren't fools. They aren't leaving any room for slip-ups and I've yet to find Jude's source, or even *witness* him make a purchase for that matter. So right now, I can't slap him with anything that sticks. For now, you—and the captain—are gonna have to be patient and have a little faith in me—unless you can nab him sooner," I added. "*Puedes hacer eso?*"

Frank looked like he wanted to argue, but he bit the bullet and just nodded his head. "So, you really think you can handle it?" He wanted to arrest Jude just as bad as me.

"I know I can. Have I not *handled* other drug dealers in the past?" I asked him. "Besides, I've already spent months doing surveillance and undercover work. I know this family inside and out. I've got their lives down pact right down to the menstrual cycles. That's how long I've been around these folks. I'm in good with these people. They know me, they trust me. You bring someone else in, and that'll just blow this whole thing up. Someone's gotta do it," I said. "Better it be me."

My real name was Diego González, and no one in Jude's camp knew that I was actually an undercover DEA agent, hired to take down him and his intricate criminal enterprise. It was indisputably the world's largest drug-trafficking organization to date—and that didn't even include whatever international supplier he'd partnered up with.

You see, Jude was just one of many prolific criminals that I worked hard to bring down. I actually had quite the track record for snaring cocaine kingpins and criminal organizations. However, the thing that set Jude apart from the rest was his political and government affiliations, not to mention his expansive network of informants and allies. The man was untouchable; clever, beyond careful, and always one step ahead. It was almost like he was laughing in the face of opposition, giving a middle finger to the DEA and CIA. Jude, his family, and his empire were well-protected.

We'd been after the bastard for years now, but we couldn't gather enough evidence to nail his ass. Jude, who was reported to have an estimated net-worth of $40 million, had evaded the authorities for over a decade now. A few years ago, the DEA put together a team to try to see if they could finally capture the infamous kingpin, and somewhere along the way, I was picked up and given a task—or better yet a role of infiltrating his circle. I had ties to Fillmore, Jude's second-in-command—and that was how I gained his trust and permission to join his team. Fillmore didn't know that I was undercover. He wouldn't know until he was tried in court and fingered as an accomplice. I knew what I was doing could easily get me killed, but it was a risk I was willing to take, over and over again.

William Conway wasn't my first alias. Before that, it was Dave Trent, and before that Iglesias Rodriguez. I'd had to impersonate countless characters, including a banker, a drug dealer, a drug user, *and* a homeless man. I had to learn and unlearn languages to fit the bill, change names, change styles, and personalities. And what made my job even harder was that none of this shit was ever rehearsed. Once I was briefed, I was given a script and I stuck to it. I'd used dozens of personas to bring down organizations, and involved in more operations than I could remember. I adopted a different identity each time, and had even seen my partner, as well as some of my closest colleagues killed during a few of these stings.

What really helped me fly under the radar was my appearance. I easily passed as a black man in his early 20s, yet I was actually a Latino man in his mid 30s, but because of my dark skin and youthful-looking face, one would never know. I'd been working for the Drug Enforcement Agency for over 6 years now, and before that I was employed with the Department of Homeland Security. I'd spent a few years in the military before that, and a brief stint as a police officer. I say all this to say, I'd been taking down the bad guys for quite some time. I liked the feeling of knowing I was doing something good for the community. I liked knowing there was going to be one less person out there selling drugs or weapons to our youth. It was a great feeling to be able to nab these guys. Jude was no different.

I could've retired a while back, bought me a beautiful bungalow on the beach somewhere and avoided the drugs, the warzones, the bullets and the criminals. But after more than 10 years in the Force, I had no intention of throwing the towel in anytime soon. I guess you could say, I was addicted to fighting crime. I wanted to see every bad guy peddling drugs tossed in a cell under the jail.

I was so close to snaring Jude that I could taste it. I'd already gained his trust; now all I had to do was be with him when he made one of his purchases, so that I'd finally have enough evidence to pin concrete criminal charges on him, and his supplier. I talked to the prosecutors so I knew what needed to be done and what needed to be said in front of me as proof.

I was determined to put Jude away for the rest of his years. I just hated to think what would happen to the kids in the process. I'd gotten really close to them over the months and they were innocent in all of this. I was also sad that Cameron had to go down with him as an accomplice. Even though she was just as guilty as her husband in the eyes of the law, I really did take a liking to her, on some legit shit. She was beautiful, sweet, highly educated, cultured, and a damn good mother. She exemplified both inner beauty, as well as outer beauty, with the brains to match. She had that strength of mind and spirit which I found both fascinating and irresistible.

I guess you could say I had a great admiration for her. It was unfortunate that she had to suffer too, but that's the nature of the beast. One thing was for sure; Jude was going down. I'd been a part of dozens of operations and stings, and almost all of them had resulted in the target being jailed, or killed. Whichever the DEA preferred. In Jude's case, I truly believed either would suffice.

"So, what do you have planned?" Frank asked.

I smiled at him. "A winning hand's only good when you keep your cards hidden."

14
JUDE

Sipping on my glass of cognac, I thought about how Eve had thrown herself at me back at the office. Then I thought about how I had almost got caught up, and I found myself questioning the strength of my mental fortitude. For over ten years, I'd been nothing short of faithful to my wife. I barely even looked at other women inappropriately, and for the first time in years, I'd almost slipped up.

I knew I had to dead this shit and I had to dead it now. I couldn't afford something like this happening again, because I might not have the strength to reject her a second or third time. Placing my glass down in the cup holder in the mini bar of my limousine, I pulled my phone out and called Eve.

She answered on the third ring, in a syrupy sweet voice like she wasn't trying to wreck my marriage a second ago. "Hey, Jude..."

"Eve..."

"I wasn't expecting to hear from you so soon."

"Yeah, well, you know, I can't let shit end on this note. I feel like, as a man, it's my place to let you know what it is," I told her. "Eve, I'm married. I'm a married man. A *happily* married man," I added. "And you're damn near old enough to be my kid. I know that you're young. And I know apart of being young is making mistakes. So I'mma chalk this up to bein' a foolish mistake and give you the benefit of the doubt this time. But you need to know that this can never happen again, Eve. Do I make myself clear?"

"I made a mistake. It won't happen again." She sounded bland and unconvincing, so I further stressed myself.

"Eve, I love my wife very much. I love my family very much. One day, when you find someone special, and you have a family of your own, you'll understand why I can't jeopardize either," I said.

"I hear you, Jude. Like I said, it won't happen again."

"I know it won't. Because if it does, I'mma have to cut the strings."

15
JUSTIN

It was a quarter after 4 a.m. when I heard the sound of soft raps on my bedroom door. Everyone in the house was asleep so I already knew who it was. We'd been doing this shit for six years now, plus her knocks were hard to mistake because they had a distinct rhythm.

"Come in, bay," I whispered.

Madison opened the door, crept inside, then quietly closed it behind her. She looked so cute in her pink nightgown and fuzzy slippers. Her long, curly brown hair was in a bushy ponytail on top of her head, and she was holding onto one of her arms like she was nervous or some shit.

"C'mere," I said to her.

Madison hesitated. "Eww. It smells like old, dirty gym socks in here."

I frowned at her. "What'chu mean? I cleaned my room hours ago," I lied. Actually, my mom had cleaned it for me.

"Well, you forgot to Febreze it," she said, wrinkling up her nose.

I grabbed her tiny wrist and yanked her onto the mattress with me. "I'mma be ya husband one day, so you better get used to it." She never saw the violent, homicidal side of me. She only saw the tender, loving side. She didn't know what I did in my spare time with Drip. I wasn't sure she ever would. I never wanted to lose her, and I didn't want her perception of me to change.

"Whatever," Madison said.

I pinched her side.

"Ow. That hurt."

"Shut up." I kissed the side of her neck. "You know I'm lightweight pissed at you for posting a pic with that black ass Djimon Hounsou lookin' mufucka."

"On the Gram? What pic?" She asked, feigning ignorance.

I quickly pulled my phone out to show her. I stalked her social media pages on the regular, so I never missed a beat. "This one. Remember that?" I asked, shoving my phone in her face.

"Ohhh."

"Ohhh," I said, mimicking her. "Yeah, who the fuck is that nigga? Ya'll lookin' mighty cozy," I noted. "You been givin' my shit away to this crispy ass nigga?"

"Oh my God, Justin."

"Man, I'm serious. Tell them niggas it's dead." I was very overprotective of her. Hell, I'd been in love with her half my life. "I ain't feelin' you flickin' it up with all these motherland mufuckas. That's bad form."

"Oh my God. That's Kwaku. He's the head of the swim team at school, jack off. That's why we're both wearing the same jackets and gold medals around our necks," she laughed. "Seriously, Justin...I swear to God, you have got to *stop* being so jealous."

"What the fuck do you expect from me when I love your ass. I can't help it." I kissed her hand, wearing an earnest expression on my face.

"I love you too...even though sometimes you make me sick," she laughed.

I pinched her again.

"Ow," she giggled. "That really hurts."

"Shut up. You like it."

"I do. Do it again," she insisted.

I playfully bit her ear. "I ain't with all that square shit. Your ass is mine, Madison." I reached a hand up her nightgown and grabbed her ass, and she laughed so loud, I had to clamp a hand over her mouth just to keep my folks from hearing her. I jumped in surprise when she bit my hand.

"Now, let's talk about you," she began. "How could you go out and get drunk when you knew I was coming into town? *That's* bad form."

"I didn't just go out and get drunk. I had some shit to handle."

"Like what?" She pressed. "Or better yet, like *who*?"

"Man, I was out and about and got distracted."

"How were you distracted when I wasn't there to distract you?"

"Man, don't do that." I kissed the back of her hand again.

"Don't do what? Call you out on your shit?"

"You really think I'd be out, messin' around, on the day you come into town? What type of nigga you take me for? I'm a genuine, real muthafucka, and I got a canine sense of loyalty." She had me in my feelings with the way she was chin-checking my shit.

Maddie rolled her eyes like she didn't believe me. "Yeah, yeah…"

"Cut it out." I drowned her protests with a peck on her lips. "I'm loyal to you. I *been* loyal to you. On hood, I be curving chicks left and right."

She fake-yawned. "Yeah, yeah. Whatever."

I sucked my teeth. "Man, whatever. Don't believe me," I said, pushing her away from me. "I'mma man. I ain't gone keep goin' back and forth with your ass."

Madison sat up to leave, and I quickly pulled her back towards me.

"Chill, chill. I'm just playin', baby. Damn. Don't do a nigga like that," I said in a softer tone, as I kissed her cheek and snuggled close to her. "Don't look for reasons to fight with me. All I wanna do is love you. We need to pause all this tension." After murdering so many people in one night, I needed her love and company to keep me sane. She brought light into my dark world.

Madison met my gaze, as she heard me out.

"I can't lie. I missed the fuck outta your ass." I swept a curly strand of hair out of the way, so that I could see her beautiful face more clearly.

"*Mhm.* You've probably been trying to replace me with one of them bum ass bitches at your school. That's why you feelin' all guilty now."

I looked at her meaningfully. "Bullshit. We share six years' worth of history. You really think that's replaceable?"

Madison paused. "You tell me..."

"Listen to me. I'm playing for all the chips here. I wanna marry your ass someday. You really think I give a fuck about these stankin' ass zero bitches out here. These bitches is zeros. You're the only girl I want."

Madison smiled like she'd hit the lottery. "Okay, Justin. We on the same page. You don't have to lay it on so thick," she joked. "I believe you."

"Am I the only guy *you* want?"

Madison shrugged. "Eh. Half the time."

I pinched her again. "Don't fuck with me."

"Ow, Justin. I'm just playing," she laughed.

Leaning in, I kissed her and she wrapped a hand around the nape of my neck, parting her mouth for my tongue to enter. She tasted like ice cream. French vanilla to be exact. Suddenly, I thought back to the first time we'd ever locked lips.

I was 11 at the time and spying on Madison, like I always did, through the tall bushes of our backyard, when I caught her torturing the neighbor's cat. She was staying with us for the summer. Apparently, Soul wanted her to stay close to her American roots so he sent her here during school breaks.

"Ooh! I'm gonna tell on you!" I threatened, making my presence known.

Madison's head snapped in my direction the second she heard me and the cat bolted from her grasp and scampered off with an injured leg.

"What are you doing here!" she yelled at me.

"The question is what are you doing here?"

"Minding my business!"

"Well, I'm sure my mom will be interested to hear about that business," I said, putting emphasis on the last word.

"No!" Madison grabbed my arm. *"You can't tell her! My step-mom already got in my ass about this. If she finds out I'm still doing it, she'll tell my dad and he'll be pissed."*

"That sounds like your problem," I said, fucking with her for the hell of it.

"Don't tell!" Madison pleaded. *"I'll give you money."*

"Ha! My parents are filthy rich, Maddie. Don't insult me with bribery," I said, quoting a line I heard from a Mafia movie I watched with my dad once.

"Well, what do you want?" she asked.

I scratched my small chin and thought about it. *"Give me a kiss and I won't tell."*

Madison looked at me like I had taken a shit on her dinner plate. *"Eww! No! Gross!"*

"Moooommmm!!!!"

"Okay, okay!" She agreed in a hushed tone. *"But you have to close your eyes first."*

Adhering to her request, I closed my eyes tightly and puckered up my lips. Madison leaned in and gave me a peck on the mouth that lasted all of four seconds. Afterwards, she stomped on my right foot and ran off.

Madison bit my lower lip, quickly snapping me out of my brief reverie. "Ouch. Why're you so rough, baby?"

"Maybe I like it rough," she teased.

I slid my hand up her nightgown. "Is *that* right? Gimme some of dat pussy then. I'll be as rough as you want me to."

She quickly swatted my hand away. "Nope! None of that." Suddenly, she reached for my journal under the pillow. "What's this?" she asked, flipping through the pages.

I quickly snatched it from her. "Nothin'," I said, tossing it on the nightstand.

"*Unh-huh,*" she said skeptically.

"Stop fuckin' up the vibe," I said, kissing on her shoulder. I snaked my hand between her thighs, but she quickly moved it away.

"No, Justin."

"Aww. Come on, baby. Everybody's sleeping..."

"I don't care."

I sucked my teeth and sighed in frustration. "When are you gonna let me hit? We've been together a while now, and I've only progressed to suckin' your tits. Nigga feel like a teenager that's still being breastfed."

Madison broke out laughing. "I don't know. Maybe after I graduate..."

"Damn. So, I gotta wait a whole 'nother year to get some of this?" I said in disbelief.

Madison bit her bottom lip. "I wanna show you something," she suddenly said, raising up her nightgown.

"Mmm. Show me somethin' then," I said, as my dick began to swell. I just knew she was about to show off her kitten.

Instead, she lifted the gown up to show me a small tattoo right above her hip. "My dad would freak if he knew I had this shit."

I flashed the light from my phone onto her so that I could see it more clearly. It was a small tattoo of my name written in cursive. The gesture really touched my heart.

"Even if you do end up waiting two years or three years or however long I make you wait...and even if you see me posting pics with guys on the Gram...this is a reminder that I'm yours, Justin."

I leaned in to kiss her and pulled her even closer. "Tell me again that's all mine."

She smiled at me in a melting fashion. "I'm yours. I'll always be yours."

I never ever wanted to let her go. "I wanna hold you all night," I said.

Madison giggled. "I would love that. But your mom would kill me if she woke up and saw me in your bed." And with that, Madison wiggled out of my arms and climbed off the mattress. "Get some sleep. We've got a big day tomorrow."

"Really?" I said, rubbing my erection. Now that she'd shown me that tat, I wanted her now more than ever. "See you playin' with a nigga. That's how you play your cards?"

"I didn't think I was playing cards," Madison smiled. "It's more like, getting up from the table and leaving."

16
CAMERON

Music was playing, people were dancing and everyone seemed to be having a good ass time at my 37th birthday party but me. "Journee, have you seen your dad?" I asked, in the midst of the celebration. She and her friends were standing near the refreshments, gossiping about shit that most teenage girls did at their age.

"No."

I sighed in frustration and looked around the ballroom again. Everyone else was in attendance; long-time friends, associates, work colleagues, and several politicians whom Jude had endorsed. He and I had nothing but rich friends, who gave us lavish gifts like money, checks, designer shit, and cars. I even had a brand-new Wraith sitting outside, compliments of the mayor of California.

"Well, if you see him walk in, call me."

"I probably won't see him 'cuz I'm talking to my girls," she said in a snobby tone, as if the favor I was asking of her was too much to handle.

"Just 'cuz your mouth is moving don't mean your eyes can't do the same. Now call me if you see him," I said, turning away.

"This lady's trippin'. He's your husband, not mine," I heard her mumble under her breath.

She was always showing out for her little friends, but she was finna fuck around and get her shit embarrassed in front of them. Ignoring her snarky comeback, I walked through the ballroom with worry lines written on my face. I looked so regal in a black gown with silver embellishments and silver heels covered in Swarovski Crystals. My homegirl Sofía had made them for me. She and I owned a chain of boutiques throughout California, which also served as a front for tax purposes. Besides Roxie and Diana, she was one of my closest friends.

Unfortunately, she couldn't be here tonight because she and her husband were in Colombia tending to her sick mother. The fact that she and Jude were both missing in action had me feeling kinda down. It was my birthday and yet I was the last person having fun. Jude hadn't returned from Atlanta, nor had I heard from him since he touched down.

An uneasy chill sat on my heart. "Where the hell is he?" I wondered. Suddenly, my phone rang and I immediately got excited because I thought it was the love of my life. Much to my disappointment, it was Diana Facetiming me from Africa. "Hey, girl."

"Happy birthday!!!" she sang. She was standing on the patio of her mansion, and I could see the mountains and exotic trees in the background. Soul really had her living good, but I expected nothing less from him. The man truly loved his wife, despite the many obstacles they'd faced in the past. "Why do you look so sad? Thirty-eight isn't that bad, is it?"

"I'm thirty-seven, bitch. And you tell me, you're thirty-nine," I laughed.

"Hoe, I'm shinin'! It ain't nothing like those menopausal years."

I broke out laughing. "Girl, bye! You on some nut shit. I have to get back to my party. I'm not finna play with you right now." I hung up the phone, then looked around and spotted Roxie and her husband Hector standing by the bar. He didn't look like he was having too much fun either, and he was throwing shots back like it was nobody's business.

"Hey, girl," I said, walking up to her.

Hector cut his eyes at me, slammed his glass down on the counter and walked off with an attitude.

"Damn, what the fuck is wrong with him? Did I say something wrong?" I asked her.

"Girl, he hates parties."

"From the looks of shit, he hates everything *and* everybody. Every time I see this nigga, he always mugging or looking like he don't wanna be bothered."

"He got laid off recently," Roxie admitted. "Things have just been hard for him lately."

Roxie was always making excuses for his tired ass. To be honest, I never liked Hector and it wasn't because he wasn't Magyc. He just had a whole fucked up disposition about himself. Anytime she brought him around us, he acted like he didn't wanna be there. Plus, I didn't appreciate the way he treated her.

"Seeing all this wealth and prosperity is just a reminder of his failures," Roxie confessed.

"Well, he better suck it the fuck up and quit acting like a little biatch," I said. "We're at a party for God's sake! No one is judging anyone by their economic or societal status. He needs to just loosen up and have a little fun."

Hector drunkenly bumped into one of the waiters, causing him to drop a tray of assorted cheeses. "I have a feeling he's loose enough for the both of us," she said.

Hector was an average Joe. He wasn't in the drug game or apart of any criminal enterprise like most of the men she'd dated in the past. When he *could* find employment, he worked a regular 9 to 5 and pretty much stayed out of the way. Ever since he and Roxie got married, she started coming around less and less. She claimed the kids kept her busy, but I knew it was because Hector didn't *want* her coming around as much. And because he was her husband and she wanted to keep him happy, she gave in to his every, petty ass demand.

One time, about four or five years ago, she showed up on our doorstep black and blue all over after a fight they'd had. Luckily, Rain was at her friend's house when it happened, so she didn't witness it. Jude was ready to beat the brakes off his ass, but Roxie begged him not to. She and the kids stayed with us for a few days and then she went right back to his trifling ass like a fucking fool. I knew that Roxie just didn't want to be alone, so she clung to Hector like a security blanket.

She'd lost 4 men she loved to violence, and now, she was desperate to keep a man, any man—even if he was a raging alcoholic and whupped her ass on the regular. I hated to see my sister putting herself through this, but it was so obvious she wouldn't leave this nigga. She held him down to her own detriment, regardless of their marriage being toxic. The cracks in their relationships were like gaping wounds, but it was so evident that Roxie wasn't going anywhere. Besides, she'd already given him a baby.

"So...How's everything else going?" I asked her.

Roxie smiled. "Pretty good. Harper will be starting first grade soon." Harper was their six-year old son. He was supposed to have a twin brother, but he died during birth due to asphyxiation. I was pretty sure that stress played a part in it too. Roxie took it pretty hard.

"And what about Rain?" I asked.

Roxie's smile faded. "Girl, she just got expelled from the secondary school I had her in."

"Another one? That makes four in less than two years."

"I know. I think I'm gonna have to start homeschooling her. The other kids are just too afraid of her."

"Can you blame them?" I asked. "I can't believe she's still having those violent outbursts."

"Yeah, and they've only gotten worse. It's like, she gets upset and totally blacks the fuck out. One time she even tried to cut me when I put her ass on punishment. I know she wasn't in her right mind, but still...the shit was pretty scary. It was like Jag all over again." She held her arms and shuddered at the thought of him stabbing her repeatedly.

I shook my head sympathetically as I listened. "You know her father, Joaquin, had the same issue," I reminded Roxie. "He'd get angry and black out just like that." I snapped my fingers to show her how fast it would occur. I'd never seen him black out, personally. I was just going on Jude's word.

"How could I forget?" she sighed.

"Try therapy," I recommended.

"Girl, I've tried *everything*. I don't know what else to do other than to homeschool her."

I felt so bad for my play sister. She had a daughter with severe behavioral problems, an abusive husband, *and* a completely different life than the one she had with Magyc. After he died, it was like everything started going downhill for her.

Roxie looked over at Justin and Madison in the center of the dance floor. They were both doing some new, hip dance that all the kids were doing nowadays. One that I'd probably pop my shoulder out of place even attempting.

"Aww. Look at Justin. He's getting so tall," she said. "And I swear, he gets more and more handsome every time I see him."

Like me, Justin had pecan colored skin, short black curly hair, and long lashes that curled upwards. Everyone called him a pretty boy, and said that he looked just like me. "Don't tell him that. He's already arrogant enough," I laughed.

"God, look at Soul's daughter," Roxie said in admiration. "She's so pretty. She looks like a little supermodel."

"Yeah, she's really stunning, isn't she? Soul told me all the boys in Ghana are in love with her. Said he almost had to kill one for showing up on his doorstep with roses."

Roxie laughed. "Them lil' niggas better move around. You know she and Justin are gonna get married someday."

I made a face at her. "Yeah, right, bitch. They grew up together. They're like cousins," I argued.

"Just look at 'em."

I peered over at my son again, and tried to see what she saw. I still didn't see it, though. "Bitch, I'm looking, but I don't see that happening."

Before she could respond, Hector walked back over, looking irritated. "I'm bored as fuck and ready to go," he told Roxie.

"Aww, but you just got here," I said, disappointed. Roxie and Hector lived in Atlanta, so I didn't get to see them often.

Hector looked like he wanted to spit venom at me. "I believe I was talking to my *wife*." He spoke with a tone of hatred and remorse.

"It's okay, Cam. We'll just get up when I'm off work," she said, once again making excuses for his sorry ass. "Tell Jude I said hi."

Hector grabbed her by the arm and snatched her out of my face. He was a real dirt bag. "If Magyc was still alive, there's no way he would stand for her getting gorillad," I told myself. Hector's broke ass wasn't even working. Roxie supported their entire family. She was a dental hygienist, and she made good money doing it. I was proud of her for going back to school to get her degrees, but sad that she chose to stay with a fucking loser. "Where the hell is Jude?" I asked for the umpteenth time.

"Mrs. Patterson, is everything okay?" Conway asked, with genuine concern on his handsome face. I hadn't even seen him approach me. "You're the guest of honor, and yet you don't look like you're enjoying yourself very much."

"I probably would be, if my husband were here," I said disappointed.

He smiled at me with wide-eyed adulation. "Well, he wouldn't want you standing around, looking like someone just died. Tell me, what can I do to replace that frown with a smile? Would you care to dance?" he offered.

Before I could answer, I heard the unmistakable sound of a live jazz band entering the ballroom.

I will never find another lover sweeter than you...

Sweeter than you...

And I will never find another lover more precious than you...

More precious than you...

Girl, you are close to me you're like my mother...

Close to me you're like my father...

Close to me you're like my sister...

Close to me you're like my brother...

You are the only one, you are my everything and for you this song I sing...

And all my life, I've prayed for someone like you...

And I thank God that I, that I finally found you...

All my life, I've prayed for someone like you...

And I hope that you feel the same way too...

Yes, I pray that you do love me too...

After the band walked in, capturing everyone's attention, a soulful singer with a mini-afro followed them, crooning his rendition of the classic 90s song. And behind him was none other than Jude carrying a huge bouquet of roses. Breaking away from Conway, I ran up to Jude and flung my arms around his neck, as he happily spun me in a circle before kissing me. Like a Disney movie, everyone broke out in a cheerful applause.

"I didn't think you were gonna make it," I said.

"C'mon now, baby. I wouldn't have missed this day for anything in the world." He placed me down, and handed me the roses. "Happy birthday, empress."

"Thank you, my king."

Jude held his hand out in typical gentleman fashion. "May I have this dance?"

"Of course, you may."

I handed my roses to the nearest patron and took my husband's hand. Suddenly, everyone in the ballroom began pairing up as the live jazz band continued to play KC and JoJo's *"All My Life"*. It was one of the most sweeting things he'd ever done for me. Jude really was the king of grand romantic gestures.

As Jude and I danced, I caught Conway staring at us from across the ballroom. We locked eyes for a prolonged beat and then he turned away.

"You look so beautiful," Jude whispered in my ear, his hands on the small of my back as we swayed from side to side.

I rested my head on his shoulder. My husband kept me grounded and I really adored him for that. We'd weathered the storm together, just to see this day. Our relationship wasn't perfect, but it was the closest thing to it. Jude was a gentleman in every sense of the word. His fierce protectiveness always made me feel so safe and secure whenever I was with him. He was compassionate and selfless. I was lucky enough to be blessed with a man who was everything I dreamed of and more.

"Really?" I looked up at him with trusting eyes. "Even after all these years, you still find me beautiful?" He always made me feel confident and sexy, but sometimes a girl liked to ask just for reassurance.

He looked at me with such glowing attention. "Baby, you're the most beautiful woman in the world."

I smiled, laughed, and rested my head back on his shoulder. "I hope you still feel like that thirty years from now, when I've got saggy tits and gray hairs all over."

Jude cupped my chin, and lifted my face to meet his gaze. "Baby, just know, I'm in this shit for the long haul…saggy tits, gray hair and all," he said without hesitating for a second.

He then leaned forward and kissed my forehead. The moment was indeed perfect, and as I rested my head back on his shoulder, I took in the sight of everyone slow-dancing around me. I was so happy to finally be holding my husband. Little did I know, our happiness wouldn't last for very long.

17
ROXIE

"Why do you do shit like that?" I asked, as me and my husband climbed into our Uber. Our driver was a chubby, balding white guy with thick-framed glasses. He looked frustrated, like he'd been picking up disgruntled couples all night.

"Shit like what?" Hector asked with an attitude.

"You always complain that we never do shit. Then when I invite you to my home girl's party, you show your ass like—"

"Like what? Like a nigga that don't like bein' around fake ass people. You know I never liked that broad or her fuckin' husband. Them bitches out here chasing fame while I'm out here chasing financial security. Their whole fuckin' lives are a joke!"

Hector had always hated mingling with high society because he wasn't on their financial tier, but that gave him no right to disrespect my friends due to his own insecurities. "That ego has to go in order for you to grow," I told him. "It's not their fault that you're in the situation you're in."

"And what situation is that?" he asked with an attitude.

"Never mind, Hector. Look, I don't wanna fight with you. Just forget I even said the shit."

"Nah, what the fuck is my situation," he slurred, spitting everywhere. "That I'm broke and jobless?"

"Hector—"

"Did you tell that bitch about my *situation*?" He yelled. "And don't lie, 'cuz I see the way she looks down her fuckin' nose at me!"

"Hector it's all in your head—"

Whap!

He slapped the shit out of me, causing my head to bounce off the window. "So now you callin' me a liar?!" He hollered.

"Hey! I won't tolerate any abuse in this vehicle! Now if you can't act like you got some sense, I'll just let your ass off at the nearest corner."

Hector quieted down since he knew he couldn't afford to be stranded. Hell, he couldn't even afford a roll of tissue to wipe his own ass, and yet he beat up on me like I wasn't the bitch taking care of him. We no longer had that same loving, respectful marriage that we used to. I was basically fighting an uphill battle.

"Keep fuckin' with me, Roxie, and I'mma be out the door on your stupid ass!" He said angrily. "You think you the only bitch I could have? I ain't never fucked with a bitch I couldn't go back and fuck. Don't make a nigga dip out on your ass."

"I'm sorry," I cried. I was desperate to keep our family intact, even at the cost of my pride. "I wasn't saying it like that, Hector. I wasn't trying to piss you off."

He sucked his teeth. "Man, whatever. You *love* to piss me the fuck off. That's why you constantly bring me around these folks when you *know* the reason I don't fuck with them!" He roared.

I wiped my tears and tried to compose myself. Yes, I knew why Hector didn't like Cameron or Jude, but they didn't.

Hector was Sanchez's great nephew. Based on what Cameron had told me, Sanchez was one of Jude's biggest rivals. He'd tried to blackmail him once, and had even threatened Cameron's life as well as her children's, so Jude was forced to get rid of his ass. What Jude didn't know, was that Sanchez's entire operation had crumbled and his entire family went bankrupt. Hector used to be a coke runner for Sanchez, but when he died, they lost everything including his coke connect. Hector had no choice but to start working a 9 to 5. Come to think of it, I had met him at Lowe's in Buckhead 11 years ago. The nigga was selling paint for a living, while the nigga who was responsible for his family's plight flourished. If it were me, I would've been pissed too.

Sadly, I never told any of this to Cameron, so she had no idea why Hector was always acting sour towards her and Jude. To be real, I didn't tell her because I knew she wouldn't approve of our union. Jude would probably kill him for self-reassurance, and I loved Hector too much to lose him. It didn't matter how terrible he treated me, or how often he put his hands on me. I didn't wanna be alone.

It wasn't always like this though. In the beginning, he was as sweet as sugar plum. He'd pick me up every Saturday, on his day off, and take me on these unordinary but super fun dates. One time he took me parasailing, then another time we went jet-skiing in Colorado. He introduced me to Hockey, and authentic Mexican food.

I fell for him fast, because he was unlike any nigga I'd ever dated. He was fun, interesting, and he made an honest living. I was tired of the rappers, the trappers, the drug dealers, contract killers, and street niggas. I had a daughter, and I wanted a family man. Someone who wanted to settle down. Someone who would come home after work, open the fridge and crack the top off a beer. Not someone who hung in strip clubs and bars all day. I wanted that white picket fence American dream lifestyle, with the kids, a dog, and a devoted husband. I thought I had found that with Hector but apparently, I was wrong. It was like he forgot what made me love him so much. Or he just stopped caring to do the things that I liked. Since he'd changed so drastically, so did my feelings.

Even though, I knew I deserved better, I didn't have the will to leave Hector. What we had wasn't great, but neither was being solo. Plus, we'd been together for 11 years now. We had a son together. A family. I couldn't just walk away from that. I always said I was over him and ended up under him. But the truth was, I was too complacent to start all over. Hell, I couldn't even imagine getting back out there on the dating scene. For God's sake, I was a woman in her late 30s with two kids—and one had severe behavioral problems. Surely, I wasn't the cream of the crop when it came to guy's pickings.

Rubbing my stinging cheek, I stared out of the window at the silhouette of palm trees, as we headed back to the city towards our hotel.

"Look...I'm sorry," Hector said, reaching for my hand. "You know how hard shit's been for me lately. Being around these rich, pretentious assholes don't make it any easier."

"Everyone was having fun though, Hector. Nobody was judging anyone based on their net-worth."

"They didn't have to. Their eyes did all the judging for them," he said. "I peeped the way everybody was checkin' me. It was like they thought they were better than me, or some shit. They see the cheap suit; the Kohl's dress shoes and they know I'm not on their level. I can't stand being around egotistical assholes like that."

"Cameron's not like that."

"Bullshit. She's the worst one of 'em all, and so are her fuckin' kids. You can just look at 'em and tell they think the world revolves around them. Little assholes."

"Hector! How can you say that?"

"I'm only bein' real. You can't fault me for bein' real."

I simply shook my head at him. "At the very least, you could have let me see Jude," I pouted.

"For what? Nigga's the same arrogant asshole he's always been. Always walkin' around with an undeserved sense of accomplishment."

My husband called it arrogant but I called it confident, and Jude had every reason to be. He was under 40 and worth more than 40 million dollars. In my opinion, he was just a boastful, charming "man of the people" type of person. There was nothing arrogant about him. Jude fed his family, and the ones closest to his family. I couldn't say that about too many people. Shit, come to think of it, I couldn't even say that about my own husband. Nigga couldn't even feed his damn self. Instead of talking shit, he *should've* been trying to get in good with Jude to see if he could get a J.O.B. I was tired of carrying that muthafucka on my back.

"I'm telling you," Hector continued. "I hate being around the guy. Nigga thinks he's Paulie Cicero, or some shit. Man, they aren't businessmen. They're just a bunch of famous nobodies. Showboating ass *pendejos*." He scoffed. "That nigga wants to be Big Meech so bad." He shook his head. "You remember what happened to him, right."

"I thought you said you hated him 'cuz of what he did to your uncle. Now it's because he's too arrogant for you." I shook my head at him. "Which one is it, Hector? Pick a side."

"Nah, that shit is just the tip of the iceberg. Real talk...I don't fuck with that nigga's character. He acts like he's some hot shot, but the nigga ain't on shit. Scary, Charmin soft ass nigga. On god, I'll smack the goofy out that guy."

"I don't think he'd let you get close enough to do all that."

"What?"

"Nothing."

Hector rolled his eyes. "You see...That's another reason, I don't like dude. You always ridin' the fuck outta slim. Like damn, is *he* your husband or am *I* your husband. 'Cuz I could've sworn *I* put that ring on your finger. Not that fake ass Frank Lucas," he spat. "Every time I speak on this clown, you come running to his rescue like some captain save a hoe. Sometimes, I think you used to fuck this nigga—"

"Oh, please. Jude is like my brother."

"Yeah, well, *I'm* like your husband," he stated in petty triumph.

I immediately dropped the subject. The last thing I wanted to do was keep arguing in front of the Uber driver. The shit was embarrassing, plus he'd already heard enough. But Hector just wouldn't let it go. He was obviously in his feelings about his failures and Jude's success.

"I know it sounds fucked up...but I'd give my left nut just to see that nigga knocked off his high horse."

It hurt me to my heart to hear my husband praying on my best friends' downfall.

18
CONWAY

Straightening my tie, I headed for my lieutenant's office after he had called an impromptu meeting the following morning. I still had a slight hangover from Cameron's party last night, but it was nothing a shot of espresso couldn't fix. *I wonder why he wants to see me,* I thought to myself. I figured it was in regards to the case, as well as my slow progression towards making any arrests.

Why else would I be at the Los Angeles police department at the crack of dawn?

"*Buenos días*, Diego," my colleague Frank greeted. He was working on the case too, and just as determined as me to bring down Jude, if not more. He was *so* determined that he might just get me killed due to his careless and impulsive actions. I was still pretty pissed at his ass for showing up to Cameron and Jude's place unannounced. That reckless ass shit could've easily gotten me murdered.

"Morning, Frank."

"Anything new on the investigation?" he asked.

"Not yet, but I got a feeling that's what the lieutenant wants to see me about."

Frank whistled dramatically, like I was about to get fired. "Good luck with that, buddy." He patted me on the shoulder. Luckily, it wasn't in the lieutenant's area of authority to fire me. If it was, I'd probably be sweating bullets right about now.

"Thanks. But I won't need it," I said, before walking off. I'd probably get a warning at best. Everyone's patience was running thin with this investigation, but I was doing everything that I could.

I continued down the hall and stopped at a door on the right-hand side of the hallway. The lettering on the window was slightly worn off, but I could still make out the name. Lieutenant Beechum was one of the finest officers the LAPD had ever seen. At 64, he now worked behind a desk in an office calling shots. He was actually the one who put me on the case. He'd heard about my extensive list of successful stings in the past, and he felt like I was the man for the job. However, when I walked in his office and saw his face, I could tell that his confidence in me was starting wane. Like Frank, he no longer had that much faith in me anymore.

"Morning, Lieutenant Beechum," I greeted in a pleasant tone.

"Diego González." His voice was flat and unwelcoming, as he pointed to a chair across from him. "Please, take a seat," he instructed.

I made my way over to his desk and sat down on the comfy chair. I already knew what he was about to say before he even started talking. "Sir, before you begin, I—"

"González, it's bad etiquette to launch into a fit of excuses whenever your superior sits you down," he said.

"I didn't call you in here to hear your bullshit. I called you in here because I wanna know if you can put together a sting before the month is over. We've been at this shit for over a year now, and as you can imagine, I've long exceeded the budget for this investigation. I'm not proud to admit that I've gotten a lot of flak about it too. So, I need you to gather some evidence *before* the U.S. Department of Justice hangs both our asses. I've come too far to be the laughing stock of the LAPD," he said. "Come on, kid. There's gotta be something. You've been babysitting these fuckers like Mrs. Doubtfire for the past twelve months. You *have* to have something."

I opened and closed my mouth several times. I couldn't say anything. He was right; it was unprofessional and unjust to sit here and make excuses, as a man and as an agent. I'd been working close to Jude for over a year now. There was no excuse for why I didn't have enough evidence scraped up to place him under arrest. But what could I say? The man was smart and proficient when it came to covering his tracks.

"I'm doing my best, sir."

Lieutenant Beechum sighed and pinched the bridge of his nose in frustration. I could sense that the investigation was finally taking its toll on him. Heck, it was taking its toll on me too. I wanted to slap the cuffs on Jude more than anybody.

"Perhaps you have," Lieutenant Beechum agreed. "But your best *obviously* isn't good enough," he said. "I'm sorry, but I'm pulling you off the case."

"No!" I sat up in the chair and slammed my fists on his table. "I've been at this shit for months! I've worked hard as hell, goddammit! I'm this close! These people trust me! Please Lieutenant Beechum! You have to reconsider!"

"What else do you expect me to do when my balls are up against the wall? I put all of my resources at your disposal. Spent millions of tax payers' dollars on this investigation, and yet you don't even have enough evidence to make a single, solid arrest."

"I have a witness," I blurted out. "The mother of the daughter who works for Jude's organization as an accountant." I spoke promptly and with purpose. I couldn't lose this case. I'd worked so hard to see these sons of bitches go down. "Just give me one more week," I pleaded. "Just one more week to put something together."

Lieutenant Beechum raised an eyebrow in skepticism. There was a doubtful look on his wrinkled face, and I just knew that he didn't think I was capable. "*One week?*" He repeated.

"One week," I said. "I'll figure something out. Even if I have to pull a rabbit out of my ass. I'll figure something out," I assured him. "I always do."

"Alright, González. I'm trusting your word. You've got one week," he agreed. "I just hope that you can nail these bastards."

Hell, I hope I can too, I thought. At this point, I needed a fucking miracle to make that shit happen.

19
JOURNEE

Wearing some Adidas shorts and a sports bra, I stood in front of my full body length mirror and admired my full-figured shape. *Damn. I'm getting wild thick out here.* I smiled, stuck my tongue out and started dancing like a slut. Just then, my phone chirped with a text message. It was from Letitia.

Will be back in town tmrw. Wanna link up?

If I'm free, I responded knowing damn well I would be. Besides, I'd been counting down the days until she came back, but I wouldn't tell her that.

Girl bye. You ain't got nothing else better to do.

Suddenly, I thought about the boy with the bushy ponytail I'd seen in school. I didn't feel like texting her so instead I called.

"What do you want, bitch?" she answered.

"Just a quick question answered," I said. "You ever seen this boy at our school? He's medium brown, has slanted Chinese-looking eyes, and long pretty ass hair."

"I think I *have* seen him around. He sells weed and pills to the kids at our school. Why?"

He sold a lot more than weed and pills, but I'd save all that for a later discussion. "Nothing...I just...thought he was kinda cute..."

"Wow, Journee. Of all the boys in our school you could like, you pick the neighborhood drug dealer?"

"I didn't say I liked him, bitch. I just said that he was cute. And stop trying to pair me up with them lame ass niggas at the academy. Those guys are fucking dweebs."

"Why, because they don't sell drugs?"

"No, they're just all spoiled. They're always walking around with this annoying sense of entitlement."

"*Hmm.* Sounds like someone I know," she said sarcastically.

"Up yours. Like I said, I had a question, that's all. Now that you've answered it, you can get the hell off my line," I said before hanging up in her face. I tossed the phone back on my bed at the same time my door cracked opened.

"Princess, you decent?" My dad called out.

"Yes, Daddy."

My dad walked in, closed the door behind him and ambled over to my desk. "You got a couple minutes to spare for your old man? I wanna talk to you 'bout somethin' that's been on my mind lately."

"Did mom ask you to talk to me?" I asked with an attitude.

My dad folded his arms and pinned me with a shrewd glance. "No, she didn't. *Should* she have?"

"No. I don't know. What do you want to talk to me about?"

"Go on and take a seat," he said.

I flopped down on my mattress and stared at him incredulously.

"You're gonna be fifteen soon," he began. "You're getting older, developing, and, uh, blossoming into a young woman." He cleared his throat.

"Dad...this is really awkward and uncomfortable."

"Just hear me out," he said. "I know that you're getting older, and your hormones are probably going crazy, but I just want you to remember the importance of self-worth. Always remember to value yourself, princess. Don't let these knuckleheads out here make you lose your sense of value or worth as a person," he said. "Value yourself, your worth and your contribution in the world because you're special, Journee. Do you hear me? You're my special little girl. And I don't ever want *anyone* to make you feel like you're anything less. You hear me, princess? It's important for you to know that, baby girl. Always remember to value and respect yourself as a young woman. That's all I wanted to tell you."

"Okay, Daddy. I promise I won't grow up and become a stripper like mom."

He laughed and shook his head, before walking over and kissing me on the forehead. "You didn't wanna go to the beach with Justin and Madison?" he asked.

"No. I was thinking about going to the Grove."

"Not with that on, right?" He asked, pointing to my meager attire.

"No, Daddy," I laughed. "Not in this."

"Okay. Be careful and be sure to take Conway with you." He turned around and headed for the door, and I rolled my eyes behind his back. I couldn't stand having Conway follow me around. It was repellent to boys who *wanted* to hit on me.

"Yes, Daddy," I murmured.

"Oh, and one more thing," he said, stopping in his tracks. "Just out of curiosity...Is Justin and Madison...a thing?" He asked.

I stifled a laugh. "I don't think so, Daddy, why do you ask?"

"No reason. Forget I even asked. I'll see you later on tonight, sweetheart. I love you."

"Okay, Daddy. Love you too."

I smiled sweetly, then let it vanish the second he closed the door behind him. Climbing off the bed, I got back in the mirror and started popping and twerking, completely disregarding his boring ass speech about self-value and self-worth. Unfortunately, it was a lesson that I'd have to learn the hard way.

20
MADISON

That day, Justin surprised me to a night out on the town, starting with a visit to the popular Santa Monica Beach. We walked along the shore hand in hand while feeding each other cotton candy, then after, we went to *Palisades Park* to take pictures. It was located atop Santa Monica's famed sandstone cliffs, providing a vantage point to see sweeping views of Santa Monica Beach and the Pacific Ocean. It was really romantic, and I wouldn't have wanted to be anywhere else with anyone else.

The fact that Justin went out his way to show me a good time had me kinda feeling bad about posting that pic. Sometimes, I just did shit for the hell of it to see if Justin would finally give me the boot, but he never did. He was in it to win it.

"I'm sorry I posted that photo," I said, as we headed towards the pier.

"Yeah, you'd better be." He kissed me. "Gettin' me all worked up and shit. You know how stingy I am when it comes to you."

"Okay, so am I. How do you think I felt when I saw that Aria bitch leaving hearts and kissy faces all over your photos? Who is she? Your little fan girl?"

"Man, chill," Justin laughed.

"You know, that's the only reason I posted that pic."

"Nah, that ain't the *only* reason," Justin said.

"Then what other reason is there?"

"The most obvious. You petty as fuck," he laughed. "You know I ain't goin' nowhere. As long as you have my back, I'll have yours. We're more than just a couple, Maddie. We're family. I would never intentionally go out my way to hurt you. I love you. I've loved you for half my life."

"I love you too," I told him. "But if I ever see that bitch commenting under your shit again, I'll rip your fucking fingernails off!"

"I'd like to see you try!" Justin picked me up and tossed me over his shoulder before running towards the shore.

Before I could tell him to put me down, he dived headfirst into the water. I crashed into an oncoming wave fully clothed, and Justin laughed like it was the funniest shit ever.

"Oh my God, Justin! I hate you!" I screamed.

He pulled me close to him and kissed me. "No, you don't. You love me."

I stared into his pretty brown eyes. "You're right. I do love you. But sometimes you drive me crazy."

"Well, I hate to burst your bubble, princess, but you're no walk in the park either," he said. "I don't give a fuck though, 'cuz I love your pretty ass anyway."

Suddenly, I put some distance in between us. "Justin, I have something to tell you."

"Wassup, baby?"

"I got a scholarship to a school in Ghana."

I watched all of the color leave his face. He was pissed because he wanted me to attend college in the same city as him. I wanted the same but my father had other plans.

"So that means we'll have to keep doin' this long-distance shit," he said sadly. "I hate doin' long distance."

"Well, what would you rather *do*, locals?" I couldn't help but take a playful jab at him to lighten the mood.

"Real funny, nigga." Justin forced a smile. "Don't get me wrong. I'm happy as hell for you, and you damn sure deserve it. You worked your ass off for it. I just thought when you turned eighteen, we'd be livin' together and doing our own thing."

"...Maybe this is for the best," I said.

Justin looked offended. "How you figure?"

"Because if we lived in the same city or under the same roof, we'd get sick of each other. But since our time together is so brief, we've learned to appreciate one another and value the moments we share."

"Madison, I would never get sick of you," he said. "I love you too much to get sick of you. Your ass may get on my last fuckin' nerves, but I could never ever get sick of you."

The depth of his comment made me smile. He always knew what to say to reassure me. That's why I loved Justin. Because with him, I never had to wonder. He was always open and honest about his feelings for me. He never tried to downplay them for the sake of looking cool or hard. "I love you, Justin. But we've already done this for five years. What's another four?"

Justin looked disappointed as he turned away from me and headed to the shore. I could tell he was upset and I hated to see him angry, so I latched my arms around his waist and just held him there in the water, in soaking wet clothes.

"I'm sorry," I whispered. "If you want, I could try to talk to my dad and see if—"

"No," Justin interrupted. "You're right. Sometimes you have to compromise in a relationship, whether you want to or not. And I would never wanna stand in the way of you accomplishing your dream. You go to that school if that's what you wanna do. I've got no problem waiting for you. Like you said, I've already waited this long. I'll just come to visit you every spring and summer break."

"I would love that! And thank you for being so understanding. I swear, I'm so lucky to have you."

Justin turned around, cupped my chin and kissed me. "You damn right you lucky," he teased.

I kissed the back of his hand and looked up into his dark brown eyes.

"I'll wait four years or five years or however long I have to. You're gonna be my future, Madison. I'm not goin' anywhere."

I gently bit his bottom lip. "Good, you better not. Because if you tried to leave me, I'd probably kill you."

"Mmm. My dick gets hard whenever you talk that crazy shit."

He squeezed what little ass I had and I broke out laughing hysterically. I really loved this boy. He was my best friend, my partner in crime, and my confidante all wrapped up in one handsome, perfect guy.

"I love you, Justin. I promise we'll make it work."

He kissed my forehead. "I know we will."

We were so caught up in the moment, we didn't notice the pair of eyes on us.

21
JUSTIN

That morning, I decided to take my dad up on his offer of shooting some hoops at the local rec center. He used to be pretty damn good in his heyday, but you couldn't tell from the way I was breaking his ankles and shit. I was happy that we were at the rec and Mom wasn't here to witness this.

"Come on, old man, you lettin' me school you," I said, after crossing him over. I dribbled down the court, then scored two more points with a smooth ass layup. "That shot was hella saucy, wasn't it?" I bragged. I had terrible sportsmanship, and an even worse habit of showboating. "C'mon pops, I know that ain't ya best."

My dad paused to bend over and catch his breath. "My knees ain't what they used to be, son," he said.

"That stomach ain't either," I said, playfully patting his abdomen. It wasn't huge. It just wasn't washboard flat like mine. I'd seen plenty pics of him when he was younger, plus I still somewhat remembered how he looked back then, and let's just say age was finally catching up to him.

"You know what, kid. One day you're gonna wake up and realize you ain't as fly and fierce as *you* once were."

"Bullshit," I said stubbornly. "I ain't goin' out like you." My dad always let us curse, but Mom Dukes wasn't havin' it.

Jude laughed haughtily. *"Like me*? What the fuck does that mean?" he asked.

"My own son schoolin' me and shit. C'mon dad, you're like Jordan."

My dad smiled proudly.

"Trying to play baseball," I added.

My dad laughed again.

"C'mon." I tossed the ball to him. "Check me." Jude passed it back, and I made a move to go right, then quickly cut left and dribbled my way down the court, before dunking on his ass like LeBron in his prime. "C'mon, pops. You lettin' me cook you. You like an old ass uncle tryin' to see if he still got it. Shit's embarrassing," I teased.

Jude gestured for a time out, then limped over towards the bleachers. There was a surgical scar that ran vertically down his back. Mom said it was from him getting shot by her ex-boyfriend, Silk. I didn't know which one I was more upset with. The fact that he'd gotten shot, or the fact that she used to date a nigga named Silk. Thankfully, this was before my time.

"Junior for the win," I bragged.

After reaching the bleachers, my dad flopped down and started massaging the joints in his legs. We were the only ones in the gym, probably because it was 8-something in the morning. Unzipping my duffel bag, I pulled two water bottles out and tossed my dad one. Next, I plopped down on the bench beside him and unscrewed the cap off of mine.

"Why you let me jimmy you though?"

My dad just laughed as he took a swig of his water. "Ah. You just got lucky."

I took another sip of my water, then gave him an inquiring look. "Is it really that hard for you to stay in shape with all that you do?" I asked him.

"What can I say? I'm a busy man. Oftentimes, too busy to hit the gym."

"Well, that's why you need to start grooming ya boy," I said, slyly.

My dad looked over at me like I was crazy. "Grooming you for what?"

"To take over the business. What else?"

My dad laughed and shook his head at me. "The only thing you're gonna be taking over is Stanford University."

"C'mon pops. What the fuck am I gonna learn in that school that will contribute to your legacy in any way?"

"*Legacy*?" he repeated.

"I already got it mapped out, pops. I could be something like your protégé—"

"Justin—"

"And I know how busy you are. You won't have to train me yourself if you don't have time to. I could like, shadow Fillmore or some shit—"

"Justin—"

"I could dedicate my whole summer to learning the business—"

"A fool is known by his speech; and a wise man by silence. Now please, son, let me talk," Jude stated. "I don't need you to carry on my legacy. I need you to get an education and make something of yourself."

"I can make something of myself. As your predecessor," I told him.

"Fillmore—"

"Fillmore isn't your son," I reminded him. Fillmore was my dad's second-in-command. I knew this because after I found out my dad sold drugs, he sat me down and broke down everything to me. Fillmore was his operations chief, in charge of his money and logistics. He was also gay, and I never knew that until my dad told me. He certainly didn't *act* gay. He and his husband were really close to the family; his husband worked for my dad, as well. Though me and Fillmore were cool, I'd be damned if he ran my father's business before me.

"You know your mom will kill you if she heard you talking like this. You're not even supposed to know what I do," he said.

I found out he was a drug dealer at 13, after I found his hidden stash of drugs under the floorboards in the basement. "Yeah, well, that's why I'm runnin' it by you and not her."

"This isn't up for debate, son."

"Why not???" I pressed. "How many niggas have degrees but can't find a job after they graduate? Nowadays them shits be just a piece of paper to hang in a fuckin' plaque," I argued. "Running your business is for sure money."

"You sound like you've only ever strived to be a drug dealer," my dad said.

"No. I'm striving to follow in your footsteps," I told him. "It's all I ever wanted to do. Besides, after uncle Magyc died you've yet to take anyone else under your wing. Why not let your next predecessor be your flesh and blood? I'll be the rightful sole heir to your empire anyway." I was determined to have the product *and* the power.

My dad laughed. "You sound like you've thought long and hard about this."

"Tell me and I forget. Teach me and I remember. Involve me and I learn," I explained. "I wanna follow in ya footsteps, pops. That's all I've ever strived to do."

"Son...Running a business is just like farming. Planting the seeds alone isn't going to make the crops grow on their own. You need to feed it foul smelling shit and spray it with pesticides before you can harvest the fruit. What I'm trying to say is...there's a lot that comes with this street shit. Things that I'm not yet ready to expose you to."

"You're the one that told me if opportunity doesn't knock, build a door. You know the world is gonna expose me to shit no matter what, pops...Better it be you than some other muthafucka in the streets." Jude sighed, like he didn't want to talk about it, but I wasn't about to let up so easily. "What about *after* I get my degrees???" I pressed. "If I can't find any work in my field, *then* will you consider it?"

My dad paused for a very long time, then scratched his beard. "Maybe I'll consider it," he said. "And that's a very strong *maybe*."

"Fuck it. That's good enough for me," I smiled.

Jude finally stood from the bleachers. "I'm tired than a bitch. Let's call it game and grab some breakfast."

My stomach started rumbling at the mere mention of food. "Sounds like a plan."

"So, um, you and Madison," he began. "Are you two like a couple, or something?"

"Did Journee tell you that?!" I asked angrily.

"No, she didn't, so don't go picking on your little sister," he warned. "It's just...you know I was your age before, once upon a time. I know how the game goes, son. I done been around the block more times than you can imagine. I'll just say that a man knows," he told me.

I hesitated with answering, because I was scared of how he might react. After all, me and Madison had kept our relationship secret for years.

"It's okay. You can be real with me," he said.

"Well...Yeah...Madison's my girlfriend...." I finally admitted, and it actually felt good to let it out. As a matter of fact, it felt like a weight had been lifted off of me. The burden of keeping our relationship secret was becoming too much to bare.

Jude smiled at me and ruffled my hair. "Some words of wisdom, son. Don't ever let Soul hear you say that," he laughed.

***

After breakfast, I met up with Drip at an abandoned skate park on the outskirts of the city. It was tagged with gang signs, and a lot of folks met here for drug exchanges since it was out of the way.

"So, I talked to my old man today about runnin' the business," I told Drip. We were smoking on some loud that smelled like thunder. I'm talkin' the whole muthafuckin' block was reekin'.

"Okay...good for you. And what about the nigga we got tied up in the warehouse? How 'bout we talk about that?"

"On five, I'mma handle it," I said, taking a pull from the blunt. I coughed a little when it filled my lungs too fast. The backwoods always blew my whole chest out.

"You know the rules of the Backwoods, man. You ain't never 'posed to hit that shit too hard," he said.

I coughed some more, then spat a mouthful of phlegm on the ground.

"So, *when* we gon' handle that?" Drip asked again, in a more serious tone.

"Don't worry about that lil' situation. I'mma clean that up real good. Why you on my dick so hard about it, though?" I asked, noticing his bad mood all of a sudden. "You gotta stick up your ass, or some shit, my nigga?"

"I just don't know why you'd come at me 'bout that bullshit. As if it has anything to do with me."

"Damn, brozay, I can't share good news with you now?"

"That's good news for *you*, my nigga," Drip said angrily. "Where the fuck does that leave me and mine?"

I immediately noticed that the vibe was off between us. "Nigga, you switch up more than a lightswitch.

What the fuck is wrong with you? All I said was me and my dad had a chat about me taking over his business."

"And all I said was I don't give a fuck. Or did you not catch that?"

"My nigga, you actin' like a whole hater right now."

"Nigga, what the fuck is there to hate on?" he asked, with suppressed anger in his eyes. "It'll just be another thing that your fucking father handed over to you. I don't see what the big deal is. You's a daddy's boy. When everything is laid out for you, you ain't really gotta do no work. You ain't never had to get it out the mud."

"So, what'chu sayin'?"

"Nigga, you 'posed to be my folks. I'm *sayin'* where the fuck will that leave me and mine? Your peoples don't fuck wit' me like that. Ain't like they're gonna recruit me, Chris, and Nahmir to join the team."

"So, that's what this is about? My nigga, you bitter 'cuz you think shit ain't gone move for you? You think I'mma have you goin' back to drinkin' sugar water and eatin' mayonnaise sandwiches?" I was only fucking with the nigga but he took the shit personally.

"Nigga, I ain't never had to worry 'bout a meal! Just like I ain't never got nothin' handed to me. Nigga, I always had to trap for it," he said, matter-of-factly, as his eyes hardened in determination. "I ain't never been nothin' *but* a muthafuckin' trapper!"

"Drip—"

"Man, whatever. I'm outta here," he said, tossing his butt.

"Drip?" I called after him. But he just kept on walking, obviously in his feelings about what the future may hold. Since he had three other mouths to feed, I couldn't say that I really blamed him.

22
CAMERON

"Cam, baby, we gotta talk," Jude said, walking into the bedroom that night. I had just stepped out of the shower and was toweling myself off when he approached me with a look of ambiguity. "I've been puttin' this shit off long enough, but now it has to be said."

"What's up? Is everything okay?" I asked, starting to grow concerned. It wasn't often my husband came to me wanting to talk about something serious. He held the business and family down, so I wasn't sure what he had to say me.

"Sit down," he insisted.

That only made me more concerned. Tightening the towel around my partially damp body, I slicked my short hair back with my hands. I then took a seat on the edge of the bed, crossed my legs and clasped my hands together in front of my knee. Jude sighed deeply, then ran a hand over his brush waves. There was obviously something eating him. "Just a disclaimer...you're not gonna be happy after I tell you this shit," he began.

I stared meditatively at him. I didn't feel like playing the guessing game. "Well, I'm not happy with you stalling," I said. "Just tell me what it is, so we can get this over with. You know I hate surprises."

Jude took a deep breath and exhaled. "Well...When I went to Atlanta about the missing ledger...Eve sorta...came onto me."

Anger and disgust rose like bile in my throat, and I could barely form the words to speak. "What do you mean she *came onto you*?" I asked angrily. I just knew it was a reason I didn't like that young bitch and it had nothing to do with her being King's daughter; a man who responsible for having me beaten and brutally raped years ago.

"Well, when I got to the building to confront her about it, she was asshole naked in her office. She was just...waiting for me. It was really strange and out of character."

I jumped off the bed, ready to swing on him. "That bitch ain't got no character!!!" I yelled; I was in a red haze, mad at the world. "I swear these little hoes have no respect for marriages nowadays!"

Jude immediately fell silent.

"So, she never even lost the shit???" I asked him. "It was all a lie then? You were all worked up for nothing???"

"It was all just a ploy to get me down there."

"And what the fuck did you do when you *got* down there???" I pressed.

Jude looked offended that I was even questioning his morality and loyalty to me. "What the fuck you think I did? I got ghost."

"Did you? Did you really?" I said with a doubtful look on my face. It was hard for me to believe him knowing his track record.

"Cameron, I didn't even have to tell you this shit," he said uncharacteristically calmly.

"Well, it sure took you some time to. I can't believe you didn't tell me this shit sooner—"

"Baby, it was your birthday. I wanted you to enjoy your party. I ain't wanna drop a bomb like this on your special day. It wasn't the time or the place."

I gaped at him like he'd just lost his mind. "Well, you should have! If the shoe was on the other foot, you'd want me to tell you ASAP! The fact that you waited *this* long feels sneaky and underhanded as fuck—"

"Really? So, I'm sneaky now?" He asked in disbelief. "I keep it solid with you and you call me sneaky???"

I could sense a rising tension, and I felt like throwing the clock on the nightstand at Jude's head just to show his ass what time it is. "I just know how shit was in the past," I said snidely. "Remember Essence? Remember her?" I was still disgusted by the shit that went down all those years ago.

Jude simply laughed and shook his head. "If you keep looking back, you gone trip going forward."

The space between us was fraught with tension. I was so angry about the situation that I was taking it out on him. "So, what the fuck you gone do?" I hounded him. "'Cuz I'm two seconds away from hopping on a plane just to drag that hoe—"

"Ain't nobody dragging nobody," Jude said with finality. "I already called and spoke to her and Evelyn about the shit."

"So, you told Evelyn before you told me?" I asked angrily.

Jude frowned in irritation.

Overcome with emotion, I screamed, "I WILL DRAG BOTH THEM HOES—"

"Listen to me, you've surpassed your years of draggin' bitches," he said.

With a look of cool distaste, I folded my arms and grilled him. "Well then, *you're* gonna fire her ass!" I told him.

"You know I can't do that—"

"Bullshit! Why the hell not??? There's plenty people out there that know math."

The silence swelled ominously. Neither of us said anything for a few strained moments. "Have some damn perspective, Cameron. It's not just about knowing math. Eve is my head accountant," he reminded me. "I'm not really in a position to fire someone who has so much intel when it comes to the business. And I damn sure can't kill her—"

"Then what the fuck *are* you going to do?!"

"I'm not gonna do shit, Cam. She's just a kid. She fucked up. I only told you this shit 'cuz I felt like you needed to know. Like you said, if the shoe was on the other foot, I'd want you to be real with me."

My heart contracted. "So, I pretty much just to have to deal with it—because she's a kid??? That's basically what you're telling me?"

"Man, that shit's dealt with over there. It won't happen again. I can assure you."

"You damn right it won't, 'cuz I'm chin-checking that bitch!"

I made a move to go to the closet to start packing my bags, but Jude thwarted my path. "Where are you goin'?"

"To LAX."

"You're not 'bout to fly to Atlanta to confront this girl."

"The hell I'm not, Jude, watch me."

"Hey. Hey. Do you know how sexy you are when you're jealous as fuck?" Jude cupped my chin and kissed me on the mouth, pulling me into his body to calm me down. I knew that he was just trying to get my guards down. And with the way he was holding and kissing me, it was working. "I know you ready to pop off, but I shut that shit down," he assured me. "It won't happen again, baby. Trust me." He removed my towel and ran his hands down the length of my arms.

"You promise," I whispered, with a hint of desperation in my tone. "I don't wanna have to maul that hoe about my husband."

Jude kissed my lips, then backed me up against the bed, where I fell and landed with a soft thud. "It's a done deal," he said, comfortingly. Reaching for his belt, I eagerly unzipped his pants, snatched them below his ass, and pulled his rigid dick through the opening of his boxers. He was so damn hard, it felt like I was gripping a steel pipe in my hand. I took his cock in my mouth and sucked and licked the shaft before tickling his balls a little with my tongue. I was a thorough, attentive lover.

He reached down, ran his hands over my breasts and pinched and plucked my nipples. "*Mmm.* Damn, Cam," he groaned, grabbing a handful of my hair, as his pre-cum shot in my mouth like an Uzi. My jaws inflated while my throat moved up and down, struggling to take every last inch of him.

Slipping a hand down my body, I played with my own clit as my pussy leaked raw desire as I sucked and gagged on 10 inches of steel. Thrusting his hips, he forced his dick down my throat as far as it could go, connecting with my tonsils every so often. I had to breathe through my nose just to keep from choking to death, as he pumped my face aggressively. His hand went to the back of my head, as he fucked my mouth until I had no choice but to come up for air. A line of spit connected his dick and my mouth. He had me spitting and slobbering everywhere like a newborn baby.

"C'mere," he said, forcing me on my back. The house was so big that we weren't worried about anyone hearing us. Plus, our bedroom was on the third level.

Jude flipped me over into a 69 position, spread my thighs and launched a tongue attack on my wet, fat pussy. We went wild together in a whirlwind of lust. Using his index and thumb, he touched and teased my swollen clit. I felt my soul leave my body when he stuck his tongue inside of me and started tickling my g-spot. I immediately went into a seizure like state of euphoria as I shook, trembled and cried out his name.

"Oooohh, Jude," I moaned. My body was covered in sweat and gripped by pleasure. "You're a fuckin' beast."

"Say I'm your beast," he whispered in my pussy.

When I didn't answer fast enough, he resorted to nibbling and chewing on my clit. Then he stuck two fingers inside of me and started rubbing my g-spot simultaneously. I squirted all on his face and beard as I continued to shake violently. "Mmm. You're my beast," I whined.

I swear, his pussy eating skills only seemed to get better and better with age. He was eating me out so good,

I couldn't concentrate on giving him head at the same time. Frustrated with my lack of enthusiasm, he grabbed my face and forced his dick down my throat, and since he was on top, that didn't take much effort. Grabbing his ass, I helped him hump my face, his balls resting on my nose. I inhaled the musky fragrance and it only seemed to make my pussy wetter as he licked me clean.

"Shit, I can't do this for too much longer without cumming. I need some ass," Jude said, rolling over onto the mattress.

He smacked my booty, then slid out of his shirt and jeans and I wasted no time squatting directly above his cock. Grabbing the base of his dick, I lowered myself onto his 10 inches of steel. He raised his hips to meet me, and locked his hands around my waist as I slid over his dick like a sword to a sheath.

"*Mmm.* Feels like I'm in another universe when I'm inside you," he moaned. His dick was perfectly handcrafted for me.

Thrusting from underneath, he began pumping erratically into my drooling pussy. I was so tight that I snatched him back into me with every thrust. He'd been working and out of town so much that it felt like we hadn't fucked in ages. And now that I knew another bitch was trying to take care of my man for me, I *had* to fuck the shit out of his ass to solidify my spot in his life.

Digging my fingernails into his chest, I bounced up and down on dick, swallowing every inch inside of my pubic mound before spitting him back out, covered in my juices. I was riding him so hard and fast, that his dick accidentally slipped out of me.

"Shit, woman," he chuckled. "You tryin' to give this old man a heart attack?"

I grabbed his glossy-coated dick and guided it towards my opening. The head of his dick pressed into my vagina, and with a shift of his hips, he entered me once again. Sliding my pussy down the length of his full hard shaft, I fell forward on his chest and we started kissing passionately. Jude grabbed a handful of my ass and slowly rocked back and forth with me on top of him. He was buried deep inside of me, his balls pressed against the outside of my pussy lips. He tenderly speeded things up, and before I knew it we were fucking and moaning like a pair of dogs in heat. I shrieked with pleasure as I felt the tip of dick brushing against my g-spot, bringing me close to cumming. My entire body began to spasm, and my pussy muscles squeezed his cock.

"I'm 'bout to nut!" He bellowed. Before he could fully get the words out, he shot a massive load of cum into my dripping cunt. Shortly after, I came too. Jude brushed a kiss over my forehead.

For a few moments, we lay quietly as I reflected on what he had told me earlier. I got a queasy feeling in my stomach just *thinking* about a dusty ass chick coming onto my man. He had another thing coming if he thought I *wasn't* about to check this crumb ass bum ass bitch.

23
EVE

Looking at my reflection in my bedroom vanity's mirror, I admired my brown and blemish free skin, and the way my perky tits sat up in my strapless dress. *What man wouldn't want to marry me?* I was pretty as fuck, and people often mistook me for a video vixen, because of my full figure and seductive looks. I'd really blossomed into quite the woman over the years. Jude would have to be blind, deaf and dumb to not notice that.

I still couldn't believe that he didn't bend me over when he had the chance. There I was, standing in his office, just as naked as the day I was born and this nigga turned me down. It was some straight bullshit. Regardless of my failed attempt, I knew his ass still wanted me. He was just too fucking proud—and scared of his wife—to admit it.

Suddenly, I heard the security system alert me to my mother's entrance. We had a cozy, luxurious townhouse tucked off in the suburbs of Marietta. It was nowhere near as plush as the house he had his family living in, and that was another thing that ticked me and Mama off. Jude moved his family to Cali, but we had to live in country ass Georgia. Why couldn't we get a beachside condo, or mini mansion in the hills. I'd been grinding for his ass for 3 years now? Did I not deserve the same luxuries?? After all, he wouldn't even be in the position he was in, if it wasn't for my father putting him on.

My mother quietly entered my bedroom, breaking into my thoughts. She was wearing a look of pure disdain, and she didn't look very happy to see me. She had a mink fur draped over her shoulders with a matching headband and Chanel sunglasses covering her hazel eyes. Long, knee high leather boots accentuated the entire fit, along with her superfluous jewelry. My mother had expensive tastes—which was one of the main reasons she wanted me to marry Jude, so that I could own half his wealth. She saw the way he had his wife and kids living and she wanted that. Hell, we both did.

"Hi, Mama. I see you're back early from Italy. Did you like it? How did it go?"

"It should've been perfect, but I had to cut my trip short after the phone call I got from Jude. He was pretty upset about that little stunt you pulled," she said, pulling a box of Marlboros out of her purse.

"Well, you told me to seduce the nigga," I reminded her.

At 6 feet even, my mother was a very tall and very broadly built woman. "Not by spreading your legs, little girl." She fired up her cigarette. "I meant to seduce him by charming him. Any bitch can throw herself at a nigga."

My mother was always trying to school me. Like I said, she'd been grooming me to become this nigga's wife ever since I was 13 years old. "You're right. My bad. I guess I wasn't thinking strategically." I graciously apologized as I put my head down in shame. I was fucking up the plan, and I needed to get with the program quick if I wanted shit to go accordingly.

"Of course you weren't. You were thinking with your pum-pum," she winked. "But it's okay. That's what you have me for, sweetie." She slowly walked up to me. "And another thing...this hair..." she gently tilted my head from left to right. "I'm sorry, baby, but this hair has *got* to go."

"Aww, mama. Not my hair." It was one of my best features. I'd never cut it a day in my life and it stretched down to the middle of my back.

"What did I teach you? You level the playing field by studying the competition," she said. "Always remember that."

Mama had told me countless tales of how men had cheated on their wives with her, just because she *looked* like their wives. It was some illogical shit, but I wouldn't have put anything past these weird ass niggas out here. Still, I wasn't a fan of cutting my hair off. "Can't I just get a wig though, Mama?"

My mother smiled and took another pull from her cigarette. "Sweetie...When it comes to success, there are no shortcuts," she simply said. "Now come on. My girl is closing shop soon, but if we hurry we can still make it."

Thirty minutes later, we were in her favorite salon in midtown. The place was scheduled to close in 20 minutes but because she was a regular who spent big money, she got special VIP treatment.

"So, what are we doing today?" Delonda asked, running her fingers through my long, silky jet-black mane.

"Cutting it all off," my mom answered for me.

"*Cutting it all off?* Are you sure?" Delonda asked in disbelief. "All this long, pretty ass hair?"

"Positive like a pregnancy test. Cut it off and give her one of those cute little pixie cuts. Kinda like Halle Berry used to rock in her prime. Remember?"

"Ooh, yeah, I remember." Delonda grabbed a pair of shears. "You got it."

Three hours later, I took in the sight of my new haircut. It actually was a good look, and it made me feel sexy, sleek and mature.

"How do you like it?" Delonda asked, smiling like she'd just finished her biggest masterpiece.

"I love it," I said.

"It's perfect," my mom smiled.

After paying Delonda, we left the salon, with me looking like Cameron's fucking twin. I really hoped this shit worked, because I needed Jude to notice me, and not just as his business associate.

"There. That'll teach 'em," my mom said, starting up her truck.

"You really think this shit will work?"

"Why wouldn't it?" she asked, fastening her seatbelt.

"I don't know, Ma. I just hope that us going the extra mile isn't for nothing."

"Your father's dead," she reminded me. "You know that for years now, I've wanted the life we used to have. *You* deserve to have the life you used to have," she stressed. "We're above living in some crappy ass townhome in Marietta, Georgia. King had us living like fucking royalty! Jude got us living like fucking peasants! You've been busting your ass for this business for over three years and *this* is the best he can do?" she said, gesturing to her surroundings. As if on cue, a homeless man stumbled up the street in a drunken stupor.

"Jude's done a lot for us too though, Mama," I tossed in.

"And he'll do twice as much when you're his wife," she countered.

"True," I said penitently. "But do you ever think about me bagging some other high roller? Like a doctor or a lawyer maybe? What if this nigga never leaves his wife?" I asked disappointedly. Don't get me wrong. I wanted Jude more than Mama wanted to see me married to him, but I wasn't trying to chase this nigga for the rest of my life.

My mother sighed and pinched the bridge of her nose in frustration. "Baby, see, this is why I have to steer you in the right direction. Because you'll be all fucked up out here if I don't," she said. "A doctor or lawyer doesn't have a 40-million-dollar net worth. Jude is beyond making the Forbes list. Shit, he could own Forbes if he wanted. These doctors and lawyers won't provide the same financial security that Jude can give you. You have to level up. Hell, *I* can fuck any old doctor or lawyer," she chuckled. "Who do you think I was in Italy getting my groove back with?"

I couldn't help but laugh myself. My mama was so damn crazy, but I knew she only wanted the best for us. She was right. We *deserved* the best.

"You're right," I agreed.

"Eve, honey, you've *got* to start thinking long-term. You're a twenty-two-year-old, beautiful ass bombshell," she said. "If you play your cards right, we'll be living like royalty again in no time."

24
CAMERON

"Heeeeyyyyy, Cameron!!! *Mamacita! Feliz cumpleaños tardío!* Muah! Muah!" Sofía hugged and gave me air kisses, then she grabbed a handful of my ass and squeezed it. *"Tienes mucho culo!"* Her Colombian accent was so thick, sometimes I *still* had difficulty understanding her even when she was speaking English.

I quickly peeled her hands off of me before my daughter saw another woman feeling up her dear, sweet mother. Sofía was my crazy ass Spanish friend. She was actually from Colombia, and she'd just gotten back in town last night. That day, we decided to link up for an afternoon of some much-needed pampering.

Sofía was one of the wildest home girls I'd ever had. At 38, she was a year older than me and bi-sexual. She had ivory skin, dark brown hair, pouty lips and a coke bottle figure. It was all paid for, compliments of her hubby. The woman had work done on every part of her body, including her hairline; fake boobs, fake lips, fake hips, *and* fake ass. Still, she was one of the sweetest fucking people that I knew and she was a boss bitch. Her husband, Raúl, was a wealthy investment broker, and he'd helped us invest in several businesses, including the chain of boutiques Sofía and I owned. We met at a charity event several years ago, and we'd been tight ever since.

"Girl, you are so damn crazy. Would you sit down so we can soak our feet? I have some shit to catch you up on!"

Sofía was stunning that day in a black dress, fur collar, and jewel encrusted Louboutins. The bitch looked like money; like a walking, talking bag of money.

Sofía and I plopped down in our chairs and dipped our bare feet into the bowls in front of us. She even enlisted a technician to file the toenails of her cream-colored Pomeranian. I swear, she treated that thing like he was her newborn baby. Speaking of babies, our children were on the other side of the salon getting manicures. Well, actually I only had Journee with me. I wasn't sure where Madison and Justin had wandered off to. Knowing them, they were probably somewhere running the streets. I'd be damned if I could keep up with those kids.

"So, what's up mamí?" Sofía asked.

"First and foremost, how's your mother doing?"

"She's doing much better now. Raúl paid top dollar to put her in this fancy ass treatment center. So, she'll be getting the help that she needs."

"I'm so glad to hear that." Her mother had recently been diagnosed with breast cancer.

"So, what's up with you, *chica*? *Qué hay de nuevo*? Is everything going well in your marriage?" she asked.

"Yeah, everything's fine—"

"Oh, I was gonna say. You know I just had Vaginoplasty done not too long ago." Her voice was a thrilling whisper. "I'm all good to go down there. Bitch don't mind third wheelin' to get you and your husband back on track, you know, in case ya'll were having *marital problems*." She winked and made air quotes at the last two words. Before I could tell her TMI, she eagerly carried on. "I just love me some threesomes, mamí. I rate it second to cuckolding." It was just like Sofía to jump head first into the topic of sex—even when no one else was talking about it. The woman was a certified freak.

"And what the fuck is cuckolding?" I asked, almost too afraid to know the answer.

"So...okay...you know how much I love Raúl, right. He's my daddy, my heart my everything. But he's just not man enough to keep me satisfied in the bedroom." She held up her pinky finger to emphasize his shortcomings. "So, we compromised, and he lets me fuck other guys just as long as he's present."

"What??? He lets you fuck other men in front of him?!" My nail technician made a face and I lowered my tone, so that others didn't hear. "Are you serious?"

"Oh, bitch, he loves it! He just sits in a chair beside the bed and beats his meat while I do my thing." She giggled. "Sometimes he even lets me do two at a time."

"And he likes that shit???"

"Hell yes! He loves it when I humiliate and belittle him. I be talking hella shit and riding the fuck out of those *pingas*." She started humping her chair like she was fucking her dream guy.

"Say what now?"

"We've been doing it for years. It's what keeps our marriage alive," she stated proudly.

"I mean to each his own. That shit just seems...kinda...tacky," I said for lack of better word.

Sofía shrugged. "You call it tacky. I call it taboo."

"I think we have different philosophies about that."

"We'll just agree to disagree."

I shook my head at her. "Jude would literally kill me before he ever let me fuck another man."

"I don't blame him." She reached over and rubbed my leg. "I'd be selfish with this *chucha* too?" She teased.

I quickly swatted her hand away. If Sofía wasn't clowning, or telling me these crazy ass sex stories, she was busy trying to fuck me. She definitely had Pocahontas beat with her outrageous antics. Let's just say, because of her, I knew why they called it Holly-weird. Sofía was always exposing me to these wild ass fetishes that only people in LA seemed to enjoy. Or maybe, I was just old school. Like really, who the hell fancied cuckolding? It seemed like nowadays, marriage was no longer a sacred union.

"Oh, before I forget. I got you a gift," she said, reaching into her oversized Fendi bag.

"Please. No more wands," I said exasperated. Last birthday, she got me a 12-inch seven-speed, sex toy. I damn near electrocuted my pussy trying to use it.

"No, mamí, it's not another sex toy," she giggled. Sofía pulled a small box from the bag and I instinctively reached for it, but she quickly pulled her hand back. "Now if you want it, you have to scissor me for it."

I snatched the gift from her hands and eagerly opened it. Inside was court-side tickets to the next LA Lakers game, along with a certificate for a fully paid for spa retreat for couples.

"Aww, Sofía, thank you! Jude is really gonna love this! He works so hard."

"You're welcome, babes. I'm still bummed I missed your party though. I know your fine ass baby sitter was there lookin' like a whole fucking snack on a stick." She licked her filler-injected lips. "Or better yet, a whole meal."

"My baby sitter?" I repeated, confused.

"Clark, or Calvin, or whatever his name is. Girl, I don't remember names, I just remember dick prints."

"Conway," I corrected her. "And he's *not* my baby sitter, bitch. He's the head of my security team." He was actually outside right now, keeping watch.

"Bitch, I don't give a fuck *who* he is," she laughed. "All I know is he can rip my ear holes out with his dick any day."

I broke out laughing at her vulgarity. "Girl, I'm still trippin' on Raúl letting you fuck other men. And that he actually *likes* the shit."

"Bitch, *like* is an understatement. I told you, he loves it," she laughed.

"That's crazy as fuck, Sofía. I think I could've gone an entire lifetime without knowing that about ya'll."

Sofía just laughed like it was the funniest shit ever. Suddenly, my phone rang. It was Jude. "Hey, baby. How's everything?"

"Pretty good. Me and Journee are at the nail salon with Sofía's crazy ass." I cut my eyes at her and she batted her long mink lashes innocently.

"Lord, don't have that woman tainting my daughter," he joked.

"You need to be worried about her tainting me," I said.

Jude laughed. "Trust me, I *am* worried."

I broke out laughing too.

"What did his smart ass say?" Sofía inquired.

"He says you make him worried."

"He should be 'cuz I don't want him. I want his wife," she giggled.

I laughed and hit her leg, silently telling her to stop. I swear her crazy ass was too much for TV. "Sofía got us floor seats to the next Lakers game."

"Alright then. That's the move right there. Tell her I appreciate it."

"Jude thanks you for the tickets."

"Well, I just wanted to check in with my favorite girls. See how ya'll were doing. I guess I'll see you back at the crib."

"Okay, baby. Love you." I blew kisses through the phone and hung up.

"Well, aren't ya'll picture fucking perfect," Sofía teased. "Ya'll don't seem to be having any problems at all. So, what the hell did you have to talk to me about?"

"Bitch, so tell me why Jude said his *head* accountant tried to give him *head* the other day?"

"The young broad? She tried to fuck him?" Sofía asked in disbelief.

"Girl, yes. The one that's fifteen years younger than me," I said miserably.

Suddenly, Journee and Sofía's daughter walked up to us, and I quickly stopped talking. Sofía's daughter was actually adopted and Guyanese, and she and Journee attended the same private academy. Even though Sofía and Raúl were a couple of real life weirdos, they really went above and beyond to give their little girl the best life that they could provide.

"Mom, can I have some money to go to the mall?" Journee asked.

"You just went to the mall the other day," I reminded her.

Journee groaned under her breath, and there was an irritated look on her face. "Okay...and I *just* want more stuff," she replied smartly. "So, can I have some money or not?"

I made a mental note to check her about her mouth later on, but for now I decided to cave into her demands, as usual. That's why she was so rotten now, because me and Jude had spoiled her most of her life. Jude more than me. She was a real daddy's girl.

"Here," I said, handing her a small wad of cash. "Don't spend it all in one spot."

Journee flipped through the bills, then rolled her eyes like it wasn't enough. "I'll try not to," she said sarcastically.

Sofía handed her daughter her black card. "You know there's a credit limit so don't you get carried away, either. *Tener en cuenta.* Alright? Be mindful."

"I won't get carried away, mom. I promise."

Damn. Why can't my own daughter be sweet and respectful like that, I asked myself.

After Journee and Sofía's daughter left the salon, I turned my attention back to my girl to continue venting. "*Anyway,* when I checked him about the shit, he totally dismissed it. Said she was just a kid and she fucked up. Can you believe that?"

"Nah, she's about to *get* fucked up!" Sophia guffawed. Anytime she laughed, her long pink tongue stuck halfway out of her mouth. "Listen, this beef will never be cooked if you two don't sit down and square shit out. And it ain't shit but a four-hour flight to ATL, bitch! I say we pull up on that ass!"

25
JOURNEE

"Five hundred dollars. What the hell am I supposed to do with five hundred punk ass dollars?" I complained, as if it were a measly 5-dollar bill. I didn't understand my mom. She and Dad made more than enough money to give me a higher allowance. I got good grades at the stupid ass school she had me in. I didn't know what more she wanted from me. She could've at least given me 2-grand. It wasn't like that would put a dent in her pockets.

With envy burning through me, I watched my friend Letitia grab bag after bag from the display shelves. "I thought your mom said her credit card had a limit." On the low, I was just being a little shit bag of hater and I wanted to rain on her parade.

"There *is* a limit," Letitia said over her shoulder. "A ten-thousand-dollar limit."

I folded my arms and grimaced as I looked over the sale items again. I attended school with some of the wealthiest kids in the city. Competition was fierce, and I couldn't have Abigail and her minions trying to flex on me.

All of the parents kept their children laced, so I felt like I had to go shopping every other day to keep up. However, I damn sure wouldn't be able to stunt with just $500 to spend. We were in the Gucci store, so that would probably only get me a wallet or a belt—and that wasn't even new edition.

"What the hell am I supposed to do with this pocket change? I don't have enough to buy anything here," I seethed in anger.

"Damn. That's all bad. Pretty girl like you should be able to buy the whole damn store if she wants it." His smooth, deep voice made the hairs on the back of my neck stand. Turning on my heel, I took in the sight of the handsome stranger standing before me.

He was tall, muscular, and as manly as a man could get. His clothes were neat and dark. He had on some fitted jeans, a Givenchy tee, designer sneakers, and several chains. His looks and his swag made my heart beat faster, but I tried my best to play it cool. I had a weakness for men with a keen sense of fashion.

Gotdamn.

He was incredibly fine with his square jaw, brown skin and thick, sexy ass lips. He had these big pretty eyes and girlishly long lashes that looked unreal. Both of his ears were gaged, and on anybody else, I would have found that weird but the piercings actually suited him. I noticed he had perfect teeth as he gave me a charming smile. He rocked a Caesar fade with the c-cut in the front, and I could easily tell from the texture that he had a good grade of hair. He was so sexy and mysterious.

The parts of his body that were exposed were completely covered in tattoos, and tatted across his throat in bold Roman letters were the numbers 666. A small serpent was tattooed above his left eye. He looked to be in his early to mid-twenties, but he could've just as easily been older. I had never seen a man like him before. He was uncommonly handsome.

I looked up at him with a sweet, earnest expression.

"How you doin'?" he asked.

"I'm fine..."

"Shit, I can look at you and tell that much..."

The depth of the compliment made me blush. "Thank you," I smiled. "And how are you?" I asked him.

"I'm great. No complaints. Even better now that I got your attention."

"Nice tats," I said in a breathless state of awe.

He looked over at Letitia standing several feet away, but I felt no inclination to introduce the two of them. Besides, she was nowhere near as interesting as me. "I got 'em all over my body," he said. "I'd love to show 'em off to you someday."

"Yeah, well, we don't always get what we want, now do we," I said, snidely. His tattoos were cool but kind of off-putting. The man was sexy yet scary as fuck. Up until now, I didn't even think it was possible to be both.

"Big facts," he chuckled. "But aye, what's your name, lil' mama? They call me Elder." He patted his chest, then stuck his hand out for me to shake. There was a demon-like creature tatted on the back of it.

"Elder?" I repeated, making a funny face. "What kind of name is that?" I shook his hand, despite my reservations about him. He was all alone, but still intimidating as fuck.

"It's my name," he laughed, showing off those pearly whites of his. "Now can I get yours, if you don't mind?" He licked those sexy ass lips of his and my clit simultaneously jumped. Before today, that had *never* happened.

I blushed under the warmth of his admiring gaze. "Journee," I said, shedding my shyness.

He kissed the back of my hand. "Beautiful name for a beautiful girl."

I gave him an intimate smile, and his dark brown eyes twinkled as they stared worshipfully at me. I don't think I'd ever seen a man with longer lashes. He made me feel weak in the knees, warm in the belly, and just a wee bit petrified.

I tried not to blush in front of him. "How old are you?" I asked curiously, my tone somewhat hesitant.

"Old enough to know you're jail bait," he said, with just the hint of a smile.

I surprised myself by nearly chuckling. "And you're still talking to me knowing that?" I couldn't suppress my curiosity when it came to his code of ethics.

Elder shrugged like it was no biggie. "What can I say? You cute as fuck. Besides, if you ain't willing to risk the unusual, you'll have to settle for the ordinary. And in case you haven't noticed, I'm not a nigga who's fond of ordinary."

He disarmed me with his boyish charm. "So, are you gonna tell me how old you are?" I pressed.

"Twenty-four. Are *you* gonna tell me how old *you* are?" He quizzed.

I felt a wave of relief that he wasn't in his thirties. It would've been weird if he was close to my dad's age. I shuddered at the thought. "Sixteen," I lied.

There was a brief unconvinced silence between us.

"Unh, unh, unh. Like I said, jail bait," he smiled, shaking his head as he looked me up and down. His eyes were round with lust, and he had a presence that was unmatchable to any other. My mind told me to run but my legs were frozen stiff. He screamed 'trouble' and I devoutly hoped it wasn't true, but then again, I was a bit of a troublemaker myself.

At only 14, I was built like a nineteen-year old. I had size C cup breasts, wide hips, and a big butt. I also had a tiny pouch to go along with it, but that was expected when you were as thick as me. My mom always said that I was overdeveloped for a girl my age, and that dad would've kept me locked in a basement if it wasn't illegal.

"Well, don't just stand there. Gone get whatever you want," he said, pulling out his wallet. "Your fine ass deserves to leave the store with whatever you had intentions of buying."

He didn't have to ask me twice. I quickly grabbed shit off the racks and display shelves, and when the cashier rang up the purchases, it came to a whopping $16,572.89. Elder didn't bat an eyelash as he slapped his card on the counter. Letitia stood off to the side, wide-eyed, as she watched a complete stranger spend close to $20,000 on me.

"All set. It was a pleasure doing business with you," the cashier said, smiling like hell off the commission she'd made. "Would you like the receipt with you or in the bag?"

"The bag," Elder answered for me.

The cashier stuck the long slip of paper in the bag and Elder grabbed them from off the counter. "Do you just go around buying chicks designer shit?" I asked him.

"First off, you're not just any chick," he said. "You gone be my little girlfriend."

I bit my lip, then forced my mouth into a smile as I reached for the bags, but he quickly moved them out of reach.

"Nah, not so fast. I need that number first, baby girl. Fair exchange, no robbery."

I was suddenly struck by a fiery wave of rebellion. Propping a hand on my hip, I caught an automatic attitude. "You think 'cuz you spent a couple dollars on me that you own me now? Nigga, I've got news for you. My daddy drops racks on me religiously. Who the hell are you?"

"Who gone be fuckin' you though? Your daddy or me," he said, in a satisfied sort of way, while looking directly at my lips.

People watched enviously as we politicked, including Letitia. A few hoes had their eyes on him, and a couple of guys were ogling me, but neither of us were paying our groupies any mind. I grabbed the bags from him and this time he let me have them.

"Besides, I like the fact that you ain't easily impressed. I can't tell you how tired I am of meeting broads like that. I already peeped that you used to boss shit, so am I," he said. "That's one thing we already have in common."

I met his eyes calmly as I lolled my head to the side. I couldn't believe how bad he was acting like he wanted me. I mean, I knew I was cute and all but I still felt like he was sorta out of my league, though I wouldn't admit it. And it wasn't just because he was older than me.

"I'm sixteen and you're twenty-four," I reminded him. "I think our distinctive love of luxury is the *only* thing we have in common."

He closed the space between us, and I could smell the enticing scent of his Tommy Hilfiger cologne. "Nah, I don't think that's true."

"I do..."

"Let's find out," he said persuasively.

I rolled my eyes like I didn't wanna be bothered.

"Look, I don't wanna hold you up any more than I already have. I'm just tryin' to get a number on you or somethin', and I'll be out of ya hair." He held his hand up, damn near blinding me with the ice on his wrist and pinky ring.

I thought about whether or not I wanted to go through with it. The man was ten years older than me. My parents would flip if they knew I was communicating with a grown ass man.

"Look, you choosin' anyway. Smilin' like a mufucka and shit. You might as well make that move. Gone put ya number in my phone." He licked his lips. "Matter fact, I'mma need *every* contact number on you."

I thought about giving him the wrong number, or maybe even Letitia's, but against my better judgment, I went ahead and gave him my own. For once in my life, I decided to throw all formalities to the wind.

"A'ight then. I'mma bang ya line later." With a great deal of elegant flare, he swaggered off. "And you bet not catch amnesia when I call," he tossed over his shoulder.

I giggled an enchanting low chuckle. "If you're memorable, you won't have to worry about that." I actually found him fascinating, but I wouldn't tell him that.

There was a triumphant look on his face, and he smiled reassuringly. "Oh, I got a feelin' I'm the realest and most memorable nigga you ever met."

***

"He looked old," Letitia said with a frown as we walked out of the mall and towards the parking lot where Conway was waiting for us.

I had to beg him to not chaperone us through the entire mall. I hated whenever he did that shit because it was embarrassing as fuck. His bald-headed ass followed me everywhere. If I went to the bathroom he would pass me the fucking toilet paper. It was like having a full-time baby sitter. However, my mom insisted. She always thought I was gonna get kidnapped and raped, just because she'd been snatched a million-gazillion times. What she failed to realize was that I could take care of myself. I wasn't as silly or simple-minded as she was at my age. I had some common sense and couth about myself.

"Well, he said he was twenty-four," I told Letitia. I could feel a chill of disapproval in the air without her even having to say anything.

"He looked older than twenty-four," she said, her tone ripe with suppressed irritation. I could also sense criticism in the sharpness of her voice. It was abundantly clear that she was jealous. She must've been salty that I showed her up in the Gucci store.

"Bitch, don't hate 'cuz he dropped them stacks on me and not you." I was a real Angelica type of bitch. I subtly bullied all of my friends because I was one of the prettiest and most popular girls at school.

"Eww. Trust me. I'm not worried about some creepy ass, old man wanting me."

"Then why're you still talking about him?" I replied brusquely.

Letitia immediately fell silent. "Whatever," she mumbled.

She knew that I had her number, but I still continued with my rant. "Bitch, nobody asked you to make your opinion known. Every time a nigga approaches me, you have some slick ass shit to say. You wanna know what I think?"

Her mouth tightened. "I really don't," she said in a grim tone. She was obviously in an irritable state.

"I think you're just mad that all the niggas you be wanting want your mom," I teased.

Her face turned beet red. "You a duck ass hoe! I hope he gives you worms!" Letitia yelled, stomping off to the truck Conway was in. I smiled to myself like the wicked little bitch that I was. At the time, I didn't know what I was up against. If I did, I might've ran the other direction. I also didn't know that Elder was watching my every move from across the parking lot. As a matter of fact, he'd been watching me for quite some time...

26
ELDER

That lil' bitch had no idea that I'd been on her head for some time now. After several of my traps were hit, I had no choice but to start doing my homework on these cats. I did some digging and found out that the nigga cleaning me out was just a 16-year old kid and his friends.

At first, I didn't know why he was targeting me, but that was before I discovered that he was the son of one of my biggest competitors in the game. The irony of it all was un-fucking-canny. Unfortunately for them, I had a way of killing two birds with one stone. There could only be one Cocaine King. There wasn't enough room at the top for two, and before Jude showed up and took over the west coast. I couldn't respect a nigga like that. A man's reputation was his most important asset, and I had to do whatever it took to protect mine.

I came from a long line of dope runners. I'd been selling drugs damn near my whole life, but it was white gold that ultimately brought me vast wealth. After all, cocaine was America's cup of coffee. I also made a nice lil' check off heroin, prescription pills, and a few other side hustles. It took a lot of stability and leadership to get to where I was. I'd been moving hundreds of kilos of cocaine from state to state for years, and this fuck nigga just comes along and fucks up my cash flow.

My Bolivian distributor was hesitant when it came to maintaining our relationship, because I wasn't moving weight like I used to. I had to negotiate a different deal with them just to continue doing business. Our product *used* to always be in high demand, then Jude came along and rewrote the script. Now his dope was the talk of the town, and he had me out here looking like a mid-level dealer. Him and his crew were like hyenas who overthrew the lion.

The shit was embarrassing, but I planned to make a preemptive strike in order to get my weight up. I'd been waiting to debut my newest strand of dope, but the fiends were so hooked on his shit, I doubted they'd give mine a try. To be honest, I had gained a bad rep for cutting my shit with fentanyl so when the users found something that they liked more than mine they stuck with it. At the end of the day, it was all about quality.

This nigga was taking all of my clientele—including a few world-famous actors. They'd been rocking with me for years. Then this fool, Jude, rolls up, and muthafuckas stop fucking with me period. Hell, I was losing invites to red carpet events and everything. I had lost half the city to this muthafucka. He was stealing all of my thunder. Playing with my money was like playing with my life. He'd ran an alpha dog out its territory, and I wasn't feeling that shit. Then on top of that, his son was running wild in the hood, killing off my dealers and torching my traps. A nigga couldn't have that shit. It was bad for business, so I did what any man in my situation would do.

I stooped to an all-time low and went for his bloodline.

"Damn. *That's* the nigga's daughter?" My shooter in the backseat asked.

I had all three of the hittaz with me, and all of my goons were clutching. Lex, Logan, and Luther were triplets, and trained to kill for me at the drop of a hat. All my colleagues were savages, but them muthafuckas were the *most* barbaric. Niggas get jealous when you're getting a lil' money, so I kept a group of mercenaries on my payroll. Along with cash comes plenty of envy. Nigga had to keep an eagle eye out on these niggas.

"I would give up everything I got for one night with her," Luther said, licking his lips.

"Bro, that ass big enough to sit a drink on," Logan said, his mouth watering at the mere sight of Journee. He fired up a blunt, took a few pulls, then passed it to me.

As I hit the weed, I studied her flawless skin, soft brown eyes and curvaceous figure. Her visual was on point. Plump breasts, a fat ass, and a waist that was impossibly small. My dick got hard just thinking about tearing up that tender, young pussy. She was a bad muthafucka, but an insufferable smart ass. But that shit could easily be corrected.

"Easy now, killaz," I said to them. My lil' niggas stayed wildin'. "I bagged her ass, and I ain't playin' no games. That right there's gone be my new lil' girlfriend."

All three of their asses laughed. They knew that I was schemin' and up to no good. I was 'bout to apply that pressure in order to maintain my turf.

I'd been doing my homework and watching Justin for some time now, so I knew where he liked to hang out, where he went to school, and where his friends liked to kick it. I should've faded the lil' nigga on sight, or had my young boys wet him up. But now that I'd seen his sister, I planned on really hitting him where it hurt. And then I would cut him and his father from the herd and continue securing the bag. The hand of fate was overpowering and it wasn't prejudice against niggas who thought they were untouchable.

27
JUDE

Where the hell is my wife, I asked myself for the third time that hour. I'd been calling her nonstop, but her phone went straight to voicemail every time. I prayed she wasn't out doing some shit she had no business doing...or even worse, stirring up drama with Eve. I knew she was still pissed after what I had told her, but I'd talked to Eve after the incident and I had already deaded the shit. It was no need for Cameron to go fanning the flames.

"Hey, Conway. Have you seen Cameron?" I asked after he and Journee strolled inside the crib, with even more shopping bags.

I didn't mind spoiling my baby girl, but it was clear that she determined her worth by the worth of her possessions. I made a mental note to talk to her later about materialism. Nowadays, these kids knew the price of everything and the value of nothing. It was partly my fault though.

"Nah, I haven't seen her. I've been with Journee all day."

I shook my head in irritation. Cameron knew better than to wander around without security, or without checking in with me periodically. I wasn't trying to be her father, I just liked to know her whereabouts and to make sure she was okay. After all, trouble was Cameron's middle name.

"Last time I saw her, she was with her home girl," Conway added. "I'm sure Sofía won't let anything happen to her."

That was what worried me. "Trust me, something definitely might happen with the two of them alone." I fucked with Sofía on the strength of Raúl, but I didn't like Miss Plastic Princess coming onto my wife 24/7. Cameron didn't seem to mind but the shit really irked the fuck out of me.

Conway just chuckled. He probably thought I was overreacting. Maybe I was just stressed about having to fly out the country last minute to re-up. In the last two years, our profits had tripled, so I was constantly making runs out of the country. The security guard who usually escorted me was currently in the hospital with his wife who'd given premature birth to their twins. Since Conway seemed to be free, I decided to have him escort me instead.

"Aye, I need you to make a quick run with me." I wasn't giving him the option of declining. "You got your passport on you?"

"R—right now?" He stuttered.

Of all the months he'd worked for me, I had never had him come with me to make a pickup. I should've had someone else doing this shit, but with the purest cocaine that money could buy at stake, I refused to trust anybody with such a responsibility. Instead, I made the coke run with a shooter to meet Soul myself.

"Um, I don't see any other muthafucka in the room," I joked.

"Sure thing, boss. Should I round up the kids?"

"Nah." I waved him off. "They'll be fine here. Cam should be back soon. Plus, you know I keep a herd of hittaz on standby." I didn't play about my family.

"Alright then, chief. Let's rock and roll."

28
CONWAY

This was it. The moment of truth. God had finally answered my prayers and delivered my miracle. After months and months of building up this case, I would *finally* have enough evidence to toss this animal in a cage where he belonged. Not only would Jude be going down, but everyone in his ring, including his supplier.

I had a tiny recording device hidden on the inside of my tie, and I knew my colleagues were listening in probably cheering with joy. Judgment day was coming and I couldn't wait to be there when the verdict came back that Jude was guilty.

"Should I send a text to Cameron, letting her know we're headed to the airport?"

"I'd appreciate it. Shit totally slipped my mind." He was so worried about his wife's whereabouts he forgot to keep her abreast to his own.

"I sent the text, but the message doesn't show that it's delivered."

"Yeah, her phone's off for whatever reason. It'll come through once she powers it back on."

I followed Jude into the living room, where Justin and Madison were playing some race car game on his XBOX. Madison was smoking a square like she was even old enough to buy her own cigarettes. I swear, these kids were grown as fuck nowadays.

"Hey. I'm heading out. I should be back in a day or two. Your mom's around here somewhere, but until she returns I'm leaving you in charge, Madison," Jude said.

"*Madison*????" Justin repeated, eyes wide with disbelief. He looked offended that his dad didn't pick him. "Why the hell does Madison get to be in charge?"

"'Cuz she's the oldest."

"She's barely two years older than me."

Journee's head was buried in her phone as she texted away, on the sofa beside theirs. She didn't even seem to care about who was in charge.

"I say we vote on it."

"Justin, I don't have time for this shit."

"That's not how politics work though. To appoint a person in charge, there has to be a fair vote. All in favor of being your own boss, raise your hand."

Everyone raised their hands, including Journee, who I assumed wasn't even paying attention. She used her other hand to continue texting whoever was on her phone.

"Fine. Everyone is in charge of themselves until your mother gets back," Jude agreed. "But I don't want any shit out of *any* of you. You hear me?" Jude snatched the cigarette out of Madison's mouth.

"Yes, dad," Justin and Journee said in unison.

"You got it, Uncle Jude."

"And I'll be sure to let the security know your curfew is 10 pm. That goes for all of you."

"But my curfew is usually eleven," Maddie argued.

"When you're under my roof, your curfew is whenever I say it is," Jude said with finality.

"Yes, Uncle Jude." She gave him a sarcastic salute then went back to playing video games.

"A'ight then, I'm outta here. Call or text me if you need anything. And I mean *anything*," he stressed.

"Safe travels, dad," Justin said.

Jude ruffled his hair and kissed his daughter on the forehead. "See you soon, princess."

"Bye, Daddy."

As I followed Jude out of the house, I suddenly felt bad about what I was about to do to him. I was tearing an entire family apart with my bare hands, but like I said before, it was the nature of the beast. If it wasn't me, it'd be someone else doing it. Unfortunately, it was something that had to be done. He and his entire organization *had* to go down.

29
CAMERON

After our flight landed at Hartsfield-Jackson International Airport, I immediately powered on my phone and saw that I had over 20 missed calls and texts from my husband and one from Conway, letting me know they were headed to the airport. I immediately got ticked off because I wouldn't have flown last minute to Atlanta if I knew Jude was leaving town.

Who's with the kids?

I reached out to Jude, but his phone went straight to voicemail. He must've been in the air already. I called Conway but his phone was off too. Afterwards, I called Journee.

"Hey, mom," she answered exasperated, as if she didn't wanna be bothered.

"Hey, baby. Where are you right now?"

"At home, why?"

"Me and Sofía had to run to Atlanta really quick. Is Justin and Madison there with you?"

"Yeah."

"Good. I need ya'll to stay inside tonight. Order take-out or movies or whatever you want, but please stay indoors. Pass the word to Justin. I'll be back as soon as I can, and *try* to be on your best behavior."

"Okie dokie, mom," she said sarcastically.

I hung up the phone on her sarcastic ass, and followed Sofía to the restaurant, where Eve was waiting to meet with me. I'd called her for a mature sit down and to get to the bottom of things. I refused to let this young hoe disrespect my marriage. Damn what Jude was talking about. I'd make it so this bitch didn't earn a single dollar. She was fucking with the right one.

"Is that her?" Sofía asked, as we neared Eve's table.

She was seated with her mother, but I wasn't all too surprised. Her mother was like her fucking sidekick; her shadow. Eve was such a mama's girl, I wouldn't have been surprised if her mom still burped her. That's why I didn't invite either one of them to my party. I couldn't stand their asses, and I didn't want them there. Jude knew how I felt about them, but he always tried to keep the peace. And he always tried to look out for the people who looked out for him. That was the only reason Eve even had a position with the organization.

"I can't tell if it's her or not," Sofía whispered.

"It's her," I replied through my teeth.

"*Dios mio*. This bitch looks just like you. Same haircut, same style of clothes, same everything. It's like she read a pamphlet on how to be you."

"Girl, please." I was too stubborn to see it. "This bitch *wishes* she looked like me."

"I don't like this weird bitch already, Cam. And did this hoe really bring her *mother* with her?" She laughed. "What in the Norman Bates hell is that?"

"Girl, every time I see this bitch, she got her mama right by her side. I wouldn't be surprised if she still wipes her daughter's ass."

Sofía opened her mouth to respond, but by then we had reached their table.

"Cameron, what a pleasure it is to see you again," Evelyn said, standing to her feet. She had a busted ass platinum blond lace front on her head and the hairline was all fucked up.

"I wish I could say the same, but I'm sure you already know why I'm here..."

"Yes. Unfortunately, I do. Your husband told me everything."

"Yeah, well, *my husband* doesn't know why I'm here so I'd appreciate it if we could keep this little meeting between us."

"Why of course," Evelyn said. "Please...take a seat. You ladies hungry or—"

"Actually, I'd like to get straight to business." I wasn't here for her fake ass hospitality. I knew that she and her daughter couldn't stand me; they never could. I took a seat and stared daggers at Eve. I could've clawed this bitch's eyes out with my razor-sharp stiletto nails, but I tried to compose myself to the best of my ability. Now that Sofía had mentioned it, Eve *did* bare an uncanny resemblance to me. Her haircut was exactly like mine, as well as her style of clothing. "What's this I hear about you coming onto my husband?" I asked her.

Eve opened her mouth to respond, but her mother quickly cut her off. "From what I understand—"

"I'm sorry, but I'd like to hear it from the horse's mouth...Unless, you're trying to screw my husband too."

Evelyn's mouth fell open. "Hold on now, I thought you said this would be a *mature* sit down."

"I am being mature. It could just as easily be a beat down."

"Look, my daughter's young. She made a mistake. We all know how it is to want someone who's off limits. We've *all* been there," she said, taking up for her daughter. "Besides, she grew up around Jude. It's perfectly normal to like the man who's been something sort of like a father to her," she explained. "And pardon me for my manners, but if you're truly secure in your position, you shouldn't be worried about another woman taking your spot. I know if I was in your shoes, *I* wouldn't be."

Well, you're not in my shoes, tired ass bitch. That's what I wanted to say, but I refrained from getting too ratchet.

"Mama, you don't have to keep making excuses for me," Eve finally said.

"Oh, so she *does* talk," I said, ready to pounce on this broad.

"Yeah, I can talk. I was just biting my tongue, that's all. You see, I respect your position as Jude's wife. Plus, my mama always said if you don't have shit nice to say then don't say shit at all."

"Nah, you might as well say what's on ya mind, mamí. Ya'll need to get this shit off or dead it altogether," Sofía said. "My girl's got kids and a business to run. She don't got time to be flying back and forth to Atlanta every time you look at her husband funny."

"Actually, he's the one giving *me* the sly looks," Eve corrected her. "Why do you think I tried my hand. I *thought* that I was catching a vibe."

My cheeks flushed in anger. "Well, you *thought* wrong, bitch!!"

Evelyn quickly jumped to her feet. "Now, Mrs. Patterson, we're all adults here. Let's keep our emotions in check and try to be measured and civil. There's absolutely no need for name calling! Now I'm kindly asking you to check your tone."

"And I'm kindly asking you to check your home-wrecking whore of a daughter!"

"Hold up, you raggedy ass bitch! I don't give a fuck who you are!! You can disrespect me all you want, but you ain't gone keep poppin' off at my mother!! Now you either gone run the fade or move the fuck on—"

Before she could finish, I lunged across the table and attacked her. So much for a mature sit down. "Disrespectful ass hoe! You wanna be me, bitch!??" WHAP! "Huh?!" WHAP! "Well, too bad, hoe, 'cuz you will never be me!!!" WHAP! WHAP! WHAP! I pummeled her face and skull, with no regards to our age difference whatsoever. I didn't give a damn if she was 15 years younger than me. I would show her ass what happens to a lil' pup when he comes for a big dog. "I do this shit for fun, lil' bitch!!!"

Evelyn tried to pull me off of her, and Sofía smacked fire out of her ass, causing her wig to fall off. The poor woman must've been suffering from alopecia because she was completely bald. I didn't give a fuck either way as I continued dragging her dusty ass daughter through the classy four-star restaurant. I looked crazier than a bat with rabies flying around in the day time.

People marveled at the ghetto ass spectacle we were creating, and on-site security quickly rushed over to break it all up. We were then escorted outside and instructed to leave the premises before the police came.

"Next time I see you, it's lit for yo ass!!!" I told Eve.

"Old ass bitch! *Estúpida puta culo*! With that dry ass frontal! Both you hoes are some fuckin' train wrecks! Like mother, like daughter," Sofía cursed.

Evelyn stared daggers at us, as she headed to her brand-new Nissan Note. She probably would've said a mouthful if it wasn't for the fact that I was Jude's wife. Sofía and I were halfway to our rented Porsche when Eve rushed over to us. I was about to drop this bitch a second time when I saw her reach inside her purse, but she surprised me when she pulled out a small handbook instead of a switchblade.

"Cameron, hold up! Wait."

Her hair was all over her head, and her face was scratched up, but she hadn't sustained any real damage. At least not as much damage as I *wanted* to inflict. I had lost some of my luster over the years. My age was obviously starting to catch up with me, 'cuz the old me would've fucked her up!

"Here," she said, pushing the book into my hands. "Take it. I don't want the responsibility anymore. You're right. I had no business coming at a married man. And to ensure it never happens again, I think it's best if I just step back from the business altogether."

I knew my husband would be pissed once he found out about this, but I wasn't about to beg this thirsty dry ass bitch to stay so I took the ledger.

"I'm really sorry about everything that happened," she said before rushing off to join her ratchet ass mama.

"Damn, you dragged that bitch into a straight submission," Sofía laughed. We hopped inside our rental and pulled out of the lot.

"Yeah...but Jude's gonna be hot as fuck. He doesn't even know I flew to Atlanta. Now Eve just quit. He's gonna be mad as hell."

"Oh well. He should've handled that shit, then you wouldn't have had to."

I flipped through the ledger and shook my head in frustration.

"So, uh...what do you wanna do now? All that cat fighting has gotten me riled up. Any chance we can get a room, and bump boxes?" She laughed haughtily, like a horny old man, sticking her long ass tongue halfway out her mouth.

As angry as I was, I couldn't help but laugh too. Sofía's ass was wild. "Girl, bye. My kids are all alone, and I miss them already. I need to get back home to my babies."

"Ah, well. Maybe some other time."

"Girl, I can't believe you beat up that old ass lady. That shit should be considered a hate crime. You know the AARP are comin' for your ass, right."

Sofía shrugged like it was no biggie. "Oh well. Let 'em come. Old ass hag shouldn't have been making excuses for her trifling ass daughter the whole time."

I ran a hand over my face and sighed. "God, I feel so immature, though. I know better than to be out here scrappin' like I'm still sixteen. I don't even condone violence from my own kids. What kind of example am I setting for my children?"

"Hey. Sometimes a bitch gotta get popped to let her know shit's not a game."

I had no idea, at the time, that my problems were much bigger than a bitch who wanted my man.

30
EVE

"Mama, are you sure I should've given her that ledger?" I asked. I regretted it the second I put it in her hands. I should've bashed her brains in with the shit, but I followed my mother's instructions. After all, she was the mastermind of our million-dollar plan.

My mom opened the sun visor, checked her reflection in the mirror, then straightened her hair before re-applying her lipstick. I was so embarrassed when they popped her wig off in front of everybody, I could've killed Cameron. That bitch was almost 40 years old, and squabbling like she was still her kids' age. The shit was sad and beyond pathetic. And to think, Jude was married to that animal.

My mom had lost all of her hair after my father died. His death really took a heavy toll on her, not to mention she had to downsize her way of living. She sold his cars and his cribs to cover his debt. My mom had tried everything to grow her hair back, but she couldn't get it to grow no matter what she did. That's why she spent so much money on lace fronts and wigs.

My mom started up the car and pulled out of the restaurant's parking lot. "Trust your mother, dear," she said. "That bitch did all that hollerin' but has no idea that the DEA are coming for her dumb ass."

My mouth fell open in shock. This shit was definitely news to me. "Mama!" I gasped. "Are you serious? The DEA is after Jude??? Oh my God, Mama." I covered my mouth. I was completely at a loss for words. "I—wh—How long have you known?"

"Long enough to know I needed to cut a deal with them. Believe you me, when the shit hits the fan you'll be happy you handed over that ledger. Right now, it's nothing but evidence."

"What about Jude? How am I gonna get this nigga to marry me if his ass is on lockdown?"

"Baby girl, just trust me. Your mother has her ways, dear. She has her ways." There was a sinister grin on her face, and I could only imagine the demented ideas running through her wicked mind. "I promised you we would be living like royalty and the time is coming sooner than you think."

31
JOURNEE

"I'm 'bout to slide," I said, climbing off the couch. I'd been texting Elder all day, and he finally invited me to link up with him at this event he was going to.

Justin paused the video game. "I thought Ma said to hold the crib down."

"Since when have you listened to Mom?"

"True. Hold up though. Where you goin'?" He asked.

"That's for me to know and you to never find out."

"Your fast ass better be going over your friend's house. Don't let me hear 'bout you linkin' up with some nigga."

"How 'bout you focus on your scoreboard. I got me," I said arrogantly.

Madison just snickered. She was always entertained by our sibling rivalry. "Be careful out here though, Journee," she said.

Before Justin could say anything else, I left the room, grabbed my keys and walked out of the house. We were strictly forbidden from allowing anyone to know where we lived so I caught an Uber to a local diner and had

Elder meet me there. I wasn't even gonna lie, I was scared as shit. I'd never hung out with any guys before. None of the boys at school were attractive to me, and only older dudes hit on me—probably because they thought I was their age.

I was talking big shit at the mall, but the truth was he made me nervous. Besides, my folks would kill me if they knew that I was even considering entertaining a man that was 10 years older than me. It didn't matter how mature I *thought* I was. I was still just a child, at the end of the day.

While I waited on Elder to arrive, I pulled my phone out and sent a text to Letitia.

Guess who I'm finna link with?

Honestly, I don't care, she responded.

Stop being a hater hoe. Remember the fine ass nigga from the mall?

The one old enough to be your dad, yeah, I remember.

Well, he's about to pick me up and we're going on our first official date, I bragged.

Technically, it was my first date ever, so I had every reason to be excited.

Letitia responded with **IDC**.

It was crazy how Letitia and I were friends *and* enemies at the same time. If it wasn't for the fact that our parents were cool, I wouldn't even talk to the girl. She wasn't popular, she wasn't cute, and she had a big ass forehead and huge buck teeth. All the boys in school made fun of her. They'd say she fell out of the ugly tree, and hit every branch on the way down. I was the only one who was somewhat nice to her.

Hating never got nobody nowhere, I texted back.

Letitia didn't bother to respond.

Suddenly, my phone rang. It was Elder. "Hello?"

"Come outside."

"Come inside. I'm hungry," I pouted.

Elder chuckled. "Why didn't you order anything?"

"'Cuz I was waiting on you," I said. "You wouldn't make a girl pay for her own meal, would you?"

"Never."

I looked up when I heard his voice. He was standing several feet from my booth, and he looked scrumptious in a pair of fitted black jeans, a black Gucci shirt with a tiger on the front and a tan Gucci logo cardigan. He had bulky diamond rings on four of his fingers on each hand, and a collection of big, gaudy diamond chains draped around his neck. Designer shades covered his eyes and diamonds glistened in his ears. He looked like he'd recently gotten a fresh cut and shape up, and it was obvious the man loved making a statement. He was the raw embodiment of being a boss, and it was inconceivable how attractive he was.

He spotted me instantly and bound over to me. "Wassup," he said, sliding into the booth across from me. His cologne smelled like the Lord's breath. It was a peppery but pleasant fragrance. "Of all the places you could eat in LA, you choose to dine here."

"I've eaten at all of the fancy restaurants already," I shrugged.

Elder tossed his hands up in mock surrender. "I forgot you one of dem spoiled ass rich girls," he teased. His voice sounded like sex. It was so smooth and deep

I shrugged. "What can I say?"

He flashed his spellbinding smile, then picked up the menu. "So, what we havin', boo?"

"*We*? Oh, you gone eat this basic food with me?" I teased.

"I'd much rather eat somethin' else. But beggars can't be choosers. Besides, I am kinda famished."

I crossed my legs and blushed.

"Hey. I'm Wendy. I'll be your waitress," a bubbly white girl appeared at our table. "Can I get you two started with any drinks, or appetizers?"

"Yeah, some mozzarella sticks for me. And for the lil' lady, a Caesar salad."

"Excuse me? Are you trying to call me fat?" I asked angrily, clutching my little pouch. I couldn't believe he had the audacity to order my food. I could easily put down a 16 oz. steak all on my lonesome.

"Nah," he laughed. "Not at all. I just don't want you to have too much on ya stomach, 'cuz of where we're going."

I figured he was taking me somewhere that already had food for our date, so I didn't put up too much of a fight about it. After ordering our food, we chopped it a bit and I found out some of his interests. He liked tattoos— obviously—dogs, rap and classic rock, and surfing and traveling in his down time. I also found out that he lived in Oakland, California and was only in LA for business. I was surprised at how cool and down to earth he was. I expected him to be many things, but likable wasn't one of them. Fortunately, I was wrong.

"You all ready to go, lil lady?" Elder asked, after paying the tab.

"Yep."

"Good 'cuz this event starts in thirty minutes."

I followed Elder out of the diner and he led me to a shiny black Ferrari with custom rims and tinted windows. While his back was turned to me, I reached in my purse and made sure my Taser was inside. He seemed cool and all, but you never could be too sure. I'd rather be safe than sorry. As fine as Elder was, he still made me nervous. Still, I decided to let my inhibitions go.

After hitting the locks, Elder opened the passenger door for me and I climbed inside. His car smelled like perfume and marijuana. I wouldn't have been surprised if he was riding 'round the city with another bitch prior to meeting me. He was certainly handsome enough to have whatever woman he wanted. He could certainly afford them.

Elder climbed in, started up the car and lit a blunt.

"So...I've gotta ask," I began. "What's up with the tattoos?"

"I thought you liked 'em."

"I do. I mean...I just never seen so much..."

"So much what? Originality? I told you, a nigga don't do ordinary," he said.

It seemed like I wouldn't get a deeper answer than that, so for now, I decided to drop the subject.

"So...Do you have a girlfriend?" I asked him next, daring to get a little personal.

He took a pull on the blunt, and looked at me with fondness. "Yeah...you."

I felt a sudden warmth fill me up inside. "I'm for real," I giggled.

His face cracked with a big smile. "I am too. You my baby. We locked and loaded." Elder pulled out of the parking lot and eased into traffic. "Say, what's the quickest way to get to the freeway from here? I don't feel like fuckin' with the GPS."

Traffic was heavy since it was the weekend. "You sure you wanna take the freeway?"

"You right. I should take the streets."

"Then again, they might be just as congested. You know you ain't the first person to think about cutting traffic," I said sarcastically.

"Yeah, well, I'm finna be the first person to pull over and fuck the shit outta you."

My cheeks flushed and I got all quiet.

"You got some mouth on you. You know dat?"

"So I've heard," I said. "Anyway, what type of event are we going to? Is it a comedy show? Or a concert? I love concerts."

"Not quite, babe. It's actually a work-related event."

"*Work-related*?" I repeated, looking a tad bit disappointed. I was also mad as fuck that he made me eat that bogus ass salad. I was still pretty hungry. *They better have good food at this work place*, I thought.

"Yeah, I gotta go grab this money real quick," he said, navigating through the streets of LA.

"You couldn't have someone else do that?" I asked curiously.

"Everybody wants to eat steak, but no one wants to kill the cow."

I didn't understand what he meant by that, but I was sure I would soon find out.

32
JOURNEE

Thirty minutes later, Elder and I arrived at a small gated brick building, that resembled a manufacturing warehouse. It was tucked off in the cut, and the area seemed somewhat sketchy. Needless to say, I was nervous as fuck.

"What is this place?" I asked, my face pale with fear. I still couldn't believe I was all alone with this grown ass man. I'd barely hung out with a boy on my own, let alone a full adult. My parents would fucking kill me.

"I just gotta go grab this money real quick. You comin'?" He opened the door and climbed out of the car.

There were plenty of vehicles parked in the lot, but the place was poorly lit and no one was standing outside, so it felt like we were the only ones there. I didn't wanna be left in the car like a dud, so I quickly snatched my seatbelt off and hopped out the car too. Suddenly, my phone vibrated in my purse. When I pulled it out and looked at the screen, I saw that it was Justin. I checked the time and saw that it was 10:30 p.m., which was well past my curfew. He must've been calling to see where the hell I was. Too bad, I didn't know myself to tell him. I'd never been in this area before. I usually only hung out in Hollywood, Calabasas, Inglewood, Ladera Heights, Beverly Hills, and all the other ritzy neighborhoods. I stayed away from all the bad parts in California. And without a doubt, that's exactly where I was now. A bad ass part of the city.

"What kind of venue is this?" I asked, rubbing the goosebumps on my arms.

Before I could answer, the steel door to the building opened and a group of guys walked out fuming mad. "Shit, man! FUCK!" One yelled in anger. "I put everything I had on that damn dog!"

Dog?

As soon as we entered the building, I heard the unmistakable sounds of canines barking and a flock of people cheering them on. So, this is what the big event is? Dog fighting.

Elder and I walked into a small stadium type of arena, and the place was crammed with thugs, gang bangers and shooters.

"Aye! Wuz good, Boss?" A tall guy with short, purple dreads dapped up Elder. "You smooth out here?"

"I'm straight, but I'll be even better once I snatch this thirty G's," Elder said, rubbing his hands together.

"Facts. Aye, where the three amigos at?" Purple Dreads asked.

"It's Garbage Day," Elder said. "I sent them lil' niggas to take out the trash. But aye, you seen Tek? I got the nigga holdin' my wolves."

"He's over by the DJ booth."

"Good lookin'." Elder patted him on the back, then grabbed my hand and led me through the rowdy crowd. On the way over to the DJ booth, I took in the appearances of all the attendees. They all looked like they belonged on the Most Wanted posters.

"I was just lookin' for you. You up next, my G." Tek walked over and dapped him up. I was surprised to see that he was the same boy I recognized from my school. The one selling drugs, who I was checking for not too long ago.

He was still just as handsome as ever with his brown-skin, slanted eyed and full lips. He looked like he was half black and half Asian, and he had a bushy ponytail under a gray skull cap. He was so damn cute and he looked to be only a few years older than me. If I had to guess, I'd probably say he was 16 or so. He wore a Bape hoodie, baggy jeans, and a pair of Jordans on his feet.

"Aye, nephew! Wuz poppin'?"

Oh my God, he's Elder's nephew! What a small ass world!

"Shit, just stayin' low-key," Tek said.

Elder laughed. "You staying in the way but out the way. I can dig it."

"Exactly. Tryin' to get this paper."

"Shit, me and you both, nephew."

I was so busy checking out Tek, I didn't notice the menacing dogs he was holding onto by their leashes. They looked ready to kill at a single command and they were foaming at the mouth like they had rabies. It was really scary and suddenly I regretted coming here with him.

"I kinda wanna go home," I whispered in Elder's ear.

"Okay. I'll take you back to the crib. Just lemme sweep these niggas real quick. I'll make it fast. I been doin' this shit for years, baby girl. I got this shit on smash." Elder took the leash from Tek and our eyes met for a brief moment. "Oh nephew...by the way, this my new, lil' piece, Journee. Journee meet my nephew, Tekashi."

"Wassup."

"Hi."

We shook hands, and I jumped when one of the dogs growled at me.

"Aye, chill Buttercup. You can't be goin' brazy on my ole lady."

"*Buttercup*? You named that beast Buttercup?" I asked Elder.

Elder just laughed. "C'mon. Let me show you what this beast can do."

Old Three Six Mafia poured through the speakers of the venue, as we neared the stage. The last match had just ended, and a couple of guys were carrying a mangled dog corpse out of the ring. When I saw its guts hanging from its carcass, I quickly kneeled over as bile shot up my throat. Luckily, I swallowed it back down before I threw up all over the place and embarrassed myself.

"Aye, you good?" Tek asked, putting a hand on the small of my back. Now I understood why Elder wanted me to eat light. He knew this shit wasn't for the faint at heart. But why would he bring me here? It was crazy inappropriate for a first date.

"Elder," I whined.

"I'll be quick," he said again. "These muthafuckas are undefeated. Most dogs can't even go two rounds with 'em. You'll see. In the meantime, all I need you to do is sit back, look pretty and enjoy the show. Can you do that for me?"

My phone vibrated again. It was Justin calling me. I could've easily asked him to come and get me but I was kind of curious to see the next fight unfold. I knew it was fucked up, but I figured what the hell. I was already here.

"Okay," I murmured.

Elder pinched my cheek, like I was a kid then prepped his dogs for their match. A stocky Mexican with face tats entered the other side of the ring with two white bull terriers. They looked just as terrifying as Elder's dogs, if not more.

"Most of the dogs are strays," Tek said to me. "So, try not to feel too sympathetic."

"I'm not sympathetic," I shot back.

"Oh yeah? Then why's there a tear coming down your cheek?"

I quickly swatted it away. Deep down inside, I *did* feel kinda bad for the poor dogs. I'd never seen something so sadistic, so maniacal, so inhumane. But at the time, I couldn't tear myself away from watching it either. My emotions were conflicted. I was sympathetic but still curious.

"Whatever. I'm not crying. There's just lint in my eye."

"You're a bad liar, you know that?" He leaned even closer. "Say, how old did you tell my uncle you were? I'm just curious."

"I'm sixteen!" I spat.

"Bullshit. I sell weed and shit to some of the kids at your school. I saw you around a few times. That academy only goes up to the 9th grade, so dat means you 'bout fourteen. Fifteen at most."

I gave him an evil eye.

"Chill. I'm not gonna say shit...yet," he added surreptitiously.

Suddenly, the DJ announced the fighters. Buttercup was going against his female terrier. In order to psyche the dog into a state of aggression, Elder started rubbing her and saying some words that I didn't understand. It sounded like some type of satanic ritual and whatever it was had Buttercup riled up. The bell rang, and Elder stepped back as Buttercup launched her teeth into the bull terrier. She went straight for her face, and her tooth impaled the poor dog's eye. I felt like I was gonna throw up again, and I had to cover my face for most of the fight. When the bell finally rang, the bull terrier was laid out in the center of the stage, with her stomach busted open and her organs exposed. Buttercup had ripped the poor thing to shreds.

"Shit crazy, ain't it?" Tek asked. You would've thought he was watching a UFC fight, not two dogs tearing each other apart. "If it's too much for you, you can always go back to watchin' the Disney channel," he teased.

"Fuck you," I spat. Tek seemed to really enjoy taking playful jabs at me.

Why can't he just be smooth, suave, and under-the-radar? Why does he have to keep fucking with me? I figured he must've had a crush on me or something. Either way, I felt like I now had something to prove. This time, I would watch the whole fight play out. I wouldn't cover my eyes no matter how gruesome it got.

"Fifteen racks. Easy money." Elder handed me the stacks that the loser had to cough up. "Hold onto that, baby. That's yours," he said. "That's *all* you."

I took the money and felt bad that a dog had to die for it.

"Next up, we got the undisputed Baxter versus newcomer Manson!" The DJ announced. Everyone in the crowd started placing bets. Manson was bigger but Elder's dog, Baxter, had more muscle.

"A'ight now, Baxter. Let's take it home!" Elder coached. "Dead this bitch, and I'll give you a juicy ass steak later on." He rubbed the dog and said the same weird, ritualistic sounding chants and just like that, Baxter was off before the bell even rang.

Baxter went straight for Manson's jugular, but the bigger dog was much quicker than I imagined. He leapt out of the way and latched onto Baxter's head. Both dogs growled and foamed at the mouth as they snapped at each other. As soon as Manson got a hold of his throat it was over. He ripped Baxter's neck open, and bit a chunk of his nose off. The bell rang again, signaling that it was a done deal. Elder had lost.

"Got damn!" he yelled angrily.

"One more round. Winner takes all," Elder's Mexican rival said.

"Bet, G," Elder agreed. "On the dead homie grave, I'm cleanin' house tonight," he told Tek. "I ain't gone lose this next one. I'm on top of my game."

Baxter was moaning in pain and kicking his leg still when Elder walked up to him, snatched his gat out and put a bullet in his head. He was completely devoid of warmth and compassion.

"Oh, God." I felt the blood drain from me, I had never seen anything more brutal.

"There's a bucket right next to you if you're gonna be sick," Tek said. He really seemed to get a thrill out of teasing me. "Whatever you do, just don't throw up on my kicks, youngin'. These shits are vintage."

He had a generous sense of humor. Instead of responding, I focused back on the ring. Besides, I didn't give a damn about his sneakers. Buttercup was going up against Manson. Girl dog versus guy dog.

"I got money on Manson."

"Fuck that shit. Buttercup is that business."

People in the crowd started placing their bets, and both men prepped their dogs for the fight. The bell rang and the dogs went at each other something fierce. As they fought to tear one another's throats out, I stole a quick glance at Elder. He was cheering his dog on like a father would at his son's football game.

There was so much excitement and insanity in his eyes. And it was in that moment that I realized he was a bad boy. It was also when I realized that I liked him a lot. The raw power and presence of him made my panties wet. There was a mysterious magnetism about him. I couldn't explain it. It was just something about Elder that drew me in. There was an air of humility with him while at the same time authority and menace. Maybe those chants of his were spells he'd casted on me. Whatever the case may be, I was really feeling Elder. The fact he was also handsome as fuck only amplified that sensation.

"Come on, Buttercup! Dead this shit!" He coached. "You got this in the bag!"

Buttercup took a final fatal bite out of her enemy's neck, and Manson was down for the count.

"Hell yeah! And *that's* how we get shit done! Gimme me money!" Elder said excitedly. "Twenty bands! That's all me!" Elder collected his winnings and tossed Tek a few stacks for keeping his dogs for him.

By then Buttercup was all beaten up, and I wasn't surprised when Elder told his cousin to give her a steak then put her out of her misery.

"C'mon, we outta here, babe," Elder said, taking me by the hand. "I told you that shit would be a quick lick."

As I followed him out of the building, I realized I could no longer suppress my curiosity. "How do you do shit like that?"

"C'mon, girl. You liked that shit. A nigga already peeped it."

"I did *not* like that," I told him.

Elder opened the passenger door to his Ferrari for me, as if he were a perfect gentleman and not just fighting dogs a second ago. I climbed in, fastened my seatbelt and thanked God that all that brutality was over.

"Whatever you say to help you sleep at night," he said. "Anyway, let me gone get you back to the crib. I already know it's past ya bedtime," he teased.

Elder started up the car, and instead of pulling off right away, he brandished a small tube filled with a white powdery substance. Dumping it onto the back of his wrist, he snorted it off and wiped his nostrils.

"Is that..." I paused. "Cocaine...?"

Elder chuckled. "Baby girl, this shit is better than cocaine."

"How so?" I asked curiously.

"It's a new strand of dope," he explained. "I'm still toying with names, but for now I call it Euphoria."

"*Euphoria?*" I repeated. "Why do you call it Euphoria?"

He pulled out a second vile and handed it to me. "Take a hit and you'll see why."

I hesitated. "I don't know...I've never done drugs before."

"There's a first time for everything, kid," he said. "A few bumps and you'll see what's up."

I mulled over the idea. A lot of the students at my school drank and did drugs even though they were underage. They all seemed to function just fine in their everyday lives, so I figured there was no harm in trying it. Besides, I'd been curious about drugs for some time now. It was hard not to be when TV and music practically shoved it down your throat.

Abandoning all rationality, I took the vile from him and screwed the top off.

"Be careful not to add too much, start small," he instructed.

"I'm a good girl. You got me cutting up," I told him. There was an inexplicable connection and imprint that he left on me. It had my ass breaking all the rules, *and* throwing caution the wind.

Elder smiled at me and licked his lips. "You can cut up for me," he said sincerely.

Heeding his warning, I dumped a small amount of cocaine on my hand like I'd seen him do. I couldn't believe how much influence he had on me. "What next?" I asked him.

"Hold one nostril shut. Be careful not to breathe out or you'll blow it everywhere. Now don't snort too hard or too soft, snort it up chasing the line as if you were taking a deep breath into your nose," he explained. "Hold your breath for two or three seconds and then breathe out through your mouth. Your nose will burn a little and you may feel an urge to sneeze but try not to or you'll sneeze out the coke."

I carefully did as he instructed, and the cocaine worked its way into my nasal passages. Sure enough, seconds later, I felt my nose burn and the impending sensation of wanting to sneeze.

"Just take a few deep breaths and relax," he said.

Suddenly, I felt a blissful feeling take over me, along with a throbbing sensation between my legs.

"How do you feel?" He asked.

"I feel..." My voice was incredibly low and deep, like special effects were being used to change my tone. "I feel good...but what the hell's wrong with my voice?"

Elder just laughed. "Yo, you tweakin' already. It's perfectly normal."

I laughed at him. "I think I know why it's called Euphoria. I really, *really* feel good."

Elder reached over, cupped my chin and brought my face close to his. His lips pressed against mine, and they were the softest thing I'd ever felt. I moaned a little as his tongue slipped into my mouth. The warm, wet sensation of his kiss penetrated through my very being. He had me feeling a little tingle in my chest, and the sensation traveled straight to my clit.

"I have a confession," I said, after we pulled apart.

"What's that, love?" He fingered the baby hairs on the nape of my neck. My curly locks were piled high into a messy bun on top of my head.

"I think I did sorta like the dog fights."

He kissed me again. "I know you did. I could tell it got you wet."

"Can I ask you a question?"

He kissed my shoulder. "Anything, baby."

"...Can I...see your gun?" The overwhelming excitement in my voice could not be disguised if I tried to. I'd been fascinated with it ever since I watched him put his dog down.

Elder pulled his strap out, and cautiously handed it over. "Be careful now. It's loaded."

I was high as fuck and still giggling, as I pretended to shoot an imaginary target in front of me.

"Have you ever killed anybody with it?" My tone carried curiosity and skepticism within it.

He chuckled. "Now you askin' *too* many questions, kiddo."

He leaned in to kiss me again, but I backed away and held the gun to his temple. "Answer me, nigga."

Elder undressed me with his cold, dark, mysterious eyes. Smiling, he rubbed my inner thigh seductively. He didn't seem the least bit fazed by me having a loaded gun to his head. "I'm finna *kill* this." His hand inched closer to my crotch region. "Damn, that muthafucka hot too. Yo ass ready." With his hand, he pulled my face up to look at him. "And you so fuckin' pretty too. You make it hard for a nigga to keep his hands to himself."

He took the gun from me, and gently ran the tip of the barrel across my lips. Ever so timidly, I stuck my tongue out and licked the cold metal. He gave me a flirty grin, then guided my hand to his erection. He was harder than a brick.

I shifted nervously in my seat. I'd never had anyone touch me so intimately, nor had I touched anyone else in such a way.

"You ever had an orgasm before, Journee?" He asked, unbuttoning my jeans.

I was in pretty deep now and not even trying to deny it. My lips quivered and I hesitated for a moment. "No," I squeaked out. I'd never had sex before even though most of the kids at my school were doing it. That's not to say I wasn't curious about it. The TV and music shoved it down my throat just as much as the drugs and violence.

"So, you don't know what an orgasm feels like?" He yanked my zipper down while keeping his intense gaze locked on mine.

I knew that I shouldn't have let myself drown in this moment. After all, I had just met this man...but he was so damn handsome that a girl couldn't resist. Suddenly, all my inhibitions about letting go evaporated into thin air.

"No," I whispered nervously.

His hand snaked into my panties and his fingers brushed across my clitoris. I trembled in my seat as he pinched, plucked and rubbed on the sensitive piece of flesh. A tiny moan escaped me, as he flicked it back and forth with his index finger, then rolled it between his forefinger and thumb. He tickled the tip of it gently with his nail, and I almost screamed out in pleasure. It was the most sensational thing I'd ever experienced in my life, and I immediately felt like a woman.

"Mmm...that...that feels so good," I said, breathing hard.

"So, you never felt that before?" he asked. His eyes roamed over my body, and he licked his juicy lips as he waited on a response. He was practically undressing me with his gaze.

I bit my bottom lip to stifle a moan, as I shook my head and sighed in surrender. He then slid a finger inside my virgin pussy. It hurt somewhat, but when I relaxed a little, the pain began to subside to pleasure.

"What about that?" He asked.

He was making me feel so good. "No," I breathed. "I've never felt that before."

Elder curled his finger and my leg began shaking. He was tickling a spot on my insides that sent me into overdrive.

"You've never felt that?" He whispered.

My voice was trembling with pleasure. "No," I cried. I felt like I was about to pee all over myself. My body involuntarily began to grind against his hand.

"*Mmm.* You so damn wet and tight," he whispered. "Can I have you, baby?"

"Yes!" I moaned.

"Can I have this pussy?"

"Yes! Yes!"

His finger continued to plunge in and out of me, as he stroked my spot. "Yeah, that's it. Let go and give me that nut, baby," he whispered. "Cum for me."

The pressure from his touch jolted my entire body and I gasped and moaned out loud. Even I was shocked to discover how wet I was down there. Suddenly, I felt myself gush all over his hand, and for some reason I was uncontrollably whimpering and crying while doing it. I couldn't even contain myself it felt so good. I didn't know if it was him, or the drugs, but whatever it was had me losing my mind.

"Now that's how you make that pussy cum. I'm glad I could give you your first orgasm," he said, pulling his hand out of my pants. He then sucked my coochie cream off of his finger.

Wow. I could not believe *that's* what an orgasm felt like. I definitely wanted to experience it again and again. "That was really something," I said, relishing in his attention.

Out of nowhere, his phone started ringing. He picked it up and looked at the caller ID. "Damn, wifey's wildin'."

My eyes grew big, and I felt a pang of guilt shoot through my body. "Hold up, nigga! You're married???" I asked in shock.

33
JUSTIN

"Where the fuck is this broad?" I asked, running a hand over my hair in frustration. I'd been blowing my sister up for the last half hour, but she wasn't answering my calls. It wasn't like her to give me the cold shoulder, and I figured she was out with some guy. Why else would she be ignoring me?

Madison ashed her cigarette. "She's out enjoying herself. Let her have some fun. We should be doing the same thing." She stretched her arms and legs. We'd been playing video games for two hours straight. I always said Madison was a tom boy at heart. "Wassup? I wanna get out of the house. Why don't we find somethin' to get into?"

"Hell, I wanna get into you." I rubbed her leg and she pushed my hand away—like she always did whenever I tried to get some ass.

"I'm serious, Justin. You have no idea how boring my life is in Ghana. My dad is so fucking strict, like you really have no idea. Plus, he likes to live by all these strict ass customs and traditions now that he's in Africa. I'm always trying so hard to abide by all his rules. Now that I'm in California, all I wanna do is just let loose, and be a teenager and turn the fuck up!"

After hearing all of this, I couldn't say that I blamed Madison. Her father kept her on a tight leash, so she was always looking for action whenever she got to the states.

"Well...I *did* get invited to this lil' party up in the Hills—"

"Fuck it, let's go," Madison proposed.

"For real? You wanna go?"

"Yeah! Take me there!"

I saw the excitement in her eyes so I didn't wanna tell her no, even though I'd much rather be doing something else. Here we were in this big ass house all alone, with more beds than IKEA, and instead of occupying one she wanted to drag me to some weak ass house party.

Damn, am I ever gonna get some pussy, I wondered. I couldn't take another year of the homies clowning me. I was 16 years old, still beating my chicken like an adolescent. Some niggas my age had kids.

"Are you positive you wanna go?" I asked again. I was hoping to get my dick wet now that we were all alone but Madison obviously wasn't on it. She never was.

"Don't look at me like that. I know what you're thinking," she said.

"You *should* know what I'm thinkin'." I wanted to knock her walls loose. Just the thought of it had me harder than a pack of frozen neck bones. I rubbed my dick through my sweatpants. "I'm tryin' to rearrange them guts. Wassup? A nigga need some ass, you bullshittin'," I said with an attitude. If given the opportunity, I'd beat them cheeks from here to Africa. I tried to stick and lick her every second of the day, but Madison wasn't on it.

"When do you *not* want some ass?" she asked. "How 'bout this? You take me to that party and I *might* just think about it." She stood to her feet. "Journee's out having fun. Why shouldn't we?"

***

I couldn't believe that I finessed the security to let us out past curfew *after* Madison had finessed me into going to this weak ass party. As soon as we pulled up to the block, I regretted it. I tried reaching out to Drip to see if he wanted to go, but the nigga sent my shit to voicemail. He must've been still in his feelings about our last interaction. I swear, the nigga was cool as fuck but mad wishy washy. I gave him a pass though; I knew he was only upset because he depended on me. He loved to brag about being a trapper, but he didn't start seeing any real revenue *until* I started fucking with him. If I removed myself from the equation, he'd be right back at square one and that's what ate him up inside.

"So, who's party is this again?" Madison asked as we pulled up to the baby mansion.

"Some nigga named Travis."

"He goes to your school?"

"Yeah, but I don't really rock with dude like that. We hang in different circles."

"His parents must be filthy fucking rich. Look at this house."

"You wanna look at it all night or you wanna go inside?" I asked, killing the engine to my Benz. My tone was laced with sarcasm.

"What the hell you think? Nigga, I'm tryin' to get zooted," Madison said, popping off her seatbelt. She climbed out the car before I did like these were *her* classmates.

Before we walked in the house, I popped a stick of gum. Trap music had the whole block lit, and people were scattered everywhere, drinking, smoking, popping pills and whatever else was the newest drug fad. A few folks had even passed out on the front lawn from going a little too hard. They were obviously some rookies. In any other hood, the police would've been here but knowing Travis, he had more than likely paid them off.

We entered the mansion and it was like walking into a drug infused orgy. People were dancing, kissing, and fucking in plain view. And the ones who weren't getting their freak fest on were sniffing coke, shooting up and ingesting expensive drugs by any means necessary. Then there were the people playing dominoes, busting cards, and shooting craps. My parents thought that they'd done the right thing by moving me and Journee out here, but they had only made the problem worse. The city had turned us out. Once you got used to the underworld, it was hard to get out.

"Damn, this hoe lit!" Madison said, bopping her head to the music.

"Man, this shit is weak as fuck. Let's go back to the crib." I would've much rather played Call of Duty.

Instead of answering me, Madison walked over to a table full of liquor bottles and fruit punch bowls. "What's in this fruit punch?" She shouted over the music to a girl beside her.

"I don't know," she held up her double Styrofoam cup. "But I'm fuckin' with it tough!"

That was all she needed to say for Madison to grab a cup and scoop some juice inside of it.

I grabbed her arm so hard, I thought it would break. "Man, chill. You don't even know what that shit is," I told her.

She pulled away from me. "Let me go. I already have a daddy, Justin. I don't need two." And with that, she tossed the drink back and scooped up some more juice.

Man, this bitch trying to flex on me.

"Here. Try some," Madison offered.

"I don't want that shit," I said, pushing her hand away.

Even though I kicked in doors for a living, I didn't fuck with any drugs. I'd tried it on a few rare occasions, and once in a while, I'd test a competitor's product to see how it compared to my father's, but that was as far as it went. You would never catch me high and out of my right mind. Drugs were a liability. Besides, I needed to stay on point at all times. With all the enemies I'd made over the last two years, I couldn't afford to get caught slipping. You never knew who was looking for you when you were tied to a crew or doing dirt.

"Fine. Suit yourself," Madison said, tossing the drink back.

I shook my head and was just about to scold her when Lee walked up and gave me dap. "Wuz good, bro? Ain't expect to see you here."

"I ain't expect to be here," I told him. "But my girl talked me into it."

Lee averted his attention to Madison. "Damn, J. This all you?" He looked Maddie up and down. "Shorty is gorgeous."

"Thank you," Madison beamed. "And you are?"

"This is Lee, the captain of the basketball team. Lee, meet my ridah, Madison."

Lee laughed. "Ole sucka for love ass nigga."

I tossed my hands up like I couldn't help it.

"I'm just fuckin' with you, man." Lee and Madison exchange handshakes and I didn't miss how his eyes lingered on her lips. "It's a pleasure to meet you," he said.

"Likewise," she replied. "So, where can we get some weed in this bitch?" she asked, looking around the party. Everyone was getting high, but she didn't know who to approach.

"Them niggas over there in the corner. They'll get you right." Lee pointed to a corner in the living room, where a group of niggas were blowing heavy. Judging from their attire and blue rags, they were Crippin'. I didn't recognize any of them niggas from school. They looked like trouble, and I wouldn't have been surprised if the blunts were laced with some other shit. Madison didn't give a fuck as she drunkenly stumbled over towards them.

I quickly grabbed her wrist, and spun her around to face me. "Hey! What the fuck are you doing? You never take shit from strangers. You don't know what the fuck them niggas smokin' on."

She snatched away from me. "Well, I guess I'mma find out, cuz," she said, throwing up made up gang-signs. She was about to get herself killed.

"Man, chill. See, this is why I didn't wanna bring you here. 'Cuz I knew your sheltered ass would show out."

"You have some nerve calling me sheltered, Mama's Boy!" She was yelling louder than Bruce Buffer, as she caused a few people to look in our direction. She was already tipsy and showing her ass. "Jesus, just let me have fun, Justin! Why do you have to be such a fucking buzz kill?" She wandered off towards the gang of Crips and I didn't have the will to stop her. Maybe she was right. Maybe I was being a Debbie Downer. Besides, who the fuck was I to pass judgment when I did the things I did and lived the life I lived.

The niggas were all over Madison the second she walked up, and she was loving the attention. That was probably another reason why she wanted to be here so bad. She knew niggas would be at her neck.

Really? That's how you comin', I asked myself. Watching her with an attitude, I chewed my gum aggressively. Madison was on some other shit.

"So...is that the *special someone*?" Aria asked.

I was so engrossed in Madison's antics, I didn't even see Aria walk up. I barely recognized her as I took in her appearance. She didn't look as nerdy today. As a matter of fact, she looked fine as fuck. She had on a slutty, little fuck me skirt with a plunging neckline, exposing her cleavage. She was thicker than Madison, but Madison had her beat as far as looks. Speaking of Madison, she was chilling and smoking with the group of niggas like I wasn't standing six feet away. It didn't take a rocket scientist to realize she was chumping me off.

I can't believe this bitch just hoed me. I'm her guy, not her groupie.

"Nah, I don't know that broad," I lied to Aria. "Don't wanna either."

"Oh. I thought I saw you walk in with her but I must've been mistaken."

"Must've been." My eyesight must've been mistaken too, because I never peeped how fine Aria really was till now. I mean, I always thought she was cute, but the bitch was bad as fuck. I'd just never noticed her full potential. She had big tits, a fat ass and the longest, sexiest, most lickable pair of legs I'd ever seen.

"So, what made you change your mind?" She asked with a flirtatious grin.

"I knew *you* would be here," I said real smooth-like.

Aria was all smiles as she blushed.

"I see somebody's finally coming around," She pinched my arm, and I grabbed her ass and pulled her closer to me, hoping Madison saw.

I knew Aria wanted me. And for the first time ever I wanted her too. Since Madison wanted to stunt on me, I would show her that two could play this game.

"I guess I just needed a lil' prodding, that's all" I said, pushing my erection against her. I looked up to see Madison watching us like a hawk. She'd taken the bait, and she didn't look too happy.

Staggering to her feet, she headed straight towards us. "*Oomf!*" She bumped her shoulder against my arm hard as fuck, like she wanted to fight me.

"I'm going to the bathroom," she slurred. "When I get back, that bitch better have vanished."

"Like your self-respect?" I countered.

"Whatever, Justin. Like I said. That bitch better be gone by the time I get back, or else." She said it loud enough for Aria to hear.

On the way to the bathroom, Madison grabbed another cup of fruit punch laced with whatever had her tripping.

"Really, Justin?" Aria folded her arms. "You used me to make your little girlfriend jealous? Nigga, go find another bitch to play head games with," she said, storming off.

Suddenly, my cellphone chirped with a text message from Drip:

Fuck you want fool?

I texted back: *At this party in the Hills.* I then texted him the address. *Pull up.*

Man, I would but I'm on the block. I'm bout to go catch something today. Maybe l8r.

That meant that he was about to rob a nigga.

I texted back: *Aight then. Fwm.*

He responded: *I'mma hit you tomorr blood*

Our beef never lasted long. We were like brothers, at the end of the day. And just like brothers, we fought from time to time, but we always made up. Several minutes passed before I noticed that Madison hadn't returned. She was drunk and high as fuck, so I immediately started to get nervous. Navigating through the crowd, I looked everywhere for her.

"Hey, Travis?" I found the guy whose party it was in the kitchen smoking hookah. "You saw a girl, 'bout this tall? Light brown, dark hair, freckles on her face? Anybody seen her? She's wearing a white t, acid washed jeans and chucks. She kinda looks Arabic."

"Nah, bro. But I'll keep an eye out."

"I haven't seen her."

"I think I just saw someone who matches that description. You said she looks Middle Eastern, right?"

"Yeah."

"Yeah, she just went upstairs with some guys."

Now I was fuming fucking mad! This bitch had touched several nerves of mine, and we hadn't even been here an hour. *I know this chick ain't out here kicking dirt on my name*, I seethed in anger. Balling my fists, I stormed off to the staircase and climbed the steps three at a time. When I reached the second level, I looked through every room. There was one last door at the end of the hall to the left, and as I approached it I heard her drunkenly calling out to me.

"Justin??? No...I don't wanna...*noooo*...stop...Justin???" She whined. "Where's Justin???"

I kicked the door open and found Lee pulling off her pants while his homeboy held her down. Madison was half-conscious as she lay there helplessly. Lee immediately stopped what he was doing and looked at me like a deer caught in headlights. "J—Justin!" he said surprised. "My nigga...on some real nigga shit, it's not what you think! We saw she was fucked up, and we were just helping her to the bed," he lied.

"Speak for yaself," his homie said. "I was helping myself to some ass."

I swooped in like an action hero and launched my fist into his friend's face, shattering the bridge of his nose. Blood gushed from his nostrils like a volcano, and he crumpled to the floor, howling in pain. Lee tried to grab me, but I scooped him up, lifting him off his feet and charged towards the bedroom window.

KSSSSSSSSHHHHH!!!!

His body crashed through the glass and he fell two stories. The people outside started screaming in horror, but I didn't give a fuck as I went into attack mode on his friend. Jumping on top of his ass, I punched him over and over until I finally exhausted myself. Then I resorted to kicking and stomping him in the head and face. His teeth flew out his mouth as I bludgeoned him into a state of unconsciousness.

Chest heaving up and down like a mad man, I stopped and turned around to see people huddled around the room staring at me in shock and disbelief. They'd never seen this side of me before. I was always so low key and chill in school. I was the cool guy. Mad as fuck, I snatched Madison off the bed. This bitch had me ready to kill a nigga about her.

"Damn, he pressed his shit," one of the bystanders said.

"Yeah, he straight baked his ass," another commented.

"All I wanna know is who the fuck gone pay for this damage? My parents are gonna freak if they see this shit," Travis said.

I pulled out all the money I had, and tossed it at Travis's feet.

"Justin," Madison whined. "Justin, where were you?"

I walked over to the bed, lifted Madison's drunk ass up, and tossed her over my shoulder. The crowd parted for me as I carried her out of the bedroom. Once we reached my car, I tossed her in the passenger seat and slammed the door with an attitude. I didn't know if I'd killed Lee or not, and quite frankly, I didn't care. He deserved worse for trying to rape Madison. And to think this was a nigga who I once called my friend.

My dad always said, "Niggas either want your life, or want your wife."

Lee was a perfect case in point.

"Justin," Madison called out to me as I started up the car. "Oh my God, Justin, I'm so fucked up."

"I know you are. Your ass was finna fuck around and get ran down on."

"Oh, Justin, I think I'm gonna be sick."

"Yo, how the fuck could you say you my bitch, then go and do some simp shit like that?! You embarrassed me, Madison! You embarrassed me with no regards to the fact that I have to face those fucking people every day!! I brought you here to have a good time! Not for you to turn around and shit all over me! I would've never done you like that. At the end of the day, I live by a code of ethics."

"Oh my God, Justin! Do you need your cervix checked?" she asked. "Seriously. You have got to *stop* being so jealous!"

"Are we together, Madison? Are we a couple? Yes or no??? Let me know now, so that a nigga don't be wastin' his time," I said. "If you gone fuck with me, I need you to stay solid. I don't have time for the shakiness."

Madison smirked tauntingly, and the shit pissed me off even more.

"How the fuck could you tattoo my name on you? Then have little regard or respect for me as your man?"

"What tattoo?" She asked, confused.

"Fuck you mean what tattoo?? This one!" I yanked her pants down enough to show her, and the muthafucka was hardly visible. The words were smudged and I realized that it was a fucking fake tattoo. Probably some shit that she drew on herself with a pen. "You fuckin' bitch," I murmured. My cheeks were red with embarrassment.

Madison started laughing even harder. "Oh shit! You should see your fucking face!"

"You think that's funny?!" I yelled at her. "You think playin' me is fuckin' funny???" I started swerving in and out of lanes erratically. "Well, let's see how funny you think shit is when I crash the fuck outta this bitch!!!!" I washed niggas up for less than the corny ass shit she'd just pulled. More than anything, I took it as disrespect.

Madison grabbed the dashboard to brace herself. She wasn't laughing anymore. Instead, she looked petrified. I got all the way up to 120 mph, and was headed straight for the back of a semi-truck.

"JUSTIN, STOP! You're scaring me!!!" She screamed fearfully.

"Good, bitch! You oughta be scared!!!!" I hollered. "You think I'm a fuckin' game?! You think that I'm some fuck nigga out here?! Bitch, you will never see your daddy or your brothers again, fuckin' with me! You won't even make it to fuckin' college!!!" I threatened. "Bitch, I'mma whole different type of animal!!! What the fuck was you thinkin' tryin' to play me?!!"

"I'm sorry!!! Justin, please! I'm sorry!!!!"

"IT'S TOO FUCKIN' LATE FOR SORRIES!!!!"

"JUSTIN, STOP!!!"

"I been loyal to your ass all this time, and *this* is how you repay me?! Now I see why niggas treat all women like shit! 'Cuz trusting a bitch will get your ass took out!" I spat.

"Justin, please, slow down!!!"

"You burnt out bum ass bitch! FUCK YOU!" I pressed my foot down on the accelerator as hard as it would go, increasing the speed.

"JUSTIN!!!!!" she screamed.

Just seconds before we rear-ended the truck, I veered into the right lane and avoided a deadly collision.

Madison relaxed and started giggling. You would've thought coming close to dying was the funniest thing on Earth to her. I surprised myself by laughing too. The light ahead turned yellow, and I gradually brought the car to a stop.

"Man, why do you do this shit, Madison?" I asked. "Why do you purposely push my buttons?"

Madison leaned over and kissed me. "I'm sorry, baby. It's just...I got bored at the airport, so I started doodling on myself. I thought it'd be funny if I told you it was a tattoo."

Her mangled reasoning instantly ticked me off. I really loved this girl. I had our whole future carved out, and I thought she wanted the same, but evidently, I was wrong. She didn't even care about me enough to respect me. I was just some fuck boy to her. "The fuck is in your head? That shit ain't funny."

"Yes, it is," she giggled.

I shot a hard look in her direction. "So it's funny to hurt me? It's funny to make me feel like an idiot? To see me sittin' here with egg on my fuckin' face."

Madison started laughing even harder.

"Man, I ain't on that square ass shit, Madison. A nigga don't like being lied to."

"Oh my God. How you gone get tight over that? Lighten up, Justin. Issa joke," she said.

"Man, you so clowned out. I'm glad I could entertain you at *my* expense," I said, sarcastically. "What the fuck else have you lied to me about? Is the nigga on your Gram really your boyfriend too? Is this really mine?" I asked, grabbing on her ass. "Or has he been hittin' that shit?"

Madison fell silent.

"Answer me," I pressed. "Did you let that nigga hit or nah?"

"Justin—"

I pushed her off like she had Malaria, or some shit. "YOU FUCKED HIM!!!" With a glare that was as hurt as it was hateful, I pointed an accusatory finger in her face. "You grimey ass bitch, you fucked him! I fuckin' knew you did!!!" I was so fucking mad that I was foaming at the mouth! I loved hard, and that shit really broke a nigga down. It fucked me up. I had been nothing short of faithful to Madison and she couldn't even do the same. "So that explains why you never wanted me to hit! 'Cuz you been giving my shit away to *this* fuck nigga!" I was ready to put hands and feet on her stupid ass. "BITCH, I SHOULD SPLIT YOUR FUCKIN' HEAD OPEN!!!!" I hollered. The chopper was in the back and I was two seconds away from grabbing that bitch and emptying the clip out on Madison. I kept it on me, and she had a nigga feeling homicidal. There was a simmering storm of hatred and rage inside of me. And beneath all that was sadness. "And to think I was down for you, all these years!!! Man, I feel like a fuckin' fool!" I yelled. "When you told me ya moms was a whore, man, I didn't believe you at first. Now I see, the apple doesn't fall too far from the tree."

At 14, Madison revealed to me that her birth mother was a former prostitute. I figured now was the perfect opportunity to throw the shit back up in her face. Her accusations sounded loudly in my mind, and all I could think about was her accusing me of fucking around when *she* was the one doing all of the cheating.

"Justin, don't you ever talk to me like that. We grew up together. Let's keep the respect level high."

"Man, that shit a dub. You ain't shit but a fuckin' jump off. You don't deserve no damn respect," I told her. "To get my respect, you first gotta respect yourself, and you clearly don't! Man, I should've let them niggas run a train on that ass! That's what the fuck I should've done. I put you on this pedestal, when in reality, you ain't shit. Man, I can't believe I ever thought I loved you!" I punched the shit out of the steering wheel to keep myself from knocking her teeth out. I could barely keep my temper in check, I was so mad. "Check this out, I'm DONE with your ass! On five, I'm cool on you!" I told her straight and forward. "You don't exist to me no more. You and me, we're over!"

"Would you calm your ass down!" she yelled. "I did *not* fuck Kwaku! Or anybody!" she added.

"I don't believe you!"

"Well, pull over so you can find out for yourself."

Her unexpected offer caught me by surprise. "You...for real?" I asked skeptically.

Instead of answering, she pulled off her top, and I was suddenly at a loss for words. I'd been practically begging to hit it every day, and now that the opportunity had finally presented itself, a nigga was stuck on stupid.

Before I could say or *do* anything, the butt of a handgun came sailing through the passenger window.

KSSSSSHHHHHH!!!

Glass sprayed everywhere, and an arm reached through the broken window, unlocked the door and snatched Madison out by her hair.

I quickly hopped out the car to help her—and was struck in the chin with a sawed-off shotgun. Dropping to the ground like a sack of bricks, I hit my head on the side of the car on the way down. We were so busy arguing we didn't notice we were being watched, and now it was too late.

When I looked up, I saw 3 niggas wearing black ski masks. One of them was standing over me with a shotgun. I didn't know who these niggas were or what the fuck they wanted. But if I had to guess, I'd say they were somehow tied to my recent chain of robberies.

"Pussy ass fuck nigga!! Let her go before I—"

My sentence was cut short after he kicked me in the head, knocking me unconscious.

34
JUSTIN

When my eyes finally fluttered open, I noticed that I was in a basement tied to a chair, with my hands shackled behind me. Across from me, Madison was tied up as well with a gag inside her mouth. The kidnappers were nice enough to give her a dirty, old sweater to put on, but her head was still leaking from a gash above her eyebrow. I figured she must've tried to put up a fight when I was unconscious. Or maybe it was from the glass that had exploded in her face.

I tried to say something, but soon realized that I was gagged too.

Suddenly, three niggas walked into the room. They were wearing ski masks and carrying heavy ass guns. I assumed they were the triplets that the drug dealer from Watts had spoken of. The ones his supplier had dropping off the dope. They were the only niggas who I could see coming after me to this degree—and for damn good reason. After all, we'd been torching traps left and right. It was only a matter of time before *someone* sought revenge.

"'Bout time you woke the fuck up, sleepy ass nigga. We got business we need to discuss," the leader said, using a voice modulator.

I tried to yell at him, but my own voice came out muffled. He signaled for one of the kidnappers to remove my gag.

"Pussy ass nigga, you hidin' behind a mask!!! Take that shit off and look me in the face! I wanna see you before I kill you!!"

Without warning, he snatched a 9 out his holster and shot Madison at point blank range. Her muffled cries echoed off the walls of the dreary basement. Luckily, he only shot her in the shoulder but it was enough to let me know that I wasn't running shit.

"Nigga, you better look before you leap!! This ain't a battle you wanna fight, homie, trust me!" The leader said in this weird ass robotic voice. "I'm packin' the heat, fuck nigga! I'm callin' the muthafuckin' shots!" He yelled. "Do I make myself clear?" He aimed his burner at Madison's head. She hadn't stopped crying since he shot her. If she didn't get help soon, she was bound to bleed out. I knew that it was probably best for me to just roll with the punches, so we could make it out of this alive.

"Yes, man! Yes, yes, I understand!" I said desperately. "Just please...please, man, don't kill her," I begged.

He finally lowered his gun.

"You been movin' around a lot lately," he said. "You and ya lil' *shooters* done did some brazy shit. Hit three of my boss's traps in less than six months. Ya'll muthafuckas been really disruptin' the cash flow. You really thought we wouldn't come lookin' for your ass? You know you can run but you can't hide from the wrath of karma," he said.

I couldn't believe that my sins had caught up with me. The day of reckoning had finally come.

"I *should* burn your ass for that shit, but for whatever reason, my boss was kind enough to spare you. But only under one stipulation." He held up two fingers. "You get us two M's by sunset and we'll call it even. No harm, no foul."

I didn't even think about where I'd get the two million dollars from. All I could think about was saving Madison. She was losing blood, and she didn't look so hot. "I can do that. Just let us go and I'll get you the money—"

He pointed his gun at Madison again. "WHAT THE FUCK DID I JUST SAY?! What the fuck did I just tell your ass???" POW! He shot her in the leg, and she cried out in agony. "Did I not just say that I was callin' the shots?!" He yelled so loud that there was static interference on the speaker. "Muthafucka, this hoe ain't goin' nowhere till I get my fuckin' paper!" He snatched the gag out of Madison's mouth. "I think you need to tell ya lil' boyfriend that shit. Or else he gone fuck around and get that pretty face of yours blown open." He put his gun to her nose. "TELL HIS ASS!" He barked.

"Justin," she cried. "Justin, please...I...I don't wanna die."

For the first time ever, I felt fear that cut to the bone. A tear rolled down my cheek. I hated myself for putting her in this shitty ass situation. "I will get you your money," I said, this time a little more submissively. "I will get you your money by sunset. I swear it."

"Meet me at the Bayshore Roadhouse in Brisbane. If you're even a second late, or a dollar short, I'mma let my boys have a field day on this hoe, and I guarantee them lil' niggas don't play no games," he said.

His homeboy put his gun by his crotch and started pumping the air with it like it was a dick.

I wanted to kill his ass for threatening to rape Maddie, but I was in no position to do anything other than what he wanted. "I understand," I forced out.

He nodded his head at one of his goons, signaling to untie me. When I was finally free, I stood to my feet. There a knot slowly forming on my head, and my chin was bleeding from a deep cut. He'd cracked my shit wide open with the sawed off he was carrying.

"Show him the way out," he told his shooter. "And remember." He walked behind Madison, shoved his finger in the bloody hole in her shoulder, and started moving it back and forth like it was a penis stabbing a pussy. Madison cried out in agony. "Not a second late or a dollar short," he said. "If you fail to fall through, I'm givin' my young niggas the green light."

I wanted to blow his fuckin skull open. Or at least, beg him to get her some medical attention, but I knew that I couldn't do much of shit in my position. I damn sure couldn't bargain with him. He'd already shown me that by putting two bullets in Madison. At this point, all I could do was try to get this money in time, and pray that she didn't bleed out on me. If I emerged from this bloody crucible completely unscathed, I would kill every single one of them niggas with my bare fucking hands.

35
ROXIE

I was back at home in Georgia, dusting the furniture in my office, when I stumbled across an old photo album in the drawer of my desk. The kids were at the park, and Hector was out only God knows where, doing only God knows what, but I was happy for the peace of mind I rarely, if ever, got.

I really needed it. Sometimes I felt like I was going to go crazy. My life was so hectic lately, I cherished each and every moment of solitude. It's what kept me sane. I was also happy that I was off for the weekend, so I had time to finally get caught up on some much-needed cleaning and reading. I planned to devour *Song of Solomon* by Toni Morrison. I'd fashioned a nice little reading nook in the basement, and I enjoyed lighting candles, playing meditation music, and getting lost in the pages of a great book. It was hard to do any of that with everyone home. If it wasn't the kids running me ragged, it was Hector. I didn't want to admit it, but our marriage was hanging on by a thread.

"I thought I put this old thing in storage," I said, blowing the dust off the cover of the photo album. I hadn't seen it in years. When me and Hector first moved in this house 10 years ago, I was certain that I'd put the album in a storage bin, but apparently, I was wrong. "I can't believe this has been in here all of this time."

I could vividly recall when and where I purchased the album book. Magyc and I had gotten it at a gift shop for tourists in Saint Tropez. He'd taken me to Paris several times, meanwhile my current husband couldn't even take me on a date. I really wished things could go back to the way they used to be between me and Hector, but I doubted that would happen. At this point in our marriage, he was far beyond my reach.

Flipping through the pages, I teared up when I saw photos of me and Magyc. There were pictures from our wedding, and when we first brought our home and of Rain's 3rd party. Everything was so perfect then.

After his death, shit seemingly went downhill for me. Rain's behavior got worse. I was in a loveless marriage with a man who didn't respect or appreciate me. And Cameron, my best friend, had moved to the other side of the country. I knew that my kids loved me and depended on me, but sometimes I felt like I was all I had. I truly believed that if Magyc was still alive that things would be different. Sadly, he was gone, and there was no use crying over spilled milk. It wasn't like it would change the past or bring him back.

I closed the photo album and put it back in the draw underneath a folder. Just then, I heard the sound of the front door opening. *Damn. I thought I had more time to myself.* Closing the door to my office behind me, I descended the stairs and found my daughter and 6-year old son.

"Oh my God, Rain! What happened to your nose??? How did you hurt yourself??? Did someone do that to you???" I fired off questions as I took in the horrifying sight of her. There was blood dripping from her nostrils, staining her pink Polo t-shirt.

"I got into a fight with one of the boys at the playground. He wouldn't let me use the swing. That's all I can remember before blacking out."

"Oh my God, girl, come here." I grabbed her by the arm and led her to the nearest bathroom. "Harper, take your shoes off and wash your hands!" I called out to him. "After you do that, you can have a snack."

He looked so much like Hector that sometimes I couldn't stand to look at his ass. He had coffee brown skin, jet black curly hair, and the same beauty mark on his cheek that Hector had. I didn't even know it was possible to inherit birthmarks before I had him. Sometimes I even caught Harper walking like him. He was Hector's twin through and through. Fortunately, he didn't act anything like his sorry ass daddy.

Harper was sweet, lovable, and he left an impression on everyone that he met. People were always complimenting me on how polite and well-behaved he was. He was only six, and already holding doors open for ladies, and I didn't even have to ask him to. I really prayed he stayed that way, because I couldn't stand to see him turn into his father one day. It would kill me.

"K, Mommy!" He sang innocently. He had no behavioral problems that I was aware of. However, he was

Hector's child, so there was no telling what mental disorders were lying dormant in him. Hector *definitely* had some issues.

"You don't remember anything that happened?" I asked Rain, as I wiped her face. She was such a cute, little girl to have severe mood swings. No one would ever know it from looking at her. She had warm vanilla skin, deep blue eyes and curly light brown hair. She was Joaquin's daughter, but looked more like Jag because of her blue eyes.

"I don't remember anything. When I came to, my nose was bleeding and there was blood all over my clothes."

I shook my head in frustration. "Mommy's gonna get you some help. You hear me?" I told her. "Mommy's gonna get you some help so you can stop having these blackouts."

After cleaning her up, I called Hector to tell him what happened, but he sent my shit to voicemail. His ass wasn't at work, so I didn't understand why he couldn't pick up the damn phone. It wasn't like he had a job or other pressing obligations. Then again, knowing him, I wouldn't have been surprised if he was laid up with some bitch. He definitely had a track record when it came to fucking around.

36
EVE

"Fuck me, Hector, shit!!!"

My tits swung and my head rolled side to side in pleasure as I rode him. Slamming my warm pussy onto Hector's gigantic cock, I fucked the shit out of him in a dingy motel bed. My ass cheeks bounced off his balls with every thrust; they were so full they threatened to explode at any minute.

"Oh, God, baby! Here it is, baby! I feel it coming! *Ungh*! Oh, shit!"

Hector grabbed my titties and started bucking his hips harder, causing the bed to shake and the headboard to rattle.

"Yeah, that's it, bitch. Ride this dick," he coached.

I was out of control and breath as I continued to slam my pussy onto his dick. Hector moaned in pleasure as his seeds released into me. There was so much of it that cum shot out the sides of my engorged pussy. I kept on riding him even though he'd already nutted. Hector grabbed my ass and grinded his hips with me, and within seconds I was flooding his dick with my juices. I never came as hard with anyone else as I did with Hector. The nigga may have been broke as fuck, but he could damn sure blow a bitch's back out. I was addicted to his sex, and loving his dirty muthafuckin' draws. My mother always said it was the broke ones who were spectacular at sex. Hector was a perfect example.

Winded and fatigued, I rolled over and laid in the cheap motel bed. I was supposed to be fucking my way into a come-up, but I couldn't resist letting Hector hit it every now and then. After all, a girl had needs. I knew his ass was married but I didn't give a fuck. I wasn't trying to break up a happy home. I just needed to get my rocks off every once in a while.

I met Hector and Roxie at a function Jude had a few years back. As a matter of fact, it was a celebration for his new magazine company, *Opulent*. I caught Hector checking me out periodically, and I hit him in his DM one night, and the rest was history.

I knew my mother would flip if she found out I was fucking Hector. She wanted to see me with a boss. Not a muthafuckin' bum. So, I never told her about me and Hector. I figured what she don't know won't hurt her.

Climbing out the bed, I headed towards the bathroom but Hector stopped me halfway there. "*Has terminado*? That's it? You done?"

He always speaking that Spanish bullshit like I understood him. "You're not?" I asked, looking at his deflated dick.

"Gimme five. I can get it back up."

"Have your wife get it back up, nigga. I've got better shit to do."

"Man, fuck my wife."

"Her pussy game must be negative, huh," I teased.

Hector slapped and squeezed on my ass. "You got all the juice. Pussy get so wet, that muthafucka spit out juices and berries." He tried to pull me back onto the bed with him. "C'mere. Let me make that pussy squirt with my tongue. That shit'll get me hard in no time."

"I'd love to take you up on your offer, but I gotta meet with Mama and the lawyer."

"About what?"

"Jude's about to go down, and I'm making a deal so that I don't go down with his ass. In other words, I'm signing my soul over to the devil." I never thought I'd see the day where I partnered up with the police, but if it kept my ass out of jail, then so be it.

"Hold up. That nigga finna get knocked off?" Hector asked in disbelief.

"Yes. Apparently so. Mama says the DEA are closing in on his ass. And I don't wanna be around when they start throwin' life sentences at niggas. I need to be prepared *and* protected for when the time comes," I said. "Look at me. I wouldn't last a damn day in a jail cell. I'm way too fucking pretty for prison."

"I won't argue with you there, but damn. That shit is crazy. So, the DEA finna take down Jude???" He asked again, just to be sure he heard me the first time. "You dead ass? No fiction?"

"All facts. He's going down, along with his ratchet ass wife, and everyone else involved in his operation. That's why I'm meeting with my lawyer today. To cover my own tracks."

"Damn. So this nigga really 'bout to get sent down the river," he cackled. "Cocky ass nigga finally finna get knocked off that high horse of his."

"Yup. Any day now," I said sadly. I really hoped Mama knew what she was doing. I still didn't understand how I'd marry him and get half his money if he was locked up in prison. "He'll probably spend the rest of his life behind bars, too."

Hector's dick quickly sprang to life. The news was enough to give him a full-hard on. "Well, ain't that something," he smiled. "That's the best fuckin' thing I done heard all year."

37
JUDE

Nineteen hours after leaving LAX, we finally landed in Accra, the city that my plug had on lock. "Brother! *Nuabarima!*" Soul greeted me in Twi the second I descended the stairs to my private jet. He looked the exact same as he did when we first met. Other than a few silver hairs in his beard, he hadn't aged a bit. "Welcome home!" he said.

"It's good to *be* home."

He pulled me into a bear hug. He was always calling Africa my home, since that's were my roots were. Too bad slavery made it impossible for me to trace those roots. I didn't know what country I was from, but that never stopped me from appreciating the beauty of Africa each and every time I came to visit. Ghana was definitely the jewel of West Africa. It was beautiful, lively and full of culture.

"Fillmore, my man, wuz good?" Soul shook the hand of my second in command, then greeted his husband. "Price, so good to see you."

"It's good to see you, sir," Fillmore said.

"Always a pleasure," Price chipped in.

"How've you been, man?" I asked Soul.

His security rushed to collect my suitcases, as we walked towards his white Maybach coupe. There was a line of army fatigue-painted trucks in front and behind the luxury vehicle. They followed him everywhere he went like he was the king of Zamunda or some shit. I was a millionaire, but this nigga was a billionaire. He was already eating good off the drug game. Then his father died and left him his businesses, tripling his net worth.

"I'm blessed, man. Look around. How can I be anything less living in a beautiful country like this?"

I took in our surroundings; the beautiful bright skies, the panoramic view of the mountains, the trees and the tropical birds. The scenery had me feeling like I had landed in paradise. Soul was right. It was nothing like returning home to your roots.

"Bro, I fall in love with this place every time I come here," I said.

Soul handed me a fresh, imported cigar. "Brother, you're gonna fall even harder," he said. "Tomorrow, we handle business. But tonight, we celebrate. And you know no one's celebrations are more festive than Africans."

"Apologies, sir," Conway cleared his throat behind me. He looked confused because he knew he couldn't fit inside the two-seater. "But I need to be able to chaperone you at all times."

"It's okay. I'm with family," I explained to him. "You can ride with Soul's security. We're all going to the same place."

"Yes sir." Conway nodded his head in agreement, and I turned back to Soul and caught him mugging the shit out of Conway.

"Who's the new nigga?" He whispered.

"His name's Conway. He's the head of the security team I put together."

"Yeah, well, you know I don't take kindly to new niggas..."

"He's just eager to do his job, man, that's all."

"Someone should tell him too much eagerness can get you fucked up," he said. "You with your day ones. If anything, I *oughta* be runnin' *his* credentials," Soul said. He was clearly offended, but tried to downplay it with humor. He was the closest thing I had to a brother, so I didn't blame him for taking Conway's statement to heart.

"Yeah, well *he* don't know that, man. He just works security. He ain't in the loop like that."

"And he won't ever be if I can help it. I don't know what it is, but there's something off with that nigga."

Together, we climbed into his Maybach and I lit up the cigar. "Let's hope you're wrong," I said. "He's been with us over a year now. And he hasn't given me any reason not to trust him."

"He hasn't given you any reason *yet*," Soul corrected. "Anyway, enough about him. If he's doing some snake shit, it'll come to light," he said. "So...tell me...how's my baby girl doin'? Is she stayin' out of trouble?"

I thought about Justin and what he'd told me the other day at the gym. I always had a feeling that something was up with him and Madison. Personally, I thought it was cool that they were dating, but I knew Soul's sentiments would be the exact opposite. Like Journee was my only daughter, Madison was his only daughter, and we'd kill a nigga 'bout our baby girls. Still, I knew my son and I trusted him implicitly. I knew he wouldn't harm a hair on Madison's head. He was a good boy, and he kept his nose clean *as far as I knew*.

"She's great. She helped Cam with the party. She and the kids really had a great time. You should've seen 'em on the dance floor," I said. "The other day they all went to the beach. I'm tellin' ya man, she really seems to be enjoying herself. And she's a good kid. Never any trouble to have, at all." I refused to tell him that she was also spending a ton of quality time with Justin. Knowing Soul, he'd probably flip his fucking lid.

"That's good to hear. I know how much she loves being in the states. It's where she was born, you know. I never wanna take that part of her from her," he said. "How's Cameron?" he asked.

"She's good. Staying out of trouble...at least as far as I know," I added.

Soul chuckled. "Cam always does seem to find herself in these bad situations," he said.

"Shit, she *is* the bad situation," I told him.

That made Soul laugh even harder. "These women of ours are something else," he said, shaking his head as he thought about Diana. "What the hell are we gonna do with ourselves?"

38
CONWAY

I didn't expect to not be able to ride in the same car as Jude, and I was somewhat disappointed that I wouldn't be able to eavesdrop on him and his supplier's conversation. I was certain that whatever they were saying was worthy of my superiors hearing.

I needed something on him to prove he was a high-level drug dealer if I wanted to arrest him. I could not slap the cuffs on him, otherwise, without probable cause.

Seated in a doorless jeep between two burly African men, I prayed that I'd be able to get the evidence I needed. I had less than a week to put this sting together, and if I failed I'd not only lose this case but my reputation as one of the most prolific DEA agents in history.

"Smoke?" Soul's security guard offered me a cigarette. I didn't smoke, but to fit the role I was playing, I kindly accepted.

"'Preciate it," I said. "So, where we headed?"

"You'll see when we get there," the man shot back.

Apparently, he wasn't as nice as I thought he was. I figured it was best to sit back and enjoy the ride. I obviously wasn't gonna get any intel from Soul's men. He had trained them well.

Sometimes you gotta play the fool to fool the fool, I reminded myself. *I'll get what I need in due time. I just have to be patient.* Soon, all my stars would be aligned.

39
JUDE

Soul wasn't bullshitting when he said that Africans were festive. He ended up taking me to some nightclub called The Bang Bang Bar in an area of the city known as Nyaniba Estates. He waited good until we pulled up to valet to tell me that he owned it. He'd named it The Bang Bang Room to pay homage to one of his old, favorite TV shows, *Twin Peaks*.

The outside was super fancy and impressive, but the inside was even more astounding. It was a converted warehouse space with trendy industrial decor and shiny disco balls throughout. A popular AfroBeats artist was performing on stage and he had the whole crowd lit. Bottle girls wearing skimpy peacock outfits walked through the crowds carrying ice buckets with champagne and sparklers. The partygoers were classy folks and almost all of them were dressed in formal attire. It was a real grown and sexy type of vibe.

"Damn, man. This is nice," I told Soul.

"Oh, it gets even better," he said. "Dhakira!" He shouted over the music to get the attention of a passing bartender. "Dhakira, come," he beckoned to her like she was a dog. "Let me introduce you to my brethren. This is Jude, of my solid day ones. I need the *best* section in the house cleared out for this man, along with the finest bottles we have in the wine cellar," he said. "It's not often my brother comes home, so we have to show him a good time while he's here."

"*Wofiri he?*" She said to me with a smile.

I didn't speak any Ghanaian languages, so I looked over at Soul for translation.

"He is from America," he told her.

Her smile got even bigger. "Ah, yes, America! Beautiful place," she said. "Such a pleasure to meet you and I will get right on clearing that section for you, sir."

Several minutes later, a group of guys walked out of the VIP section looking pissed and talking shit since they'd gotten the boot. They were draped in designer clothes and chains and probably a bunch of scammers. They reminded me a lot of how I used to be. Rowdy and reckless.

"Right this way, sir," Dhakira said. She led us to the VIP section that was almost as big as a second club. It featured modern decor, a mini bar, and a private dancer on a stripper pole.

"Wow. Is wifey cool with all this?" I asked Soul, making myself comfortable on a red leather couch. Dhakira came and placed a tray of Cuban cigars in front of us.

"It pays for her lavish life so she better be," he winked. "Oh, a couple of mint flavored hookahs for my men here too, Dhakira," Soul told her. "Almost forgot you guys don't fuck with that imported shit," he said to Fillmore and Price.

"Yeah, cigars give me a headache," Fillmore said. He and Price were the only white boys in our section, but they weren't the only white people in the club. As a matter of fact, there were tons of Caucasian people in The Bang Bang Bar. I figured they we transplants, and in the country for work. But they could've just as easily been born here, for all I knew.

"So...straight to business," I said, reaching for a cigar. I handed one to Conway, who was eerily quiet today. He must've been nervous being in front of my supplier for the very first time. I chalked up his odd behavior to jitteriness. "As you know, profits have tripled in the last two years. The magazines are selling out the ass, and print sales are going through the roof. The consumers are goin' crazy, man. It's getting to a point where the shelves are empty in every store."

"Say less, man. I'll have my company start printing up more issues right away. Can't have those consumers angry," Soul said.

He and I always talked in code, referring to drugs as magazines, just in case anyone *was* listening in, God forbid. When I looked over at Conway, I noticed he was breaking out in a sweat. "You hot, my man?"

"Yeah, I am kinda hot," he said, fanning himself. "I guess I'm not used to this dry heat."

"Yeah, Africa's like walking into a sauna," Price agreed. "I'm still trying to figure out how all these white people don't get sunburnt."

"Lots of sunscreen," Fillmore laughed.

"Dhakira!" Soul called out. "We need water. And up the central air, please." He cut his eyes at Conway. "We can't have your guard dog passing out on us," he said taking a cheap shot at him. "So, um, where is it you're from...Conway, is it?"

"Yes."

"You look black, but Spanish too. It's hard for me to tell." Now that Soul had started his interrogation there was no stopping him. "Which one is it?"

"I, uh, I'm black, and part Honduran. My great-grandmother was Honduran," he added. "Never got to meet her though. She died before I was born."

"Ever been?" Soul asked.

"Excuse me?" Conway looked confused.

"To Honduras?"

"Never. But I'd love to go someday. Get in touch with my roots."

"Yeah," Soul agreed. "It's nothin' like getting in touch with those roots," he said. "So, what made you want to join the squad?"

"Fillmore brought me on board actually. He saw that I was hungry, and he knew that I was a hard worker."

Fillmore and Price were feeling so good off their drinks, they'd started dancing and throwing dollars at the girl on stage. Their asses didn't even like women, but they were obviously in their zone, just having a good time. Meanwhile, tensions were at an all-time high between Conway and Soul.

"So, where'd you grow up?"

"Austin, Texas."

"You went to school there?"

"Yeah, I did."

"If you don't mind me asking, which university? And what degree did you obtain?"

"I don't mind at all, sir. I attended The University of Texas at Austin," Conway said. "And I got my Bachelors in Communication and Leadership."

"*Leadership*," Soul repeated, tossing back his shot. "So, do you consider yourself a *leader*, Conway?" He asked next.

"C'mon, Soul. You gone interview the man all night?" I finally cut in.

"I just wanna know who this *head of security is*, that's all? If he's spending a lot of time with your family, you should too. I'm sure he's been around my daughter on quite a few occasions. I just wanna make sure the nigga's good."

"He's good. Fillmore vouched for my guy already. Cut him some slack, man," I said.

"*Fillmore*???" Soul laughed, causing the skin around his eyes to wrinkle. "You must not remember the intense interrogation I put *him* through when you first introduced us," he reminded me. "A nigga just be wanting to know who he dealin' with. That's all."

"Mr. Asante, I can assure you, you're dealing with an honest and level-headed man," Conway said. He didn't seem bothered by Soul's questions at all, and I was really impressed that he was able to remain calm in the face of opposition.

"That's good to know." Soul stood to his feet, and snatched out the gun that was tucked in his waist. "Then you should have no muthafuckin' problem strippin'," he said.

"Soul, man. Chill. What the fuck is you on? You really think this nigga's wearing a wire?" I asked him.

"We finna find out," Soul said. "You heard me, muthafucka. STRIP!!" He cocked the hammer.

Conway slowly stood to his feet and proceeded to unbutton his dress shirt.

"Soul, sweetie, I usually agree with your sense of judgment, but this is getting a little out of hand," Fillmore said.

"Soul, don't do this. Please put the gun away," Price said.

Soul's security watched in silence. We were all on pins and needles, praying that he didn't pull the trigger.

"Nah. Out of hand is me blowing his gotdamn head off!" Soul spat. "I don't know what it is, but I don't trust this muthafucka. There's something off about him. And my pops always told me intuition never lies. So, unless he wants a bullet to the dome, he better prove me otherwise."

Conway came up out of his pants, and all I could do was sit there and feel embarrassment for the kid. There was no stopping Soul whenever he was on a roll. And apparently, he felt like he was on to something.

A few people in the club stopped what they were doing to marvel at the spectacle we were creating. By then, Conway was in his tighty-whities. The shit was mad humiliating.

"There, you happy, my nigga? No wires, no nothin'," I stated contemptuously.

"May I put my clothes back on, sir?" Conway asked Soul.

Soul looked defeated, but nodded his head anyway.

Conway graciously redressed, keeping his cool well for someone who'd just been snubbed. If it were me, I'd be ready to open Soul's head on a curb. A nigga definitely didn't play that shit.

"You gotta chill, man," I told Soul.

Instead of saying anything, he poured himself another shot, never once taking his eyes off Conway. For some odd reason, he just wasn't fucking with the nigga.

40
CONWAY

After having my ass handed to me in front of everybody, I snuck off to the restroom to gather myself and make sure my tiny, dime-sized listening device was still intact. It was tucked away in the folds of my tie, so when Soul stripped me in the VIP section, he didn't see it since he was too busy looking for a wire.

"We'll see who gets the last laugh when the judge throws the book at his ass," I said to my own reflection. I was surprised that I was actually able to remain calm after the shit he pulled. I prided myself on my composure, plus I knew I had a roll to fulfill. So, for now, I would have to take my L like a man.

After making sure I was good, I stepped into an empty stall, pulled my phone out and called Evelyn, Eve's mother. She answered on the fourth ring, despite the time difference. It was 12:58 a.m. in Accra, which meant in Atlanta it was almost 6 in the morning.

"Conway." She cleared her throat, and I could hear her wiping the sleep out of her eyes. "How can I help you?" She asked, in a less groggy tone.

She and I had started working together some months back. I enlisted her help when it was clear that I'd need insider to take down Jude. In exchange for her assistance, she and her daughter would get immunity. That was the deal.

"I need to know if you have something I can use as evidence?" I whispered into the phone. With Jude and Soul talking in codes, I wasn't sure I'd get what I needed on the trip to pin drug charges on them. "Anything at all? Emails? Documents? A book or some other type of collection of financial accounts and sales?"

"A ledger," she suddenly said. "Jude keeps all his accounts, transactions and sales in there. But it's only one problem. It's written using codes and symbols, so I'm not sure how helpful that'll be in a court of law."

"Unless the judge is a fuckin' symbologist too, it won't be very helpful at all."

"What if my daughter testifies? She can break down the codes."

"That could work," I said. "Where is this ledger?"

"Cameron has it now. She and my daughter had a little...spat. I made her give it back so that she won't incriminate herself. You said this sting was gonna happen any day now, so I just thought it'd be best if we cover our tracks."

"Totally understandable. And if Cameron has it, that means it's even closer to being in my possession," I said. "That's all I wanted. Get some rest." I hung up the phone and started putting my plan in motion. If I couldn't gather enough evidence on this trip, then at least I had another means of taking down Jude and his empire.

41
CAMERON

It was a quarter after 7 a.m. when I finally walked through the doors of my home and I couldn't have been happier. If there was a flight leaving to LAX sooner, I would have been back here hours ago.

The house was eerily quiet, and I figured everyone was sleeping, but when I looked in Justin and Madison's rooms, I saw that their beds were empty. Jude hadn't returned either.

"I told these kids not to go anywhere," I fumed. "It's okay. A hard head makes for a soft ass." I planned on grounding Justin until he turned 18.

Cracking Journee's door open, I poked my head inside to see if she was in bed. She was. I smiled as I admired how cute she looked sleeping. She had one leg sticking out from under the covers and her hair was all over the place.

Ever so quietly, I entered her room and sat on the edge of her bed. Now that she was getting older we hardly, if ever, had any bonding moments. She felt like she was too old to be up under me. It didn't matter how old she got, Journee would always be my baby girl.

I gently pulled the sheet out and covered her bare leg. She slowly stirred awake, looked at me and smiled.

And for once she didn't have an attitude or anything smart to say. I ran my fingers over her baby hairs.

"Morning, Mommy's Angel," I smiled.

"Morning, mama."

"I didn't mean to wake you up. I just couldn't resist. You looked so peaceful," I told her. "It seems like yesterday I was just watching you sleep as an infant. Now you're all grown up. You're practically a young lady now."

Journee smiled.

"Mom, dad already talked to me about the birds and the bees. You can spare me part two of the speech."

"Oh, he did now, did he?" I was so proud of Jude for taking the initiative to speak with her. That was usually every parent's worst nightmare.

"Yeah. It was kinda uncomfortable," she laughed. "But I understood the point he was making."

I leaned down and kissed her forehead. "We only wanna see you do well in life, princess. That's all. We just want what's best for you."

Journee smiled. "I know, mama. And I'm sorry I've been a little mouthy to you lately."

"*A little?*" I laughed.

"Okay, a lot," she said. "You're my mom—and a great mom at that—you don't deserve a drop of disrespect. And I promise to do better."

"Thank you, baby. That's all a mom can ask for."

I slowly stood up from her bed and prepared to leave her room.

"Hey, mom!" Journee called out to me.

"Yes, angel?"

Journee bit her bottom lip as she hesitated with her question. "Was dad a bad boy when you met him?"

Her question took me by a surprise, and I immediately had a flash from the past as I reminisced about the night me and her father met.

The PlayPen was a hood, but classy-looking strip joint in Columbus, Ohio. It was a tan brick building with the pink neon lettering that spelled its name. It was only ten o'clock and the parking lot was already packed to capacity when me, Pocahontas and Juicy pulled up to the spot.

"See, I told you this bitch would be rockin'!" Poca boasted.

After she parked the car, me, Juicy and Poca sashayed towards the building. There were a few guys standing outside conversing. They were all dressed to impress in expensive clothing and jewelry, and they didn't miss a beat to try to flirt with us as we entered the club.

"Shorty in the white, what's up?" A guy called out to me.

"Me?" I asked with a playful smile. Poca and X strolled inside while I chose to stay behind and mingle for a bit.

"Yeah, you. Come here, let me talk to you for a minute."

If it wasn't for the fact that he looked like money and smelled like money, I might've passed him by without so much as a second thought.

He stood at 6"3, and was thick and light skinned with a beard that resembled Rick Ross's. He had a freshly tapered haircut, and covering his eyes were a pair of designer shades. Each ear sported a large square diamond stud and draped around his neck was a single diamond chain with a cross pendant.

"What's up with you?" he asked.

"As you can see, I'm actually on my way inside," I told him. "It's money to be made with my name on it."

He nodded his head in agreement. "I dig that. My name's Jerrell. What's your name, sexy?"

"Nice to meet you, Jerrell. They call me Hypnotic."

"I can see why they call you that. Well, look I ain't gone hold up ya' hustle. I know you a woman about ya' paper and shit. I'll just holla at you in the club," he said.

"Good. 'Cuz I'll look a whole lot sexier in the outfit I'm planning on wearing."

There had to have been at least 40 girls on the roster at The PlayPen. I didn't see a possibility of everyone getting a turn to go up on stage. The competition was beyond fierce so I definitely had to stand out if I wanted to be noticed. A lime green metallic bikini suit embroidered with rhinestones had been my outfit of choice. With matching garter belts to go around my thighs, I made sure to pull them extra high underneath my ass to make it sit up just the way men liked it. I had already removed my hand brace while in Poca's car, so I finally felt like my old self again when I stepped out the dressing room. A few weeks ago, I'd been jumped by a pack of hating ass strippers.

2 Chainz featuring The Weeknd's "Like Me" blared through the speakers as I walked into the crowded club.

Jerrell waved his hand towards me, beckoning for me to join him at the bar. When I reached him, I noticed he was sitting with four other guys. One of them was already getting a lap dance from Juicy. Poca was nowhere in sight, but knowing her, she was probably in a dimly lit corner somewhere giving up the pussy for the right price.

"You lookin' good," he said before pulling out a wad of cash from his pocket. "Lemme see what you workin' with though."

He didn't have to ask twice and I quickly went to work popping and gyrating my ass in his lap.

Meek Millz "Errrday" began playing and Jerrell began sprinkling bills over me as I danced for him. A couple of his friends joined in and began throwing money as I did my thing. I quickly became conceited all over again. I had been out the game for a month but I was glad that I hadn't lost my touch.

Once the song ended, Jerrell pulled me close and whispered, "Aye, you see the nigga right there, two seats down from me?"

I looked in the direction he was pointing to and sure enough there a guy sitting in a bar stool with one finger plugged in his ear while attempting to talk on the phone in the loud club.

"That's my lil' brother, Jude. Go give that nigga a lap dance." He pulled my garter belt back, placed a fifty-dollar bill inside, and slapped my ass I walked away towards his brother.

"Hey, what's up?" I shouted over the loud music.

Jude was so engrossed with his conversation that he either didn't see me standing there in front of him or just didn't care.

"Um...Hello?!" I yelled waving my arms around so I could get his attention.

He finally looked at me, rolled his eyes, and continued shouting into the receiver of his cell phone.

Oh, no he didn't, I thought. If it was one thing I hated, it was being ignored. Jarrell had already paid for his lap dance, and dammit, I was going to give it to him! Without deliberation, I quickly snatched his iPhone out his hand.

"Aye, what are you doing?!" he yelled.

I hit the END button, and placed his phone down beside him at the bar.

"That was a business call," he said annoyed.

Ignoring him and his aloof attitude, I slowly maneuvered in between his legs.

He grabbed my shoulders, stopping me halfway. "Nah, I don't do lap dances, lil' ma."

"Your brother already paid for it. It's free anyway. Why don't you just sit here and let me do my thing?" It was a pride issue now. I had never had a man turn me away.

Jude grimaced and looked in Jerrell's direction, who smiled and ushered for us to continue.

"I'm not gonna bite you," I teased, climbing into his lap.

I caught a generous whiff of his fragrance. He smelled so good and I took a brief moment to admire him. He was actually a sexy guy even through all the uptightness he displayed. Jude would probably be considered a "pretty boy" to most women. He was light skinned, with dark eyes complemented by long, thick eyelashes. His lips were full.

Not too thick. Not too small. Perfect. His mid-length dreadlocks were pulled back into a ponytail underneath his Cincinnati Reds hat.

I saw the uneasiness all in his expression, so I couldn't help but tease him a bit. Taking his hands, I placed them on my waist as I did a sexy, little seductive dance. His expression quickly turned from tense into pure lust as I worked my magic on him.

"See, that wasn't so bad, was it?" I asked after the song ended.

He didn't say anything as a slight smirk tugged at his lips.

Climbing out of his lap, I walked back over towards Jerrell to collect my money off the floor.

"What was up with your brother?" I asked Jerrell the minute I reached him.

He waved Jude's behavior off. "Aww, that nigga just be actin' funny sometimes," he laughed. "But for real though...I think he likes you."

"Your father was a bad boy, but he was also a good guy," I told Journee.

She gave me a confused look. "How can he be a bad boy *and* a good guy?" She asked.

"Well," I paused. "Because of his actions. You see...He was hood, but also a gentleman. Stern but selfless.

Savage but sweet. In short, I'll just say he was a bad boy with good guy tendencies."

"That sounds like the perfect combination," she said listlessly.

"Why all these questions about bad boys? Are *you* fancying a certain bad boy?" I asked, giving her the side eye.

Journee blushed. "No, mom. I was just asking."

"Okay, baby girl. Go ahead and get your rest. I'll be starting breakfast soon."

"K, Mom."

"Oh, by the way, do you know where Justin and Madison are?"

"No..."

Journee was known to cover for her brother. They never ratted each other out. And because of that, I'd probably be grounding her ass, as well. Even people who *didn't* snitch weren't impervious to punishment. "Okie dokie," I said, walking out of her room.

As I headed to the kitchen to make breakfast, I pulled my phone out and FaceTimed my husband. Jude answered on the third ring. He was already up and at 'em but that was because of the 8-hour time difference. It was a little after 3pm in Accra.

"Wassup, babe? Everything good? What happened to you? I was blowing your phone up like crazy. Your ass went AWOL. That ain't like you."

"I know...I'll tell you about all that when you get back."

"I'll prepare myself," he said unenthusiastically.

"Well, I'm calling you because our son is AWOL now. Him *and* Madison. I told them not to leave the house, but they went ahead and did what they wanted to anyway. You know he gets that stubborn shit from your side of the family," I said, knowing damn well I was just as bullheaded.

Jude didn't seem the least bit bothered by the news. "That makes sense..."

"Um, what do you mean *that makes sense*? Is there something I don't know about? 'Cuz my son going against my word doesn't make a lick of sense to me."

Jude sighed and ran a hand over his hair. "I probably shouldn't tell you, but if it'll keep your hair from falling out, fuck it. Justin and Madison are dating. Have been for some time now," he said. "They probably just stepped out to have a lil' privacy. You know how teenagers are."

"No. Apparently, I don't know shit!" I was at a complete loss for words. I had no idea Justin and Maddie were an item. The idea never even popped in my head. I guess because I didn't want them to see each other in that way. Madison was like my niece, and Justin was my son.

"Look, don't make a big deal about it, a'ight," Jude told me. "It took a lot for our son to come clean. The last thing we want to do is make him feel guilty about it."

"I won't say anything...for now," I told him. "But since we're dropping bombs about our son, there's something you should know. The other day, I found a journal under Justin's pillow. It was filled with every hood and borough in the area of Los Angeles. Most of the names were crossed off. Do you have any idea what that means? I figured I'd ask since Justin obviously trusts you more than he does me."

"Cut it out, Cam. You know a father and son's bond is unbreakable."

"I know," I sighed.

"How 'bout this? I'll talk to him about the journal when I get back. How's that sound?"

"That's *if* I don't kill him first," I mumbled.

I was feeling some type of way about Justin keeping all these secrets from me. I was also disappointed in Madison because I felt like I'd been misled. They were only putting on an act this whole time, and while their intentions were innocent, I took it as deceitfulness. I probably would've respected their relationship a whole lot more if they'd just been upfront and honest about it. I wouldn't have banned Maddie from coming over just because she was dating my son. But I'd definitely keep a closer eye on her.

"Let me know when he returns," Jude said.

"You got it, babe."

"Love you, Queen. Try not to stress."

"Love you too. I'll talk to you later."

I hung up the phone, ran a hand over my hair and shook my head in disbelief. These kids of mine were really gonna be the death of me.

42
ROXIE

Since Hector had stayed out all night doing only God knows what, I decided to step out and do my own investigating—and I wasn't talking about finding whatever bitch Hector was laid up with. Quite frankly, I'd given up on putting forth an effort to keep him all to myself.

The old me would've tracked him down, bust his windows out and raised hell, but I was no longer invested in our marriage to do all that shit. At this point, I was simply going through the motions. Happy to claim that I had a man even if I didn't fully *have* him.

I knew I should've just left his ass, but I didn't have the will to walk. Not yet anyway. I wasn't ready to be alone. I tried to call Hector to tell him about Rain's little incident, but he ignored me like I was a telemarketer. He'd been running the streets for 2 days straight, and I already knew when I asked him about it, he'd claim that he was out looking for work. He must've thought I was stupid.

I wasn't stressing him or his whereabouts. Instead, I was more concerned with finding a remedy for my daughter's violent outbursts. If that trait followed her into adulthood, she could live a very fucked up life. She'd probably wind up in prison for hurting someone, or worse, in a casket. To avoid such a thing from happening, I had to find a cure for her blackouts.

Last night, I did some digging on the internet and found a holistic daughter in New Orleans who specialized in anger management treatment. I decided to take the next few days off work to drive down to Louisiana to meet him, and see if he could help me better understand how to help my daughter. He had tons of positive feedback, so I prayed that he'd be able to shed some light on these anger outbursts, and that he knew of a way to conquer it. I tried to let Hector know that I was leaving, but his phone was off, and I wasn't about to stick around to see why. Rain was counting on me and I had her future to take into account.

After leaving the kids with their nanny, I got on the road and prepared for the seven-hour drive to New Orleans. I could've just as easily flown but I needed the ride to clear my head, and to rethink my reasons for staying with a no-good ass dirty dick dog of a husband.

43
JUSTIN

The yellow ball of fire changed to hues of orange, and then almost tangerine as it settled beyond the horizon. Gripping the heavy duffel bag in my hand, I made my way to the dilapidated building the kidnappers had instructed me to meet them at.

Bayshore Roadhouse was one of the last roundhouses left, and it was barely standing at that. Originally, there was over two hundred roundhouses in the state of California. Trains used to run through there, then after they went obsolete in '58 they stayed open to stable diesel locomotives. However, now it was just a spray-painted landmark that people often claimed was haunted.

A sliver of sweat ran down the bridge of my nose despite it being relatively cool outside. I was nervous than a bitch about meeting these niggas—*if* they even decided to show up. What if they'd already killed Madison? A dozen doubtful thoughts ran through my mind and my nerves were on edge.

Nah. I saw the greed in them niggas' eyes. *They want this money*, I told myself. *They damn sure want this money.*

I would've come sooner and just waited for them to arrive, but I ended up having to take a 2-hour trip to San Diego, where my father's emergency stash was hidden under the floorboards of an abandoned house on the outskirts of the city. When I turned 14, he showed me where it was in case of an emergency. And because of the situation, I definitely considered this a state of emergency.

Me and Maddie's life depended on it. I knew my father would be upset and that I'd probably have to come clean about what I was doing, but it was an issue that I would resolve when the time came. Right now, I could only focus on one thing, and that was getting this money to these niggas and getting Madison back in my arms. It'd been several hours since she'd been shot and I could only imagine the condition she was in—*if* she wasn't already dead.

"Nah. Don't think like that," I said to myself as I climbed over rocks and debris. "Don't think like that. She's alive..." In the distance, I saw four silhouettes standing under a pavilion that looked like it was about to cave in at any given moment.

They were all still wearing their masks like a bunch of pussies, each one toting a different gun. I breathed a sigh of relief when I saw that Madison was still breathing—and they'd even taken the liberty of bandaging her up themselves to prevent her from bleeding out. She was still in a pretty weak state of health, seeing as how she could barely stand on her own without their help.

I'mma gonna fucking kill every single of their asses, I promised myself. They fucked with the wrong one.

"I was startin' to get worried there," the leader said, using that same stupid ass modulator. "I was actually afraid you wouldn't show up. Then me and my niggas would've had to fuck every hole on this bitch," he laughed, with a possessive grip on Madison's shoulder.

I wanted to rip his fucking arm off for even laying a finger on her. I hated to see anyone touch her that wasn't me. All that shit I said to her in the car was just my anger talking for me. I loved this girl more than I loved myself, and I'd do anything to protect her, even give my own life if it came down to it.

"Like you said, not a second late or a dollar short," I reminded him, handing over the duffel bag.

He nodded his head to his shooter who walked over towards my extended hand. He was carrying a .45 cal.

The leader shoved Madison in my direction at the same time and she slowly walked over to me. She and I made brief eye contact, and I saw something I didn't expect. She no longer looked frightened or intimidated. She looked downright pissed!

Suddenly, and without warning, she turned around and speared her good shoulder into the leader's midsection, knocking him to the ground. I joined her in action, knocking the gun from the other guy's hand with my duffel bag. He went to grab it but I swung the bag and hit him in the head, sending him sprawling to the floor. He hit the ground with a hard thud, and I quickly grabbed his weapon and cracked him in the skull with it. The third guy was obviously overwhelmed by everything happening. He didn't know what to do so he pointed his pistol at Madison's head as she wrestled with the leader for his gun.

POW!

I shot his ass in the stomach with the .45 before he could squeeze. I was still on top of the second guy, and he was unconscious from the blow to his head.

"GET THE FUCK OFF ME, BITCH!" The leader yelled. Now that the modulator had been knocked out of his hand, his voice was strangely familiar.

"Drip?"

He shoved Madison off, but she was able to grab his shotgun and she wasted no time using it on his ass.

BOOM!

Bullets tore through the side of his midsection, and he went flying backwards from the impact.

"What the fuck?" I quickly walked over to the guy I'd knocked unconscious and snatched his mask off. It was Nahmir. And if I had to guess, the person I'd shot in the stomach was actually Chris.

With everything happening, I'd almost forgot that I sent Drip the address to the party we were at. That's how he knew where to find us. Madison and I were so busy fighting, we didn't notice that we were being followed after we left the house. That's how they were able to easily ambush us at the red light. All that time, I thought he was out trying to catch a lick when I was the lick all along.

Ain't this about a bitch, I thought. My mom always said to watch the company you keep, and that betrayal usually comes from the people you trust most. And my dad would always say, *laugh with many but don't trust any.*

"WHAT THE FUCK, DRIP?!" I hollered at him after I saw that he was miraculously still alive. Writhing in pain, he held the side of his stomach to stop the blood flow. "Yo, you tried to line me, my nigga??? Really, though? Ya own brother? We done ate off the same plate, grew up shootin' hoops in the same hood! We supposed to be fam!"

Madison used the shotgun like a crutch to stand to her feet. She was far stronger than I'd ever given her credit for. And she had impeccable aiming skills.

"I ain't 'een gone front," Drip laughed through the pain. "A nigga wasn't tryin' to go back to sugar water and mayonnaise sandwiches."

"You fuckin' fool! I told your ass I'd make sure you ate! Have I not done that these past three years???"

"Nigga, that shit is breadcrumbs! I got a whole fuckin' family to feed and no rich ass parents to help me! I only did what I had to. It's a dog-eat-dog world out here. It was only a matter of time before you got on some funny ass shit, anyway," he said. "A mufucka was just tryin' to survive, my nigga. You either eat or you get ate. It ain't shit personal."

"Oh yeah?" I pointed the .45 caliber at him. "Well, neither is this!"

POW! POW! POW!

Drip leapt to his feet at lightning speed, grabbed the duffel bag, and took off running for the car that was parked several feet away. I tried to run after him, but he jumped inside and peeled off. The recoil on the caliber made it hard as fuck for me to hit my target, but I still kept shooting at his car anyway. I soon realized it was pointless as he disappeared into the night with all of my father's emergency cash. Ironically, he had exactly 2 million dollars under the floorboards. Now that 2 million was in the hands of a sneaky ass, backstabbing son of a whore.

On everything I love, I'mma murder that nigga when I see 'em.

After remembering that Maddie needed my help, I turned around and ran to her aid—but she violently shook me off with an attitude. "I'm fine, Justin! I'm okay."

"The hell you are, Madison. You've been shot," I reminded her.

"Yeah, well, my pain tolerance is pretty high," she said, grabbing Chris's gun off the ground. "All that shit in the basement...it was all an act. I just wanted these assholes to *think* I was weak," she said. "I already knew I was gonna make a move the second I got an opening. I wasn't gonna just sit back and let these bastards get away with shooting me."

"So, you risked your life just to pull this shit? Things could've ended so much differently," I told her.

"Yeah, well, it didn't," she spat. "And I had to do what I had to. They shot me, Justin! I'll probably never be able to swim again after today," she said miserably. I watched as she limped over to Nahmir who was just waking up from his temporary coma. "That means no scholarship." She pointed Chris's handgun at Nahmir's head. "Can you imagine how that feels, Justin? How devastating it is having your dreams ripped away in a matter of seconds by people you don't even know?!"

POP!

She blew Nahmir's face open, then limped over to Chris who was surprisingly still breathing with a hole in her stomach. Madison was just about to pull the trigger when I snatched the gun from her.

"Gimme that," I said. I didn't want Madison to have to carry this heavy burden on her own. Besides, I'd taken many lives. What was one more? When I looked down at Chris, it suddenly dawned on me that I'd never taken a friend's life, and that made all the difference.

"Damn, kid. I underestimated your ass," Chris smiled through the agonizing pain.

"I could say the same about you," I said, kneeling down beside her.

"Yeah, well, like my cousin said it wasn't shit personal. Niggas get grimey when money's involved. You should know that. That's just how this street shit go, fam. Everybody tryin' to eat." Chris coughed up a mouthful of blood, then wiped it away, and reached for the inside of her jacket. She pulled out a blunt and patted her sides for the lighter. "Gotdamn," she sighed in disbelief.

"I got'cha covered, girl." I pulled out my lighter and lit the end of her blunt.

She took three long, hard pulls then tossed it with a flick of her fingers. "Alright, J Money. I'm ready to meet my creator, or the Devil. Whoever welcomes me with open arms," she struggled to laugh.

I smiled and my eyes became blurry with tears.

Madison turned her back to us, as I slowly stood to my feet. Cocking the hammer, I pointed the gun at Chris's head and squeezed the trigger.

POP!

After putting her down, I quickly wiped the tear away that was rolling down my cheek. I never thought the day would come when my own day ones would turn on me. I guess money really was the root of all evil.

44
MADISON

"You're a lil' crazy. I'm startin' to see that now," Justin said.

"What?" I was confused.

He momentarily took his eyes off the road to look at my fingers rooting around my own wound to find the bullet lodged within. "Are you sure you should be doin' that?" Justin asked. "That shit looks painful."

Of course, it hurt like hell but I tried my best not to show it. "It is. But I have to. If I go to the hospital, then my father will find out. And he won't be too happy once he hears about what you've been doing..." I added.

Justin was as quiet as a church mouse.

"So...?" I pressed.

"So, what?"

"Are you going to tell me what you've been doing?"

Justin kept his eyes on the road. "You were in the basement. You heard what was said."

"So, it's true then?"

Justin's silent said it all.

"Wow, Justin. I had no idea you were about that life."

"I could say the same about you," he said. "With the way you shot Nahmir, you'd think this wasn't your first rodeo."

"What can I say? I was mad as hell," I stated. "They shot me. How else was I supposed to react?" There was a long period of silence before I spoke again. "Justin...My dad really can't find out about this. If he does, he'll never let me come back here to see you."

Justin was silent for a few moments. "I guess I didn't think about all that," he said. "But I just want you to get professional help. I don't think you should be doin' that on ya own."

"I'll be...fine." I winced in pain when I located the bullet and pulled it out. "See...now all I need is some alcohol, bandages, and a pack of smokes." My fingers trembled uncontrollably, as I held the bullet. I was still in shock from being shot, but if my dad had gone through worse things and still survived I knew I'd be alright. He always told me I was as strong as him, if not more.

"What if he still *does* find out?" Justin asked. "You really think he'd keep you away from me?"

"I don't think so, Justin, I *know* so," I said "You obviously don't know my dad. He doesn't play about me."

He sucked his teeth dismissively. "Man, I'll drop your father on his fuckin' head if he ever tries to keep you away from me. I don't play about you, either."

I laughed in spite of the pain I was in. I couldn't even imagine Justin's frail ass slamming my dad.

"Here's a CVS right up here," he pointed out.

"Awesome…" My face was dotted in sweat, and my body on fire. It would probably be so much worse though, if it wasn't for Drip patching me up.

Justin pulled into the parking lot, dug in the middle console for some loose dollars, and kept the engine running. "I'll be right back." I watched as he hopped out and ran in the store.

Damn, my baby is such a rider.

I knew that he wouldn't have left me stranded, but still, I was pleased to know that he'd risk his own life to save mine. *I'll never try him again after today*, I told myself. *From here on out, I'm gonna be the greatest girlfriend a guy could ask for.* Today Justin had showed and proved. Now it was my turn.

Several minutes later, Justin emerged from the store with a bag of supplies. He opened the door, climbed in and turned on the dome light.

"How you feelin'?" He asked with a look of sincere concern on his face.

"I'm managing," I said, through gritted teeth.

"Want me to pull out the other slug?" He offered.

"No, that one went clean through. Thank God."

"Good, let's get to the crib then, so we can properly clean these wounds."

"No!" I quickly said.

"What'chu mean no?"

"I'm saying, we can't go back now. What if Auntie Cam is there? If she sees I've been shot, she'll tell my dad and he'll never let me come back to visit you."

"Damn, Maddie, you act like you're scared of your father."

"If you knew the things he's done in his past, you would be too."

"Well, you finna be eighteen. He can't control you forever."

I laughed through the pain. "I keep saying you don't know my dad. He's a power figure and he makes shit happen. And if he finds out I've been shot while under Cameron's supervision he will *never* let me come back to Cali—let alone America. He doesn't give a fuck about me being grown or not. He damn near runs Africa. Whatever he says goes. He can't ever know about this, Justin. Not ever. Just trust me."

"But what about swimming—"

"I'll just tell him that I'm no longer interested. Find a different hobby or something. I'll figure it out. But he can't know this happened, do you hear me?"

"Okay, I hear you," he agreed. "Now take your shirt off."

"What?" I asked confused. I almost thought he was trying to get fresh until I remembered that I was shot.

"Take your shirt off. I'll clean 'em right here then."

After helping me out of my tee, he poured alcohol over my wound and I had to bite my tongue just to keep from screaming out in pain. It was the most agonizing feeling that I'd ever experienced in life. Even worse than being shot. Once he cleaned my wounds, he dressed them, and applied heavy-duty bandages. It would probably still leave a nasty scar without stitches, but I'd be alright.

As Justin patched me up, I couldn't help but to admire him. He was so damn handsome with his pecan colored skin, curly black hair and girlishly long lashes. He looked up at me and smiled, and his dark brown eyes melted my heart. I swear, those eyes of his were always my weakness.

I knew that he said it was over between us earlier, but I wasn't about to let that happen. He would always be mine, no matter what he went through or how bad we got under each other's skin.

"I'm sorry," I suddenly said.

"'Bout what?"

"Tryin' to play you at the party. The tattoo. Everything," I said. "I'm such a shitty girlfriend sometimes. I don't know how you put up with me."

Justin chuckled and shook his head at me. "Man, I'm not even on that shit, Madison. I'm just glad you're okay."

"And I'm glad I got you."

Justin grabbed me by the nape of my neck and kissed me. "I can't quit you," he said. "I love you."

"I love you too." A tear fell down my face as I closed my eyes and thanked the Lord that we still had each other. Justin was right. Things could've gone so much differently back at the roundhouse.

"What I tell you? As long as you got my back, I got yours. Ain't nothin' change," he said, letting me know I was still his girl.

45
CAMERON

Flipping through the pages of Justin's journal, I sat on the edge of his bed and tried to make sense of what I was seeing. *Where did Jude and I go wrong*, I asked myself. Journee was a selfish spoiled brat at times, and Justin, a secretive and deceitful liar. Still, I couldn't help feeling like I was to blame. After all, children become spoiled when parents substitute presents for presence. And me and Jude both had been lacking in the presence department. We were too busy focusing on fame when we should've been focusing on family.

"What the hell am I doing?" I asked myself, running a hand through my hair.

We'd moved them out here for a fresh start and better opportunities in life, but now I was second guessing the decision. Trying to live life in the fast lane was tearing my family apart.

I knew this parent shit didn't come with a manual, but some days I thought chasing a toddler around would be far less exhausting than parenting older kids. Oh, how I missed the days when their cheeks were fat, their thighs were chubby and they could barely walk or talk. Now I had two teenagers and I hardly knew what to do with either of them.

Before I had teenagers, I used to think I would be the most empathetic parent in the world. That I would understand and sympathize with my teens since it wasn't that long ago when I was young, dumb, and full of cum myself. I thought I would be the cool parent and that my kids would share everything with me and hang onto my every word.

Boy, was I wrong.

Sometimes, I felt like I was losing my sanity trying to raise them to be decent people. But this was a job I signed up for 17 years ago, and dammit I would see it through come hell or high water.

Pulling out my cellphone, I called Justin for the twelfth time that morning. On the fifth ring, he finally answered and I couldn't have been happier. His ass had me worried sick.

"Justin, where the hell are you? Did you and Maddie stay out all night?"

"Yeah, you and dad were out all night. I figured it wouldn't be a big deal."

"*Me and dad* are grown," I reminded him. "See, that's ya'll muthafuckin' problem. Ya'll think ya'll asses grown but it's 'bout time I brought you back down to size."

"Ma, chill. Me and Maddie went to a friend's party. I had a few drinks and I didn't wanna get behind a wheel, so we crashed at his place."

"So, you staying out past curfew, getting drunk and shit. Tell me, Justin, what else have you been doing?" I asked, looking at his journal.

"Ma, I haven't been doing shit. Why you ridin' my back so tough?"

"Hold up, boy. You need to watch that tongue of yours when you talk to me. I'm not them lil' girls in your school, I'm not your sister, and I'm not Madison. I'm your mother. And when you talk to me, you'll talk with respect. Do I make myself clear?" I said harshly.

Justin sighed. "Yes, Ma. My bad."

"Speaking of Madison, why didn't you tell me about the two of you? Why did I have to hear it from your father? Why did you feel the need to deceive me? All this time, you had me thinking you two *barely* shared interests. Come to find out, ya'll been dating for years—under *my* roof," I added.

"We weren't fuckin' under *your* roof though," he replied smartly.

"Justin!"

"You was thinkin' it, so I spoke on it," he said plainly.

"Where are you?" I asked again. "We need to talk about this journal I found in your room."

"Why you snoopin' through my room?" he asked offended.

"Why are you deliberately disobeying me?" Before he could answer, I cut him off. "You know what. I'm not finna sit here and argue with my child over the phone. You're sixteen, you're not grown, and you're not running shit but your mouth right now. Now you bring your muthafuckin' ass home, before I come looking for you. Do you understand me?"

"Maddie's got a hangover," he quickly said. "We gone chill here for a lil' while."

"I'm your mother! You don't go against what I say—"

"Look, Ma, I gotta go. Everything's fine, a'ight. We'll be there later on."

"Justin!"

"What, Ma?" he whined.

"What the hell is going on with you? You've never acted like this before. When did you start changing?"

"Whose fault is it for not noticing the change till now?" he said. "Face it. You don't pay attention to us anymore. That's not my fault. That's on you."

"Justin—"

"Look, Ma. I gotta go—"

"Justin, I swear to God! I don't want any babies, you hear me?" I said. "I'm not ready to be a grandmother!" I blurted out absentmindedly.

"Ma, what are you even talkin' about? It ain't even that type of party. Look, I'll just hit you later on," he said before hanging up.

"Justin!" I hollered into the phone. But it was useless. The call had already disconnected. "I can't believe this boy had the nerve to talk to me like that. I got a half a mind to rip his fucking vocal cord out. Who the fuck does he think he is??? I'm his mother! Not his bitch! I brought him into this world, and dammit, I can take him out!!!"

"Mom?" Journee lightly tapped on Justin's door, interrupting my breathless rant. I turned around and saw that she was already dressed with her keys and purse in hand. "Is everything alright?"

I cleared my throat and tried my best to compose myself. "Everything's fine," I lied.

"Well, is it okay if I meet up with Letitia? Or is now a bad time?" she seemed weary of asking me in the state that I was currently in.

"What about breakfast?" I asked disappointed. "I was just about to cook." I was also looking forward to spending more mother-daughter time with her. It was rare that we got to chill and just talk. We used to be so close until she grew up and started to believe that hanging out with your mom was uncool.

"We'll just grab something while we're out," she said.

"Okay, but I want you to take one of the security guards—"

"Mom, please don't make me walk around with an escort all day. It's embarrassing. You don't make Justin have a babysitter and we *see* how that went."

I narrowed my eyes at her, and Journee quickly backpedaled. "It's just...I'm getting older, mom. I can take care of myself. I'm not as simple-minded as you may think. I know how to watch out for danger, how to avoid bad situations, how to choose my battles. And how to avoid trouble. I'll be fine," she assured me.

I looked at my only daughter and tried my best to sympathize with her. "Okay, baby girl. I'm holding you to that."

Journee smiled. "Thanks, mom," she said before skipping off.

Because of the moment we shared earlier, I decided to cut her some slack. Besides, she was right. I'd been so strict with her and so lenient with Justin and now it had come back to bite me in the ass. However, if I'd known that Journee was only finessing me to see some grown ass man, I would've been nipped that shit in the bud.

46
ELDER

I knew I had this young bitch the minute she took that shopping bag from me in the Gucci store. I knew I had her when she gave me her math. But the fact that she didn't get ghost after finding out I had a wife *really* let me know she was down. It solidified the impact that I had on her. Journee was right where I wanted her, and I wouldn't release the vice grip I had on her *until* my job was finally finished.

That morning, I decided to hit her up and invite her out to breakfast. She agreed, and I knew it was only because she was feening for another hit of this good dope, and for me to touch on her little love box again.

"I'm over here," Journee called out after seeing me walk into Roscoe's House of Chicken and Waffles. The place was packed as always, and I found her seated in a booth not too far from the entrance.

I swaggered over towards her table and she stood to her feet to hug me. She was rocking a pair of black leggings, a gray cropped sweater and Vans and she looked good enough to eat. It didn't make any sense that a 14-year old could be so thick.

After the dog fight, my nephew 'Kashi hit me up and told me her real age. He said he'd bumped into her a few times in her school and that she'd lied about her age. I didn't give a damn; and I knew he was only telling me to discourage me from fucking with her 'cuz *he* wanted her. I'd peeped the chemistry between them back at the dog fight. He couldn't keep his eyes off her. Too bad, he wouldn't get the chance to have her after I was finished, because today, I planned to send Journee on a trip to meet her maker.

"Hey, lil' baby. You look and smell so good," I said, hugging her curvy frame.

"Right back at'cha."

We took our seats and the waitress returned to our table with a tray of waters and a strawberry lemonade for Journee.

"So, did you end up getting in trouble with your wife?" Journee asked.

"C'mon, you know I ain't here for all that," I said. "When I'm with you, I wanna focus on *you*. So, tell me. Wuz poppin' wit'chu?"

"Nothing much. I'm just trying to figure out what we're doing. 'Cuz you told me I was your girlfriend then come to find out you got a whole wife at the crib. Are you expecting me to be your side chick?"

"I'm expecting' you to roll with the punches, baby girl. Shit ain't gotta be as complicated as you makin' it seem. Didn't you enjoy yaself with me last night?" I asked her.

"Yes..."

My tone got even lower. "And didn't I make that lil' pussy feel good?"

She crossed her legs and smiled. "Yes."

"Then that's all that matters." I couldn't wait to run my fingers between her thighs and have her pussy dripping wet for me again. I figured since I planned on killing her, I may as well get another taste. "Just know I play for keeps though. Me and you, this ain't no temporary shit."

"But your wife doesn't know about us, right? I mean, she doesn't *let* you cheat on her, does she?"

"First of all, a bitch don't control me. And I'mma tell you somethin' my father told me. A nigga with money can afford to cheat."

***

After breakfast, I surprised her with a trip to Palm Springs, California to ride the Aerial Tramway. It was something she said she wanted to do during our first date so I figured what the hell. I'd grant the girl one last wish, plus it served to get her guards down so that I could strike.

"Oh my God! This is incredible!" Journee said, taking in the sight of the mountains and desert 8000 feet below.

The twelve-minute ride began at the Sonoran Desert and through the breathtaking cliffs of Chino Canyon, before transporting us to the wilderness of the Mt.

San Jacinto State Park, and arriving in the alpine forest. Because of its rotating function, we could see in all directions without moving. I had to admit that it was pretty dope. I'd definitely pulled all the stops to impress her and impress her I did.

When we got back to the car, she was ready to return the favor. "What are you doin'?" I asked, as she unbuttoned my Trues.

"You taught me how to have an orgasm, and how to snort cocaine. Now, I want you to teach me how to suck dick..."

I laughed and pulled her hand away, thankful that there wasn't anyone in the parking lot to see this underage girl trying to blow me. The last thing I wanted was to be registering as a sex offender.

"Hold up, lil' lady. Let's get a room first. That way we'll be more comfortable," I said.

"Alright," she agreed. "Do you have some coke, too?"

I reached over and squeezed her thigh as I pulled out of the parking lot. "Baby, I got good dope. Good dick. Whatever you need. A nigga got it," I laughed arrogantly. Too busy feeding my own ego, I didn't notice that someone was following us.

***

An hour later, we were in a pueblo suite with a private pool at the 4-star La Quinta Resort surrounded by palm trees and the Santa Rosa Mountains. I made sure we got the best room the place had to offer. There'd be no slacking until the deed was finally done. I would show Journee that I was a true gentleman all up until she took her very last breath.

"Wow, this is really beautiful," she said, walking through the suite. She stepped out onto the furnished patio with mountain and pool views. "Do you take your wife on lavish trips like this?"

"There you go with that shit again," I said, flopping onto the king size mattress. I dropped my MCM bag at the foot of the bed.

Journee stepped back into the room. "I just never thought I'd be in a hotel room with a grown ass *married* man. My parents would kill me," she said.

They won't get the chance to, I thought to myself.

I grabbed Journee by the waist of her leggings and tugged her roughly onto the mattress with me. "My wife ain't here. Ya parents ain't here. So, stop trippin' and come up out them clothes. You be frontin' like you a big girl and shit. Now it's time to show and prove."

I saw that she was somewhat nervous, so I pulled out a small vile of dope and placed it in front of her. Journee's eyes automatically lit up when she saw it. She was obviously addicted to the feeling it gave her—which was exactly why I offered it to her in the first place.

Journee went for it, but I quickly moved it out of her reach. "First them clothes," I said. "Fair exchange, no robbery," I reminded her.

Journee slowly pulled her top off, then her leggings and sat back on the bed in nothing but her bra and panties.

"That too," I whispered.

For the first time ever, Journee wasn't so mouthy. In fact, she was the quietest and most shy she'd ever been. Standing to her feet, she slowly removed her bra and panties and sat on the mattress with her arms covering her chest. I gently moved them out of the way and pinched her small, erect nipple.

"Can I have it now?" She asked like a fiend.

"This dope or this dick," I teased.

"*Elderrrr*," she whined.

"I'm just fuckin' wit'chu. Here you go, kiddo," I said, handing her the vile. "Remember. Just like last time..."

"I know. I remember."

"Use this," I said, handing her a tiny stick to scoop the coke out with. "It'll make it easier."

Journee scooped the cocaine out and snorted it up like a vet. Her face contorted a little as she fought the urge to sneeze.

"C'mere," I said, pulling her close. "How you feel?"

She smiled as her high took over her. "I feel really, *really* good."

I kissed her shoulder. "Oh yeah?" I softly laid her back onto the bed and spread her legs. "Let me make you feel better..."

"Wait," she said nervously. "I'm scared."

"Don't be," I said, placing tender kisses on her inner thigh. "Wasn't I gentle last night?"

"Yes," she whispered.

"Just relax," I said, spreading her pussy lips.

"Wait—"

"I'll just do two licks," I told her.

"O—okay," she nervously agreed.

I ran the tip of my tongue from the bottom of her tight, little pussy hole to the top of her clit, then peeled the hood back to nibble on her bud. Journee moaned and writhed beneath me, but I firmly held her in place.

"One," I counted.

I blew cool air onto her pussy and she started squirming uncontrollably.

"Are...you...really...twenty-four?" She asked in between pleasure spasms.

"Don't matter," I said. "You already got my tongue in your pussy now."

Journee yelped as I parted her lips wider, and slid my tongue over her tender and ripe young pussy.

"Two." I looked up at her, and she was breathing hard and staring at the ceiling as if she'd already came. "You want two more?" I offered her with a tempting grin.

She smiled shyly. "I—I don't know," she stuttered. "Can I take another hit and think about it?"

"You gone want a hit every twenty or so minutes. You know the high from coke doesn't last very long. You may as well fuck with this other shit I got," I said, reaching for my MCM bag.

"I—I don't know. My brother always said I shouldn't take drugs from strangers. I can't believe I'm even doing coke. I'm not sure if I should further experiment."

"I'm not a stranger," I told her. "I already told you, we locked and loaded. You mine now, Journee. I done already had a taste of you."

"What is that?" She asked curiously, rubbing the goosebumps on her arms.

"Heroin"

Her eyes lit up in awe. "*Heroin?*" She repeated.

"You fuck with the coke, so you gone love this shit right here. One hit of this shit, and you'll be on cloud nine."

"Are you gonna do it, too?" She asked naively.

"Of course. Daddy ain't gone let you take that trip solo," I lied. In reality, I was getting ghost the second she overdosed. I planned to pump her lil' ass with enough heroin to kill her. It was also laced with an untraceable poison to help speed up the process.

Journee watched as I carefully pulled out the supplies. "Now it has to be injected straight into the blood stream for an instant effect."

"Okay," she said nervously.

I'd just tied a cloth around her arm to make her veins pop out more when I heard a knock on the door. "Housekeeping," a Spanish woman called out.

"Come back later," I shouted back.

"Housekeeping!"

KNOCK!

KNOCK!

KNOCK!

"Didn't you hear me? I said come back later!" I said, getting irate.

"*Yo no habla ingles.*"

Climbing off the bed in anger, I stormed to the door and swung it open. A pudgy Mexican woman was standing there with her housekeeping cart in front of her. I was about to tell her off when Tek appeared from behind her with a glock pointed right at me.

"Go on. You're done here," he told the housekeeper who scampered off in fear. "Where is she?" he asked me through clenched teeth.

"What the fuck are you doin' here, nephew?"

He cocked the gun. "Nigga, I'mma ask you one more time. Where the fuck is she?"

I pointed to the bed and Journee was sitting there looking just as confused as I fucking felt. I'd put bread on this lil' nigga's table time and time again and he crosses me over a piece of pussy. Like there aren't a million other hoes in LA.

"Get your shit on and let's go," Tek told her. Journee didn't move and he yelled, "NOW!!!"

She quickly jumped to her feet and started getting dressed.

"I think you makin' a mistake, nephew," I said.

"I don't give a fuck what you think. You got daughters her age, man! That's a fuckin' child!"

I scoffed and shook my head at him. "This ain't got shit to do with you," I said.

"Well, I just made it about me. How 'bout that?"

"Muthafucka, yo ass better go back to babysittin' dogs. You meddlin' in affairs that you don't know shit about!"

"I know you a grimey ass nigga. And that's enough for me."

"Lil' nigga, I just tossed you racks the other day and *this* is how you do me? Your own family? You ain't ever supposed to bite the hand that feeds you."

Tek pulled the rolled up bands out of his pockets and tossed it at my feet. "Fuck your money and fuck you," he said. "Journee, let's go!"

She quickly climbed out of the bed and followed him out of the room.

"I'mma make you wish you'd pulled that trigger," I told him.

Tek and Journee disappeared in the elevator and I quickly rushed to my phone to make that call. I didn't give a damn if he was my dead sister's kid. His ass was going down! You never cross your loved ones—especially the ones who looked out.

Luther answered on the second ring.

"Wuz poppin', Big Man?"

"Aye, ya'll handled that lil' situation for me, right?" I asked him.

A couple days ago, I had them find and kill the nigga Justin had kidnapped from my trap in Watts. I couldn't risk him talking so I silenced his ass for good. That's why the triplets weren't able to come with me to the dog fight. Because they were busy taking care of unfinished business.

"Yeah, we handled that situation real proper-like," he said, careful not to say too much over the line.

"Good. I need ya'll to see about my nephew now. Nigga gettin' a lil' too cocky out here."

"We all over that shit," Luther agreed.

I wanted my pound of flesh; I was entitled to it. Then after Journee was dead, I'd started wiping out the rest of her relatives, one by one, starting with her faggot ass brother.

47
JOURNEE

Tek and I were back on the interstate when I decided to finally break the silence. I still didn't understand what happened or why he felt the need to come and get me. We didn't even know each other. Sure, he was cute and all, but he was way out of line.

"Um..." I cleared my throat. "I'm sorry but I have to ask...why did you come to the hotel? And were you following me this whole time?"

"You're Jude's daughter, right?"

"Um...yeah...how do you know my dad?" I asked, wiping at my nostrils in an attempt to make sure I looked decent. If he knew my dad, then he could easily tell him about me snorting drugs and cozying up with a grown ass man.

"Your dad is who pays me. I been slanging dope for him for the last three years," he said. "Not that you'd know all that—"

"I know what my father does. I've known for some time now," I said. "So, you're one of his foot soldiers?"

"Yeah, somethin' like that."

"So, wait. You sell drugs for my father at the school his *daughter* attends?"

"I'm not *supposed* to," he clarified. "But a nigga be tryin' to eat, and them rich white boys are a gold mine."

"So, if my father knew you were selling drugs to kids in my school—"

"He'd probably kill me," Tek said. "So, let's keep that lil' secret between us, a'ight?"

"When I met you at the dog fight, I assumed you sold drugs for your uncle."

He sucked his teeth. "Man, I just fuck with him on the dog tip," he said. "I'm smart enough to know no one's buyin' that garbage he's pushin'. That's why he's tryin' to knock your old man off. He's been fuckin' up the cash flow for years now," he explained. "*Now* do you see why I had to get your fast ass away from that nigga? It's because he ain't have shit good planned for you. He was gonna kill you, Journee."

I dropped my head in shame. I felt like a total fool. And I'd just told my mom that I could take care of myself. Evidently, I couldn't because I wasn't smart enough to make knowledge-based decisions. "I...I didn't know," I said, disappointed in my own naivety and childish ways.

"It's all good. Luckily, I got there when I did. Who knows what would've happened if I *wasn't* following you," he said.

"Do you know if my dad..." My voice trailed off as my hands began shaking erratically. Suddenly, the tremors ran through my body, and before I knew it was seizing and foaming at the mouth.

"Journee!!!" Tek quickly pulled over at the same time I bit my tongue hard enough for it to start bleeding. "Journee, what's wrong? What is it?" He grabbed my shoulders. "WHAT DID HE GIVE YOU?????"

Before I could answer, I blacked out.

48
JUSTIN

"So, what's the plan?" I asked Madison as I changed her bandage in my homeboy Nick's bathroom. We were laying low at his crib in Ladera Heights. He was the same cat who helped us with the lick we pulled in Watts.

"I just need time to rest." She winced in pain. It seemed like she needed her bandages changed every thirty minutes; she was soaking them so fast.

"Maddie, baby, I don't think we gone be able to hide this shit from my folks," I finally told her. "If your dad finds out, then he just finds out. But trust and believe, there's nothing he can do to keep you away from me. But we have to go to the hospital."

Madison looked away and frowned. She was so stubborn. I could see the disapproval all in her hazel eyes. "I don't know..."

"We have to, baby. This is crazy. You *need* to go to a hospital, and I love you too much to watch you suffer. If your dad flips, then he just flips. I can't stand to see you suffering."

Madison slowly looked up to meet my gaze. "So, you really think we should just go?" She asked, fearful of what my mother's reaction would be. I didn't blame her. I was somewhat fearful of her myself after talking all greasy to her on the phone. I'd never talked to my mom so disrespectfully, but I was only trying to cover for Madison. But just like her, I knew I'd have to face my mom's wrath eventually.

"Okay...we'll go," Maddie agreed. "Just let me catch some Z's first. You have no idea how much energy being shot takes out of you. I'm really tired...and sore." I watched as she popped the cap off a bottle of painkillers and tossed two in her mouth. "I just need to rest my body first...then we'll leave..."

"A'ight then. That's a bet." I was grateful that she'd finally come around.

After changing her bandages, I helped her up and carried her into Nick's spare bedroom. Gently laying her on the mattress, I pulled her shoes off and tucked her in. "You gonna chill with your friend for a while?" she asked.

"Yeah. I'll come back in a lil' bit to check on you," I said before closing the door behind me. I found Nick in the living room rolling a blunt on the coffee table. The weed he had was so fresh, it was sticking to his fingers as he broke it down. It had the whole crib smelling like dank.

"Damn." Nick shook his head when he saw me. He was a slim, dark skinned cat with nappy dreads to the middle of his back. "Nigga still can't believe ya boy jugged you," he said.

I sat beside him on the couch and reclined my head, letting the weight of Drip's betrayal take over me. "Yeah, well, believe it. Nigga got me for two M's too."

Nick whistled dramatically. "Shit." He handed me the blunt. "You do the honors," he said, passing me the lighter. "Besides, you need it more than me right now."

"I swear, it's over for that nigga. When I see homie, it's light out."

"You went to homie crib?"

"Yup. The nigga wasn't there. His crackhead mama was though. I thought about putting the bitch out of her misery, but my beef's with Drip. Nobody else."

"Damn, my nigga. That shit is fucked up."

"Fucked up ain't even the word for it, man. That shit is foul." I lit the blunt and inhaled. It was still damp from his saliva. "That nigga got lucky today. But when I catch his ass, I'm playin' target practice with his head. That's on me." I passed Nick the blunt and he hit it and coughed.

"You say it's open season on ya boy, huh?"

"Man, he shot my girl. Shot at me—I can't let that shit ride. That nigga Drip is a dead man walking."

49
ROXIE

"Well, well, well. Look who finally brought their ass back home," Hector said in a nasty tone when I walked in the house. He was sitting on the sofa sipping a beer and watching Sports Center.

I pulled my coat off, hung it on the coat rack and placed my bag on the accent table beside me. "Don't start, Hector. I've been on the road for over seven hours. I'm not in the mood for your bullshit."

"I wasn't in the mood to come here and see that my wife was gone—or that she couldn't even leave a nigga a decent home cooked meal."

"The nanny was here, Hector. She could've cooked for you."

"I didn't put a ring on our nanny's fingers. I didn't stick my dick up in a nanny and make a son with her. You're my wife. You consult with me before taking some self-discovery road trip."

"It wasn't about me. It was about Rain! I tried to call you to tell that I was meeting with a new doctor! But you were too busy discovering some woman's insides!"

Hector jumped to his feet in a fit of rage! "Fuck you talking to?! Who you talking to like that?!" He yelled. "Bitch, I'll fuck around and be out the door on your ass!!!"

"Then go!!!!" I screamed.

Usually, I begged, pleaded and kissed and licked his ass for him to stay. But not this time. After 11 years of miserable matrimony, I was finally fed up with being treated like shit.

"Just go. I can do bad all by myself."

"What?" Hector looked offended.

"Who the fuck in Louisiana put that simple shit in ya head? Bitch, you won't be anything without me! You need me to hold this family together! To hold you together! Hoe, you're nothin' on your own! When I found your ass, you were one step away from suicide! Remember that! I picked you up and breathed life into your black ass! Took care of you! Held you down! Now that I'm fucked up, you gone turn your back on me? Where the fuck they do that at?"

Now he was turning the tables to take the blame off of himself. It was a tactic that he'd been doing for years, but it no longer had the same effect.

"You turned your back on us a long time ago, Hector."

Instead of saying anything, he just stood there speechless.

"I tried to call you to tell you about Rain's latest incident. You didn't even answer. You're never here—and when you are you're broke and pissy drunk. You don't work. You don't care. You ain't faithful, and you ain't shit. I'm tired, Hector." A tear rolled down my cheek. "I am sooo, so, so unhappy. And I'd rather be lonely than unhappy."

"So, what the fuck is you sayin'?"

I wiped my tears and stood strong. "I'm saying I want a divorce."

In the blink of an eye, Hector rushed me and slapped me hard in the face. Losing my balance, I crashed into the accent table, knocking my bag to the ground.

"A divorce?? Bitch, you really think I'mma let you leave me after eleven fuckin' years! You really think I'mma let you take my kids away from me?!"

Without warning, I grabbed my bag and snatched the pistol out. It was just a small, little handgun, but if I squeezed that muthafucka, it would still do damage.

"It's not your decision!" I screamed. "Now back the fuck up!"

"You gone shoot me, you tired ass black bitch?" He said. "Go ahead," he taunted. "Shoot me! Pull the fuckin' trigger!!"

"Kids!!!!" I called out. "Rain!!! Harper!!!!"

Our children ran downstairs when they heard me call them but quickly froze once they saw the gun.

"Get in the car!" I told them.

"Ya'll get in that car and I'm beating ya'll ass," he said.

I rested my finger on the trigger. "You aren't gonna lay a hand on me or my babies ever again," I said. "Kids, get in the car!"

Rain and Harper ran out the door and Hector looked ready to kill me. "Really? You just gone take the kids and dip?"

"Isn't that what you threatened to do to me for years?"

"Nigga was just talking shit, Rox. You knew I wasn't goin' nowhere."

"That's 'cuz you ain't have nowhere else to go," I said. "You haven't held me down! I held you down! And I'm tired, Hector! I am fucking tired!" I placed the keys to the house on the accent table. "I'mma leave you with these since it's all you'll get in the settlement."

"Roxie, don't do this shit."

"It's already done."

"Roxie, if you go through with this shit, I swear to God I'll fuckin' end you."

POW!

I blew a hole through his leg and he dropped to the floor crying like a little bitch. "If you ever threaten or come near me again, the next one *will* be fatal." And with that, I walked out of the house and away from a broken marriage. At this age, I was only interested in consistency, stability, loyalty and respect. And if my man couldn't provide that, then I had no problem being alone. After all, a season of loneliness is when a caterpillar gets its wings.

50
CONWAY

By the grace of God, I managed to make it out of Accra, and with enough evidence to uphold in a court of law. Try as he might, Jude couldn't talk in code forever and he made a few slip ups, incriminating himself and his supplier. Now I had something I could run with to prove that Jude was buying kilos from Soul.

He'd moved with precision for quite some time now, but it was only natural to leave room for error. The incident in the club didn't help his case any, either. Soul's blow up was more than enough evidence. If they were only selling magazines, it wouldn't matter if I was wearing a wire or not. He'd pretty much incriminated himself by pulling a gun out on me and making me strip in front of everyone. I took petty jabs at me, because I knew he was going down. He was going to pay for emasculating me, with his life.

There was no way I wouldn't be able to pin charges on these assholes with everything I'd overheard. And as luck would have it, they never even found out they were being recorded. If Soul had located the tiny listening device hidden inside of my tie, I'd be flying back to the states in a box and not on a luxury jet with the man I planned to arrest in just a few short hours. Luckily, the department had given up on the use of wires and upgraded our technologies. If they hadn't, I'd be a dead man. These cocaine dealers were far smarter than they used to be. We had to stay one step ahead.

"Everything good?" Jude asked, as his jet landed on a private runway near LAX.

"Yeah. Everything's good," I told him.

"My bad about my man. He's got trust issues," Jude said casually. "Nigga been through a lot of shit. Don't hold it against him."

"Of course not. I know it's only business, never personal."

"You did good though," Jude said with a smile that a father would usually give his son once he made honor roll. "I'm pleased with the way you handled yaself. Especially in the club."

"Yeah, well, how can I be your security and keep shit leveled if I'm not level headed myself. I don't blame him for being cautious. Like I said, I knew it was only business. I respected his reproach."

Jude nodded his head in agreement. "We on the same page then."

"Always."

The private jet finally landed and Fillmore and Price were the first ones to deplane. "Will it be okay if I run to check on my girl later on?" I asked him. "She been givin' me grief ever since we been in Ghana." It was the best excuse I could come up with to see the captain.

"*A girl*? I'm surprised you had one," Jude said.

"Why'd you think I didn't have one?" I asked curiously. In real life, I was actually single but I still wanted to hear his reason.

"You been on Cameron so tough, I didn't think you had eyes for anyone else."

My cheeks flushed in embarrassment after he called me out on my shit. All this time I thought my sly stares and subtle flirting went unnoticed, but Jude was obviously up on game. I never realized that he'd caught me looking at his wife inappropriately on several occasions. I guess I was too busy looking at her to notice he was looking at me. As thoughts of Cameron flooded my mind, I suddenly felt bad about her having to go down too. But she knew what she signed up for when she married her drug-dealing husband.

"It's all good," Jude laughed, clapping me on the back. "I've been with Cam long enough to know that she's a looker. Just as long as you remember to *look* and not touch." There was no humor in his tone when he threatened me.

"I hear you loud and clear, sir. And I promise to present myself in a more professional manner."

"I think that'd be best," Jude said. "Now, back to you. I don't mind you checkin' in at home. Just be sure to be back at the post come morning."

"Absolutely, sir."

After our bags were collected, we were escorted to a Cadillac Escalade with tinted windows. I opened the door for Jude and climbed in the backseat with him. In silence, I watched as he pulled his phone out and called Cameron.

"Hey, babe. I'm on my way home—hold up, baby, slow down. What do you mean the kids are gone? WHAT?! Journee's been missing a whole day???? Fuck you mean, you went to Atlanta? Okay, okay, slow down. Just calm down, Cam. Look, I'm on my way to the crib right now." Jude disconnected the call, then pinched the bridge of his nose.

"I take it everything is not okay."

"Justin and Madison are holed up somewhere, and Journee hasn't been home or answering her phone for a whole day now. Cam is at the crib, freaking the fuck out but Sofía is there, and for once, I'm actually happy about that," he said. "I knew I shouldn't have left their asses home alone. I just figured they could handle it until she got back. Now I feel like shit. What type of father am I? What type of man puts wealth over the well-being of his loved ones. This shit is crazy. I've been too focused on the streets, and not focused enough on what's important."

"Hey, now don't go blaming yourself," I told him. "You carry your business and your family on your back.

That's a lot for any man to handle. Don't worry, we'll find them." I had no choice but to help track them down, because after today they'd be the government's problem.

As soon as we got to his crib, we found Cameron in the living room crying her eyes out. Sofía and Letitia were on either side of her, rubbing her back for moral support. "Oh, Jude, I'm so happy you're back," she said, hugging him.

He held her tight. "What the hell is going on?"

"I just don't know where I went wrong!" she cried. "I just don't know where I went wrong!"

While everyone was distracted with Cameron's theatrics, I decided to slip off and look for the ledger. Meanwhile downstairs, Cam repeated the last conversation she had with her children, and told them about some journal she found under her son's bed. I didn't stick around to get the full details as I crept inside their bedroom, and quickly started looking through the drawers. The evidence from the recordings should have been more than enough, but just as a safety measure, I'd take the ledger too. It would be the nail in the coffin...or in this instance, the case.

Speaking of the ledger, I finally found it on the top shelf in the closet. Flipping through the pages, I saw that Evelyn was right. The book was filled with symbols and codes that I couldn't make out. But as long as I had Eve to testify, it didn't matter. Slipping the small book in the waist of my dress pants, I slipped out of the room and went back downstairs, where everyone was now arguing and pointing the finger.

"If you hadn't taken your ass to Atlanta, none of this shit would be happening!" Jude yelled.

"If you'd handled that bitch when you should've, I wouldn't have *had* to go to Atlanta!" Cameron hollered.

"Grow the fuck up, Cameron! Grow up and take some responsibility!"

"Don't talk to me about responsibility! Nigga, I've been cooking, cleaning, feeding and taking care of *your* kids while you run the streets!"

"*Run the streets*? Muthafucka, I'm putting food on the table!" Jude yelled. "What the fuck have you been doin' other than bumpin' pussies with this bitch!" he pointed to Sofía.

"Hold up! Don't go disrespecting me! I'm only here to help!"

"Yeah, you helped alright. Helped instigate the shit," he said.

"Everyone, just calm down. Arguing isn't gonna solve anything and it damn sure ain't gone bring the kids back. Let's all split up and look for them; check with their friends from school, the parents of those kids, and anyone else that might know where they are," I said. In all actuality, I just needed an excuse to dip off now that I had what I needed.

They all stopped arguing long enough to listen.

"Maybe one of us should stay here in case they show up," Cameron said.

"Me and my daughter will stay," Sofía said. "If that's okay with Jude."

Jude nodded his head, and we all went our separate ways. Cameron and Jude sought out to look for the kids, while I hightailed it to the precinct so that I could hear what my superior thought about the recorded footage *and* to give him the ledger I'd just found. He'd been listening in the entire time I was in Africa, so I knew he'd have a mouthful to say.

***

I made it to the station in less than forty minutes tops and as soon as I walked in, Frank was practically breathing down my neck. "Welcome back, James Bond. I see you takin' international trips and shit with the plug. I know you've got something by now."

"*No lo sé*. I'm about to find out," I told him.

Frank frowned like that wasn't good enough, but instead of entertaining him I headed straight to Lieutenant Beechum's office. I figured Frank was trying to undermine me and crack the case first, but I had no time to quarrel with him. I had to hear Lieutenant Beechum's thoughts on the recording. Speaking of Lieutenant Beechum, he was already waiting for me when I walked inside of his office. I immediately noticed that he'd finally gotten the lettering on his door replaced.

"Afternoon, González. Take a seat," he gestured to the chair across from his desk. "First and foremost, I wanna thank you for sticking to your integrity and convincing me to let you carry out this case. Secondly, I want to apologize for doubting you in the first place," he said. "You're a fine, *fine* officer."

"Thank you, sir. It's a real honor to hear that from you."

"Now that we've got the dick sucking out of the way, let's get to business," he said. "I've distributed the tapes to the U.S. Department of Justice and the DEA, and they're certain that it's enough to pin drug charges on these assholes."

I breathed a sigh of relief. "And to ensure the charges stick, I have this," I said, pulling out the ledger.

"What's that?"

"The book containing every cocaine sale, and drug transaction that our guy has ever made. And what's even better, I have a witness to testify," I added.

Lieutenant Beechum reached for the ledger, but I quickly pulled it away. "No offense, captain, but I went through hell to get this thing. I want to deliver this to the USDOJ personally."

Lieutenant Beechum smiled. "Of course you do."

I was so happy with the news he'd given me, I wanted to kiss him. Working for Jude had become extremely draining. I was so glad that this shit was finally over.

"I'm gonna start making some calls now. Let's get these animals in a cage where they belong," he said. "Go have a drink and celebrate, and pat yourself on the back while you're at it. These assholes are going down and it's all thanks to you." Beechum extended his hand, and I couldn't have been happier as I shook it. Over a year's worth of hard work had finally paid off.

Smiling my ass off like I'd hit the jackpot, I made my way to my car parked down on Santa Monica Blvd, just a few blocks from the precinct. I couldn't risk parking my car at the station, just in case Jude did have eyes on me.

Pulling out my key, I hit the locks and opened the driver's door—

PFEW!

PFEW!

The sound of suppressed gunshots rang out and when I looked down, I saw that there were two holes in my stomach. I'd been shot. Before I could figure out by who, I was shoved into the car so hard I slammed my head into the dashboard.

Lieutenant Beechum quickly looked around to make sure no one saw him, then climbed in and slammed the door shut.

"You just couldn't give up, could you? Not even to save your own ass," he grilled. "I tried to pull you off the case! I tried to save your fucking life, kid, but you just wouldn't listen!"

I felt dazed, weak and confused. I was bleeding out, incredibly fast, but I still mustered up enough strength to mutter the word, "Why?"

Lieutenant Beechum snatched my car keys and started up the Cadillac. "Why?" He chuckled, pulling off. "Why not? I'm only bringing in thirty-three thousand dollars annually. This job pays shit. And after so many years of being the good guy, I realized being a bad guy is so much more rewarding," he said.

"So...you've been...working for them all along?" I struggled to say through the pain. It hurt even more to know that I was never going to take down Jude and his drug empire. All of my hard work was for nothing.

"Yeah...well...technically, I work for Soul. Jude still has no idea about you. And lucky for you, he never will." Lieutenant Beechum smiled sinisterly. "Don't worry, kid. I'll make sure you go down in history as one of the most courageous and forthright officers the DEA has ever seen. I'll make sure your service is grand and your family is well-compensated for your death. You'll be a hero," he said. "But you can't win 'em all, kid. You should've stopped while you were ahead."

I tried to lunge at him, but a shot to the chest halted my efforts. Slumped in the passenger seat, I felt my life slowly slipping away. I wanted to take these guys down so bad, I never thought about *them* having an insider. Someone to keep them abreast to the police dealings. Since Lieutenant Beechum worked for Soul, that meant the DEA never even heard the recordings. Beechum was just feeding me a bunch of bullshit.

I figured Soul must've contacted him while I was in Africa to run my credentials past him, and that's when the truth came out. And to think, all this time I thought Frank would've been the one to betray me for the sake of cracking the case first, but it turned out to be my own superior. A man of the law. Someone who'd been working for the precinct since before either us thought about becoming cops.

"I'll be taking that," Lieutenant Beechum said, pulling the bloodstained book out of my hands that contained all of Jude's information. "And that," he said, claiming the recording device. He was simply waiting on me to gather the evidence so he could confiscate it. That's why he was pressing me so hard about the shit. He never cared about fighting crime. He was only out for self. "You won't need either where you're going..." he put the suppressed barrel of the loaded gun to my head. "I really meant what I said, kid. You're a fine, *fine* officer."

POW!

51
CAMERON

If there was an award ceremony for the worst parent of the year, I'd probably win with flying colors. I had neglected my children, and tried to make up for it by over-spoiling them and giving them way too much freedom for their age. I guess, in a sense, I was just trying to be the cool mom, but now they were rude, angry, materialistic and distant. Justin was always in the streets coming home late, and whenever I tried to talk to Journee or show affection, she got smart and pushed me away.

No one ever told me parenting teenagers was one of the hardest jobs in life. It started out with just Journee being argumentative, now Justin was back talking, staying out all night and keeping secrets. I couldn't even have decent conversations with them anymore without being lied to, deceived or disrespected.

I tried to blame this all on Jude for being an irresponsible parent, but truthfully, I was no better. Jude was as supportive as he could be for someone who worked *all* the time and was almost always traveling. It was up to me to raise them to be respectable young adults. Not the hooligans they were acting like now. Still, I felt like I was fighting a lonely battle, and I didn't know what to do make things go back to how they used to be, or if going back to how it used to be was even possible, at this point.

Me and my children used to be so close. We used to do lots of things together. I couldn't even remember when shit changed. And I didn't know what to do to get that back. I loved my babies very much, more than I loved my myself, more than I loved my own husband. All I wanted was to have our old relationship back.

God, please let my babies be okay, I prayed. *Just please, let my babies be okay.*

I'd driven through Downtown Los Angeles, East Los Angeles, Culver City, Venice, Inglewood, Compton, Santa Monica, Van Nuys, and other known gang areas looking for Justin but I didn't see him or his Benz anywhere. I even went to Watts, but I came up emptyhanded.

I was on my way back to the city when Jude called me. Thinking he had good news, I answered on the first ring. "Did you find them????"

"I just got a call from one of my guys. He's with Journee right now at the Desert Regional Medical Center."

"Where the hell is that?!" I asked furious.

"Palm Springs, California. About an hour and a half away from LA."

I immediately started making up negative scenarios in my head. Was my baby kidnapped and dragged to a different city? Was she raped? "Oh my God, Jude. What was she doing out there?" I asked in a shaky and fearful tone. My words came out muffled due to the tears backed up in my throat. "Is she okay?"

"I don't know. But we're about to find out."

52
JUDE

Cam and I made it to the hospital in record time, and as soon as we reached her room, I found Tek sitting next to her bed. He was a low-level dealer who'd been working for me for three years now. I took one look at Journee sitting in the hospital bed and flipped.

"What happened?" I snatched Tek towards me by the collar of his shirt.

"I found her with my uncle," Tek said.

"AND??? WHAT HAPPENED???"

"Daddy, stop! He saved my life!" Journee cried.

"You must be the parents," the doctor said, walking into the room. He was an older, balding white guy with liver spots all over his face and hands.

"Yes," me and Cameron said in unison.

"Well, then I must say you're the luckiest parents that have come through here in a while. It could've been so much worse if that young man hadn't gotten her here when he did. We had to pump her stomach. She'd ingested an almost lethal amount of poison, along with other narcotics—"

"NARCOTICS???" Cameron repeated in shock.

"Cocaine," the doctor specified.

"You ingested cocaine???" Cameron asked. She looked ready to kill our daughter, and I had to hold her back to keep her from doing so.

"I'm guessing whoever supplied it must've laced it with the poison."

"Oh my God." Cameron covered her mouth and cried silently, as I held her close and rubbed her back.

"I would highly recommend following up this incident with a police report...and maybe some drug rehabilitation," he added.

"Thanks a lot, doc," I said.

"I'll give you all some privacy," he said before leaving the room.

I turned to Tek. "And thank you for saving my daughter's life."

"Well, he won't be able to save your ass from me!" Cameron lashed out at her. "What the hell was in your head?? Snorting cocaine?? Lying to me about meeting your friend??? I wanna know everything! Right here, right now! Starting with where you got the coke from!"

Journee shuffled about nervously, then rubbed her arms and looked down in embarrassment. "I met him at the mall. He told me he was twenty-four but it turns out he was older—"

"Twenty-four??!!!" Cameron screamed.

"Baby, let her finish." I encouraged Journee to continue even though I wanted to lay hands on her myself. And I needed to know who this 24-year old was so I could lay hands on him too.

"Anyway, we met up the other night at a diner. He took me to a dog fight, then after he snorted some powder. I wanted to know what it felt like so I tried some too," she said in a small, timid voice.

Is that all she tried, I wondered.

Cam must've read my mind because she started firing off the same questions. "You were taking drugs with this man! What else were you doing with this man??? This GROWN ASS MAN!!!" she yelled.

Journee looked up at me in sadness. She didn't even want to say it in front of me, and I already knew what that shit meant. And to think I'd just had a talk with her about self-value and self-worth.

I could feel the hatred and resentment bubbling up inside of me and before I knew it, I exploded and snatched up Tek in anger. "WHERE THE FUCK IS HE????" I hollered. His ass didn't answer fast enough, so I put my 9 to his head to further encourage him to speak.

"I don't know where he is now. But tonight, there'll be more dog fights at the spot. He always goes and cleans house so he can re-up on cocaine," Tek said. "He might be there. Now can you get that fuckin' burner outta my face if you ain't gone use it."

I released Tek and stormed out of the room, punching the wall on my way out. Cameron called out to me, but I completely tuned her out, as I headed towards the elevator. I couldn't focus on shit else but killing this muthafucka!

53
JUSTIN

The sound of my phone vibrating, interrupted my somewhat peaceful slumber. When I looked to my left, I saw Madison sleeping soundlessly. She'd bled through her bandages again, and the sheets and the mattress. I checked her pulse to make sure she was alive, and by the grace of God, she was still breathing.

My phone continued ringing and I picked it up while it was on the charger. It had died hours ago, but now it was fully juiced.

"Hello," I answered in a groggy voice. "Who dis?"

"This is your father. Where the fuck are you? And why haven't you been answering your phone?"

"Some shit came up and I lost my phone—"

"Is that all? You sure it ain't got shit to do with that journal your mother found—"

"I don't know why she was going through my shit—"

"Cut the games. What the fuck are you into, son? Talk to me. Haven't you and I always been able to communicate?" he asked. "The bond between a father and son is unbreakable," he reminded me.

"You right. Our bond is unbreakable," I agreed. "That's why I did what I did. I was doin' it all for you, pops. I wanted to make you proud; show you that I'm a man. That I'm able to carry on your legacy."

"What the fuck are you talkin' about, son? What the fuck did you do????"

Suddenly, I heard Nick talking to someone in the background. I hung up on my dad, grabbed the gun from beneath my pillow case and listened closely.

"He gone piece me off for this shit, right?" Nick asked.

"Don't worry, man. Elder gone take care of you," an unfamiliar voice said.

So, this nigga called in the cavalry while I was sleeping. Just like a pussy ass nigga. I didn't know what the fuck was in the air, but whatever it was had all my homeboys double crossing me.

All of a sudden, I heard the sound of footsteps approaching the room. As soon as the door was kicked open, I shoved Madison off the bed and took aim.

POP!

POP!

POW!

POW!

A pair of twins lit up the headboard and pillows with automatics, but I was lucky enough to get down on the floor in time. I managed to hit one of the twins in his arm. The other raised his gun to shoot Madison, but I shot him in the neck, causing him to stumble backwards. Blood sprayed the walls like cheap CGI effects, and his twin pointed his burner at me, but Maddie tackled him.

I was about to help her when Nick grabbed his gun off the ground and pointed it at me. I threw a pillow at him before he could squeeze, and jumped out the way just before he pulled the trigger.

Before he could squeeze again, I rammed my shoulder into his midsection, slamming him up against the wall. He elbowed me in the back, but I lifted him off his feet and dropped him on his head. To be so small, I was incredibly strong. Or maybe, I was just acting out of fight or flight mode.

"MADISON, RUN!!" I yelled, after taking down Nick. Holding both his arms, I tried my best to restrain him. But she couldn't do anything after the twin slammed her on her back and kicked her in the chest.

"You fuckin' bitch, you gone die for that shit!"

I head butted Nick and grabbed the gun before the twin could, then emptied the clip on his bitch ass. He staggered backwards, and tripped over his dead brother's body before falling to the floor dead.

"Madison, are you okay?" I asked her.

She grabbed her injured shoulder and grimaced in pain. "Yeah...I'm good."

"Don't kill me, man," Nick cried. "It wasn't nothin' against you. Them niggas promised me a bag, homie. You would've done it t—"

I shot him in the face, silencing him forever.

"Come on. Let's get out of here," I told Madison.

Putting her arm around my shoulder, I helped her walk to the front of the house and out the door. My car was parked just across the street.

"You straight?" I asked Madison, as I helped her down the front steps.

"Yeah," She said in a strained voice. But I knew she wasn't. She needed medical attention and bad.

We were halfway across the street when an Acura sped towards us at breakneck speed. The driver had the same exact facial features as the twins I'd just killed—and in that moment, I realized they were the infamous triplets I'd heard so much about.

In the blink of an eye, I pushed Madison out of the way and took the brunt of the attack myself. My body cracked the windshield before rolling over the hood. I landed on the concrete in a dazed and bloodied mess, and I was too sore and stunned to move for a moment.

"JUSTIN!!!" I heard Maddie scream at the top of her lungs.

The triplet climbed out of the car, reached for his strap, and slowly approached me. Because I was unable to move, all I could do was lay there helplessly and watch this man kill me.

The second he raised his gun, Maddie jumped on his back and bit the side of his neck like a wild animal. She spat out a chunk of flesh and he screamed in agony, before elbowing her in the face. She fell to the ground with a bloody nose, and seeing that shit was enough to will me to my feet.

Screaming like a madman, I ran straight at him, ready to tear his ass apart for putting his hands on her. He raised his gun and shot me, but the bullet grazed my right arm. Before he had the chance to try again, I charged him and knocked his ass off of his feet.

WHAM!

WHAM!

WHAM!

WHAM!

I punched him over and over again until Maddie finally pulled me off of him. By then, his face was a bloodied, distorted mess. "Justin, we have to go before someone sees us!"

I slowly climbed off his unconscious body and followed her to the car. I was slightly dizzy from being hit by a car, but I still climbed behind the steering wheel.

"I'm takin' you to the hospital," I said, wiping the blood off my chin. The gash on my face had reopened and was now bleeding profusely.

"And where are *you* going?" she pressed.

"To the greyhound station," I told her. "I have to catch his ass before he skips town. And Drip got too many fuckin' felonies to board anybody's plane."

Madison looked shocked by the fact that I still wasn't giving up on my revenge. When I said that nigga was a dead man walking I meant that shit. This muthafucka was supposed to be like my brother. It wasn't even about her anymore. It was about the fucking principle!

"Well, I'm going with you—"

"No," I said, through puffy lips. "You're already in bad shape."

"And you're not?" She countered. "No funny shit, but we're in this together. I don't care how bad I'm hurt, I'm not leaving your side, Justin. I ride for you, you ride for me, and I want in on whatever you got planned," she said. "What'chu tell me? As long as you got my back, I got yours. Ain't nothin' change."

54
JUDE

I told myself I'd handle Justin later. Right now, I had some unfinished business to handle with Elder. With a team of hittaz at my heels, I made my way inside of the building that was known for hosting dog fights. It was also where I hoped to find this nigga Elder to dead this shit. As a grown ass man, he had no business even *looking* in the direction of my baby girl!

I always thought having a positive father-daughter relationship would have a huge impact on a young girl's life and that maybe she'd respect herself more if I taught her to be strong and confident. I thought that I would be the standard against which she would judge all guys. But all it takes is one manipulative ass man to come and tear down everything you've instilled.

Just the thought of some grown ass nigga putting his hands on my daughter had me ready to massacre everybody in this bitch. Fucking with my daughter was like fucking with my livelihood.

"Hey," I grabbed some kid with purple dreads as he was passing me by. "I'm lookin' for a nigga named Elder. Is he in here?"

Purple Dreads looked me up and down. "Who wanna know?"

I placed my gun under his chin. "My nine, nigga."

With a shaky finger, he pointed to the stage. I roughly released him and made my way over to Elder who was surrounded by a pack of guys cheering on the dogs. He was a real life clown, and I was so disappointed in my daughter for choosing a nigga like him.

"Elder!" I called out.

He barely had a chance to crane his neck, before I punched him in the face with everything I had in me. His boys went to make a move, but my security pointed their guns at them stopping them in their tracks. The dogs continued to fight, as I grabbed Elder by the head and snatched him so hard to his feet, I tore his earlobe.

"You touched my fuckin' daughter?!" I slammed my fist into his stomach, then his face again, knocking out a few of his teeth. He fell to the floor, alongside the ring. "Gave her coke!" I stomped him in the ribs hard as fuck. "TRIED TO KILL HER!!!" I spat on him, and kicked him over and over till I felt his ribs crack underneath the brutal force of my assault. Messing with my daughter had caused me to break out into a whole new level of crazy.

"Get the fuck up! Get your bitch ass up, so I can fuck you up some more!" I grabbed him by the collar of his shirt and lugged him to his feet. His weak ass had the audacity to try to take a swing at me, but he was simply no match against an anguished father. I blocked his cheap shot, and kneed him in the gut, making him spit up blood.

He dropped to the ground like a sack of bricks, I slammed my foot down on his leg, shattering his kneecap. Without an ounce of sympathy in my heart, I climbed on top of him and commended to beating the shit out of his ass until he was no longer recognizable. Almost everyone in the building were now watching us—except for the two Pitbulls that were still trying to maim each other to death in the ring.

Even when I felt my knuckle dislocate, I didn't stop punching Elder. All I could think about was the way my daughter had looked at me in that hospital. The pure shame and embarrassment all over her face flashed in my brain every time I launched my fist into his face.

"You fucked with the wrong daughter!" I said, grabbing his hand. He cried out in agony, when I snapped two of his fingers back. I then took it a step further by breaking his wrist. Just thinking about those same hands being on my daughter had me ready to rip his arms off completely.

"Damn, low-key this shit better than the dog fight," a bystander said.

Grabbing Elder by his shirt, I dragged him towards the stage and threw him into the ring with the menacing and over aggressive animals that were still fighting. They instinctively went for Elder's neck, ripping his throat open with their bare teeth, since it's what they were trained to do.

For a few seconds, I watched in admiration, as they tore him apart like a fresh slab of steak from the deli. Blood, pus and other bodily fluids painted the stage as the dogs went to work tearing him apart. Now that my work here was done, I turned around and walked out of the building just as quietly and mysteriously as I'd come.

55
JUSTIN

An hour after the incident at Nick's place, I arrived at the Greyhound Station on E. 7th Street in downtown LA. My body was sore, I was covered in blood, broken glass and debris, but I was determined to see this shit through as I parked and killed the engine.

"Justin, wait!" Madison quickly said, having a change of heart. "I don't think we should do this. Besides, he may already be gone."

"Well, I won't know that until I see for myself."

"Justin, we can't do this. Look around. There's too many eyes."

"I thought you said you'd ride for me. If you were gone flip the script, I could've dropped your ass off at the crib."

"I am riding for you! That's why I'm telling you we shouldn't do this! It's over. We won."

"We didn't win shit. That bitch ass nigga got me for over two M's! And put *two* bullets in you in case you forgot."

"We still have our lives and our futures to think about! And your father still got bread in the bank. Like it don't even matter, Justin. Let's just go."

"It does matter!" I argued. "It's the fuckin' principle. Fuck you mean it don't matter?"

"Justin—"

I climbed out the car before she could finish and made my way to the entrance of the station. Madison was hot on my heels. Pushing my way past pedestrians, I headed straight for the terminals in search of my former best friend. I didn't give a damn how many eyes there were, I was determined to finish the shit I'd started. There was no way in hell I'd let him get away with crossing me, and even if he did leave the state, I'd hunt him down like a predator in the wilderness. Like I said, it was about the principle.

Drip was someone who I looked out for, put money in his pockets and food on the table. We were more than just friends, we were brothers. It was one thing for Lee to cross me, but Drip's betrayal hurt on a whole other level. We'd grown up together, shot hoops together, popped bottles together, laughed together. I'd even gone to his brother's funeral and poured liquor on his casket when he died. Apparently, none of those things meant shit to him. I was just a meal. Nothing more, nothing less. That shit tore at my soul.

All of the color rushed from my face, and my heart stopped beating when I saw Drip and his siblings standing in line K. They were still in their pajamas and he had them all huddled close together so that they didn't get lost in the busy bus station.

Without empathy, I reached for my gun—but Maddie quickly stopped me. "Justin, don't do this. For God's sake, he's with his family. Just let him go. It's over," she said. "Let's go back home. It's over..."

I looked in her pretty hazel eyes and saw utter desperation. She wanted me to walk away and avoid a possible life sentence for what I was about to do. And while I knew she had my best interest at heart, I just couldn't let the shit ride. Snatching away from her, I walked swiftly in his direction. A few people stopped to ogle me and how crazy I looked covered in cuts, blood and broken glass, but I didn't care.

"Deacon!" I called out Drip by his government name. The moment he saw me, his entire face went blank. You would've thought he was staring at a fucking ghost. But I wasn't a ghost. I was instant karma.

"Nothin' personal, my nigga," I said before blowing his brains out all over his brother and sisters.

Bystanders screamed and security rushed to restrain me and remove the gun from my possession. They then slammed me to the ground busting my face wide open. A crowd quickly gathered, and through the mass of people, I saw Madison looking disappointed in me...and then she collapsed.

"Madison!!!!" I screamed with a mouthful of blood. "MADISON!!!!!!"

Security quickly called in the incident, and several onlookers rushed to Maddie's aid. "She's not breathing!" one called out.

"Madison!!!!" I cried.

Oh no! No! No! No! No! No! *What did I do?* I should've listened to her and just left when we had the chance. Why didn't I just do what she wanted? Why did I have to be so fucking stubborn? Why did I have to let my ego get in the way of rational thinking? This is all my fault. This is all my fucking fault. This is all on me. *If only I'd gotten her the help she needed then none of this shit would be happening*, I told myself. But I wanted to live life fast and make decisions like I was a man. Now it was time to face the repercussions of those very decisions like an adult.

56
EVE

"Mama!" I called out. "Mama, come quick. Look at the news." I was in the living room, watching channel 2 news when I saw the coverage about a dead DEA agent, whose body was recently discovered in a lake.

My mother rushed to the living room with a wig and tweezers in hand to pluck the part. She took one look at Conway's picture on the screen and froze up. "Oh my God! That's the cop I made the deal with!" She said. "The one who promised us immunity whenever Jude's ass went down."

"So, does that mean the sting's not happening?" I asked.

My mother was silent as she stared at the screen in shock.

"Mama, answer me! Does that mean the sting's not happening???"

My mother looked over at me slowly, and her expression was all I needed to know that our plan was a bust.

"They must've found out," I said, panicking. "They had to have found out! And if Jude killed his ass, it's only a matter of time before he comes to kill us. Don't shit get past that nigga! He'll discover our involvement and then tossed our asses into a lake somewhere. I don't want that mama," I cried. "I should've never listened to you. I should've never given his wife that ledger! Now he'll know that I was trying to frame her! What the hell are we gonna do, mama?"

She grabbed her left arm and made a painful face. "There's nothing we can do, baby," she said disappointedly. "I had this grand scheme, but it could only work *if* Jude got arrested."

"And what was this grand scheme?" I asked her. I was starting to think she didn't have a plan all along, and that she was just improvising, but my mother quickly proved me wrong.

"I was gonna have the lawyer draft up divorce papers and trick Jude into signing what he thinks is an NDA while in prison. I was then gonna have him do the same with Cameron, and process the divorce papers. Afterwards, I'd have the lawyer whip up some fake documents citing that the two of you are married, and you're entitled to his assets and possessions. The plan would've been perfect if Conway hadn't gone and gotten himself killed! Fucking crash dummy! Now all my hard work was for nothing!"

"*Your* hard work???" I repeated. "You were *not* about to suck his dick in that office, mama."

"You know what I mean, lil' girl. Look, it doesn't even matter. Now that Conway's dead, the deal is null and void. We're pretty much back at square one." She rubbed her arm again and grimaced in pain.

"Mama, are you okay?" I asked her.

"I'm fine," she said.

"So, shouldn't we get ghost in case Jude *does* know about us. If he did kill Conway, then it's only a matter of time before he comes to kill us, right. You really think Jude would kill us, mama? After all the years he's known us? You really think he has it in him?"

"Chile, would you relax? You're 'bout to give yourself a nervous breakdown. We don't even know if Jude killed the man."

"But mama," I broke in anxiously.

Suddenly, and without warning, she dropped her wig and collapsed on top of the glass coffee table in front of her, shattering it into a thousand tiny pieces.

"MAMA!" I screamed in horror.

Distraught that her plan had fallen apart in front of her very eyes, my mother suffered a heart attack right there in the living room of our townhome. They always say stress is a silent killer.

I tried to pull her off the shattered remains of the table, but I cut the fuck out of my hands really badly. "Mama, oh my God! Mama!" I cried hysterically. She was my best friend, and partner in crime, so it hurt me to my core to see her suffering like this. She took a few last ragged breaths before ceasing all movement. Her eyes were still open as she stared up at the ceiling. I checked her pulse and saw that she was dead. "Mama, no!" I cried, burying my face in her bosom. "Oh, mama, no!!!"

I wanted to stay right there with her forever, but then I remembered that Conway was dead. And that if Jude had, in fact, killed him then I was more than likely next.

Staggering to my feet, I ran through the house, grabbed my gym bag from the closet and haphazardly filled it with clothes. Next, I opened the safe and grabbed my passport and every dollar I had to my name, then went back into the living room where my mother was sprawled out on a bed of broken glass.

Kneeling beside her, I placed a gentle kiss on her forehead, before leaving the house with no intentions of ever returning here or to the states, period. If Jude wanted to kill me, his ass would have to catch me first.

57
CAMERON
ONE YEAR LATER

Every catastrophic thing that ever could have happened in my life did. My 14-year old daughter dabbled in drugs and almost fell prey to one of our biggest rivals, and Justin got slapped with a second-degree manslaughter charge. Because he'd used a firearm, he was initially looking at a minimum of 25 years, but due to our close relationship with the mayor he was able to pull some strong strings and get his sentence cut in half. The judge knocked off a few more years since Justin had shown genuine remorse at the trial and this was his first major offense. After promising to join a rehabilitation program, he was stuck with serving an 8-year sentence but it could've been so much worse. He could've been locked down for life.

We never did find out what happened to Conway. He just up and vanished out of the blue, and I figured the pressure of being our security guard must've gotten to him—along with the drama that came along with working for us.

"Have you been brushing your teeth every night before bed?" I asked my 17-year old son through a glass window in a prison visitation room.

"Yeah, Ma," he said blandly.

It hurt me to my heart every time I came to see him, and it hurt me even more to know that I didn't do anything to avoid this from happening when I saw the chance. Justin was my first born; the first life I'd brought into this world. Losing him to the prison system felt like I'd lost a part of myself.

"And you've been flossing too?" I asked.

"Yeah, Ma."

"What about praying? Have you been praying?"

"Every night, Ma," he said. "Hey, have you talked to Soul again about letting Maddie come to see me?"

Jude and I exchanged looks. "Because of the situation, he's still pretty upset, so he needs time," Jude said.

After Madison fainted in the Greyhound station, she was rushed to the emergency room and given a blood transfusion. She'd gotten a minor infection from trying to treat her gunshot wounds herself, but after a few weeks in recovery, she was back on her feet and Soul wasted no time bringing her home.

When he and Diana found out what happened, they were understandably livid. Madison was supposed to be under my care and supervision and she'd almost died because of my negligence. They were so upset, they didn't talk to us for 6 months but they still came to support us at Justin's trial. They even paid for one of the best lawyers that money could buy, but all the money and support in the world couldn't stop Justin from having to atone for his sins. It was such a wake-up call that Jude took a step back from the drug game and started grooming Tekashi to take over. Since he'd saved Journee's life, Jude felt like the kid deserved a shot. I was more than cool with that. We had a ton of money in our bank accounts, CD, businesses and investments. It was time for the both of us to slow down. If not for our sake, for the sake of our children.

"I understand," Justin said, breaking into my thoughts.

"Son...I told myself I wouldn't ask but I gotta know," Jude began. "When you went in that station and shot that boy..." a tear fell down his cheek. "Did you do that for me?"

Justin scoffed. "Nah, pops. I did it for me."

"One more minute!" The security guard called out.

"We just got here," I complained. "Doesn't it feel like we just got here?" I asked my husband.

"That's how this shit works," he told me. "But don't worry. We'll be back next weekend. And the week after that, and the week after that."

"Don't cry, Ma," Justin said. "At least now you don't have to stress about my whereabouts."

He tried to make a light joke but it only made me cry even harder.

After visitation ended, Jude and I walked hand and hand out of the prison. We never brought Journee with us because we weren't prepared for her to see her brother locked up like some caged animal. We didn't want anything to stress her into experimenting with drugs again. Maybe when she got a little older, we'd start allowing her to come and see him but for now we'd put a rain check on it. She was fine with it too, seeing as how they wrote each other religiously.

"It's so hard...every time I see my baby behind these bars, it's gets harder and harder," I said, after we climbed into the car.

"I know." Jude kissed the back of my hand, and rubbed it against the prickly stubble on his face. "But just like every obstacle we've ever been faced with, we'll get through this, Cameron. I know we will."

EPILOGUE
CAMERON
FOUR YEARS LATER

Running around the house like a chicken with its head cut off, I did some last-minute preparations in time for my son's arrival. Not only was he getting out, it was also his 21st birthday, so this was something like a double celebration. He ended up serving half of his sentence and getting out early for good behavior. I couldn't have been more elated. He paid his dues to society. Now it was time to move on with our lives.

We had the balloons, a nice spread, presents, and the best gift of all Madison. Of course, Soul and Diana were here too. Four years had passed since she was shot under our supervision, and they were still leery of sending her alone to the states. At 22, Madison had blossomed into the beautiful, smart and headstrong woman I'd always known she would be. After graduating from high school, she went off to study abroad and was currently working on obtaining her Bachelors in Sports Management.

I was so proud of her. Just as proud as I was of my now 19-year old daughter, Journee. She was enrolled in Mount St. Mary's University, a private college in the Catoctin Mountains near the historic Emmitsburg, Maryland. There, she majored in Liberal Arts. She kept her head in the books, and we hadn't had any more problems out of her since her run in with Elder. Jude and I settled down in a quiet suburban neighborhood in Old Greenwich, Connecticut. We bought a beautiful house on the water and lived low-key, away from the streets, the trouble and the drama.

"Oh my God! Here he comes!!!" Roxie said excitedly. "Everyone, get in place!"

Roxie had ended up moving her family to New Orleans, so that Rain could be closer to her doctor. She hadn't had any outbursts in over 3 years now. Old Hector never gave up either, and Roxie ended up having to get a restraining order on him. He'd probably realized that he'd never get a woman as great as her. I was so proud of Roxie for finally coming to terms with the fact that she didn't need a man to be happy. She had two awesome kids.

As we waited on pins and needles for Justin to walk through the door, I noticed Tek and Journee giving each other the eye. I made a mental note to check their asses later on. We had a strict No Boyfriends policy, and she couldn't date *until* she graduated.

Suddenly, Justin twisted the knob and walked in and we all shouted, "WELCOME HOME," at the same time.

Justin was so big now, I hardly noticed my own flesh and blood. No longer was he skin and bones. He was all muscle with a few prison tattoos.

"Boy, I told you not to ink yourself up in there!" I chastised.

"Sorry, Ma. I tried not to, but I got bored."

"Look at you, man. What were they feeding you in there?" Jude asked, hugging him.

Justin patted Jude's stomach. "Same thing they feeding you, pops."

We all laughed.

"Welcome home, bro," Journee said, squeezing her way in for a hug.

Justin ruffled her curly hair. "I see you still just as ugly as ever."

Sofía hugged him next, then Letitia. She and Maddie attended the same university, and they were now closer than ever. Sofía and I still owned our chain of boutiques, and business was thriving, especially since we launched the online store. Me and my girl were getting money, but she still tried to screw me every chance she got. Her husband, Raúl, was also present to offer his support, and he shook Justin's hand the minute he got an opening.

Soul walked over next and dapped up Justin, and Diana hugged him. Justin saved the best of his love for Madison, as he took in the sight of her all grown up. Running over to her, he picked her up and spun her around. "Damn, I missed you girl."

Soul cut his eyes at Justin, and he quickly put her down when he saw the look on Soul's face. Maddie may have been grown, but he was still overprotective of his only daughter.

"Yo, who are these clowns?" Justin asked, pointing to two teenage boys leaned up against the wall.

Madison hit his arm. "Boy, stop playing! You know that's Aseem and KJ."

"I'm just fuckin' around. I know. Wassup, ya'll. Man, ya'll asses done got big." He ruffled KJ's curly hair. He wasn't Diana's biological son. Soul had him out of wedlock, but she still adopted him and took him in. It was one of the most commendable things she'd ever done.

"So did you," Aseem said. "Did they shoot steroids up your butt while you were in there?"

KJ chuckled.

Justin just looked over at Madison and she shrugged. "Welcome to my world," she laughed. "Now you finally get to see how annoying they *really* are."

"So, what do you wanna do first, baby? You wanna eat first or you wanna open your presents first?" I asked him.

Justin patted his stomach. "After five years on lockdown, I really *could* use a decent meal," he said. "But it's something I have to do first."

"What's that?" Jude asked.

Justin walked over towards Madison, dropped down on one knee and grabbed her hand. "You're my best friend, Maddie. You got me through so many bad days in that prison, whether you know it or not. I waited five long years to do this, and I don't wanna wait another second. Madison Janelle Asante, will you marry me?"

THE END

ABOUT THE AUTHOR

Jade Jones discovered her passion for creative writing in elementary school. Born in 1989, she began writing short stories and poetry as an outlet. Later on, as a teen, she led a troubled life which later resulted in her becoming a ward of the court. Jade fell in love with the art and used storytelling as a means of venting during her tumultuous times.

Aging out of the system two years later, she was thrust into the dismal world of homelessness. Desperate, and with limited income, Jade began dancing full time at the tender age of eighteen. It wasn't until Fall of 2008 when she finally caught her break after being accepted into Cleveland State University. There, Jade lived on campus and majored in Film and Television. Now, six years later, she flourishes from her childhood dream of becoming a bestselling author. Since then she has written the best-selling "Cameron" series.

Quite suitably, she uses her life's experiences to create captivating characters and story lines. Jade currently resides in Atlanta, Georgia. With no children, she spends her leisure shopping and traveling. She says that seeing new faces, meeting new people, and experiencing diverse cultures fuels her creativity. The stories are generated in her heart, the craft is practiced in her mind, and she expresses her passion through ink.

www.jadedpublications.com
https://www.facebook.com/author.jones
Facebook Fan Group:
https://www.facebook.com/groups/JadedBooks/
IG: authorjadejones
Twitter: authorjadejones
Snapchat: Jade_Jones198
Email: jade_jones89@yahoo.com

BIBLIOGRAPHY: www.jadedpub.com/books

Made in the USA
Las Vegas, NV
26 November 2023

81584359R00225